EDMOND HAMILTON RESURRECTED

Classic Stories of Edmond Hamilton

By Edmond Hamilton
Edited by Greg Fowlkes

Includes the Special Bonus Story
AND NOW A MESSAGE . . .
By Greg Fowlkes

EDMOND HAMILTON RESURRECTED

© 2010 Resurrected Press
www.ResurrectedPress.com

Published by Resurrected Press

This book of classics was handcrafted by Resurrected Press. Resurrected Press is dedicated to bringing high quality classic books back to the readers who enjoy them. These are not scanned versions of the originals, but, rather, quality checked and edited books meant to be enjoyed!

Please visit ResurrectedPress.com to view our entire catalogue!

ISBN 13: 978-1-935774-65-5

Printed in the United States of America

FOREWORD

The world of the period from which these stories are taken, the 30's and early 40's, was a much different place than today. There were still places in the world that were unexplored and the planets were known from blurry view through a telescope. It was easy in such a world to imagine that Venus was covered with cloud-shrouded swamps that were the homes to giant reptilian creatures; that Mars was covered with the canals of a dying civilization, and the moons of Jupiter and Saturn supported strange life forms and served as bases for space pirates.

This was the world in which Edmond Hamilton wrote his tales of adventure and wonder. His heroes could take off in their rocket ships to battle monstrous aliens with atomic pistols in the jungles of the asteroids or the swamps of Venus. Space pirates might prey on luxury liners bound for the moons of Saturn and secret cults might try to establish a gateway to another dimension, but in the end the hero would survive, and, if appropriate, get the girl.

By today's standards, these stories may seem a little "corny"; the was science dubious at best and just plain unbelievable at worst, but the purpose was not to predict the future, but to serve as a spring board for the imagination. They were, most importantly, about the action, of which there was plenty. The best way to approach these stories is to accept them for what they are — tales of adventure and imagination — and enjoy them on that basis rather than try to over analyze them.

Edmond Hamilton was one of the leading authors of this period, and Resurrected Press is happy to be offering this collection of his works.

About The Author

Edmond Hamilton (October 21, 1904 - February 1, 1977) was one of the leading science fiction authors of the pulp era of the 30's and 40's. He specialized in the "space opera" style of writing, but also produced works of horror and detective fiction. Later in life he wrote for DC Comics, especially for the characters of Superman and Batman. He was married to the author and screen writer Leigh Brackett.

Greg Fowlkes
Editor-In-Chief
Resurrected Press
www.ResurrectedPress.com

Table Of Contents

THE SECOND SATELLITE
ORIGINALLY PUBLISHED IN *ASTOUNDING STORIES OF SUPER SCIENCE,*
AUGUST, 1930

The Second Satellite

Earth men war on frog vampires for the emancipation of the human cows of Earth's second satellite.

Norman and Hackett, bulky in their thick flying suits, seemed to fill the little office. Across the room Harding, the field superintendent, contemplated them. Two planes were curving up into the dawn together from the field outside, their motors thunderous as they roared over the building. When their clamor had receded, Harding spoke:

"I don't know which of you two is crazier," he said. "You, Norman, to propose a fool trip like this, or you, Hackett, to go with him."

Hackett grinned, but the long, lean face of Norman was earnest. "No doubt it all sounds a little insane," he said, "but I'm convinced I'm right."

The field superintendent shook his head. "Norman, you ought to be writing fiction instead of flying. A second satellite—and Fellows and the others on it—what the devil!"

"What other theory can account for their disappearance?" asked Norman calmly. "You know that since the new X type planes were introduced, hundreds of fliers all over Earth have been trying for altitude records in them. Twenty five miles—thirty—thirty five—the records have been broken every day. But out of the hundreds of fliers who have gone up to those immense heights, four have never come down nor been seen again!

"One vanished over northern Sweden, one over Australia, one over Lower California, and one, Fellows, himself, right here over Long Island. You saw the globe on which I marked those four spots, and you saw that when connected they formed a perfect circle around the Earth. The only explanation is that the four fliers when they reached a forty mile height were caught up by some body moving round Earth in that circular orbit, some unknown moon circling Earth inside its atmosphere, a second satellite of Earth's whose existence has until now never been suspected!"

*   *   *   *   *

Harding shook his head again. "Norman, your theory would be all right if it were not for the cold fact that no such satellite has ever been glimpsed."

"Can you glimpse a bullet passing you?" Norman retorted. "The two fliers at Sweden and Lower California vanished within three hours of each other, on opposite sides of the Earth. That means that this second satellite, as I've computed, circles Earth once every six hours, and travelling at that terrific speed it is no more visible to us of Earth than a rifle bullet would be."

"Moving through Earth's atmosphere at such speed, indeed, one would expect it to burn up by its own friction with the air. But it does not, because its own gravitational power would draw to itself enough air to make a dense little atmosphere for itself that would cling to it and shield it as it speeds through Earth's upper air. No, I'm certain that this second satellite exists, Harding, and I'm as certain that it's responsible for the vanishing of those four fliers."

"And now you and Hackett have figured when it will be passing over here and are going up in an X type yourselves to look for it," Harding said musingly.

"Look for it?" echoed Hackett. "We're not going to climb forty miles just to get a look at the damn thing— we're going to try landing on it!"

"You're crazy sure!" the field superintendent exploded. "If Fellows and those others got caught by the thing and never came down again, why in the name of all that's holy would you two want—" He stopped suddenly. "Oh, I think I see," he said, awkwardly. "Fellows was rather a buddy of you two, wasn't he?"

"The best that ever flew a crippled Nieuport against three Fokkers to pull us out of a hole," said Norman softly. "Weeks he's been gone, and if it had been Hackett and I he'd be all over the sky looking for us—the damned lunatic. Well, we're not going to let him down."

"I see," Harding repeated. Then—"Well, here comes your mechanic, Norman, so your ship must be ready. I'll go with you. It's an event to see two Columbuses starting for another world."

*   *   *   *   *

The gray dawn light over the flying field was flushing to faint rose as the three strode out to where the long X type stood, its strangely curved wings, enclosed cabin and flat, fan like tail gleaming dully. Its motor was already roaring with power and the plane's stubby wheels strained against the chocks. In their great suits Norman and Hackett were like two immense ape figures in the uncertain light, to the eyes of those about them.

"Well, all the luck," Harding told them. "You know I'm pulling for you, but—I suppose it's useless to say anything about being careful."

"I seem to have heard the words," Hackett grinned, as he and Norman shook the field superintendent's hand.

"It's all the craziest chance," Norman told the other. "And if we don't come down in a reasonable time—well, you'll know that our theory was right, and you can broadcast it or not as you please."

"I hope for your sake that you're dead wrong," smiled the official. "I've told you two to get off the Earth a lot of times, but I never meant it seriously."

Harding stepped back as the two clambered laboriously into the cramped cabin. Norman took the controls, the door slammed, and as the chocks were jerked back and the motor roared louder the long plane curved up at a dizzy angle from the field into the dawn. Hackett waved a thick arm down toward the diminishing figures on the field below; then turned from the window to peer ahead with his companion.

The plane flew in a narrow ascending spiral upward, at an angle that would have been impossible to any ship save an X type. Norman's eyes roved steadily over the instrument as they rose, his ears unconsciously alert for each explosion of the motor. Earth receded swiftly into a great gray concave surface as they climbed higher and higher.

By the time the five mile height was reached Earth's surface had changed definitely from concave to convex. The plane was ascending by then in a somewhat wider spiral, but its climb was as steady and sure as ever. Frost begin to form quickly on the cabin's windows, creeping out from the edges. Norman spoke a word over the motor's muffled thunder, and Hackett snicked on the electrical radiators. The frost crept back as their warm, clean heat flooded the cabin.

Ten miles—fifteen—they had reached already altitudes impossible but a few years before, though it was nothing to the X types. As they passed the ten mile mark, Hackett set the compact oxygen generator going. A clean, tangy odor filled the cabin as it began functioning. Twenty miles—twenty two—

*   *   *   *   *

After a time Norman pointed mutely to the clock on the instrument board, and Hackett nodded. They were well within their time schedule, having calculated to reach the forty mile height at ten, the hour when, by its computed orbit, the second satellite should be passing overhead. "—26—27—28—" Hackett muttered the altimeter figures to himself as the needle crept over them.

Glancing obliquely down through the window he saw that Earth was now a huge gray ball beneath them, white cloud oceans obscuring the drab details of its surface here and there. "—31—32—" The plane was climbing more slowly, and at a lesser angle. Even the X type had to struggle to rise in the attenuated air now about them. Only the super light, super powered plane could ever have reached the terrific height.

It was at the thirty four mile level that the real battle for altitude began. Norman kept the plane curving steadily upward, handling it with surpassing skill in the rarefied air. Frost was on its windows now despite the heating mechanism. Slowly the altimeter needle crept to the forty mark. Norman kept the ship circling, its wings tilted slightly, but not climbing, Earth a great gray misty ball beneath.

"Can't keep this height long," he jerked. "If our second satellite doesn't show up in minutes we've had a trip for nothing."

"All seems mighty different up here," was Hackett's shouted comment. "Easy enough to talk down there about hopping onto the thing, but up here—hell, there's nothing but air and mighty little of that!"

Norman grinned. "There'll be more. If I'm right about this thing we won't need to hop it—its own atmosphere will pick us up."

Both looked anxious as the motor sputtered briefly. But in a moment it was again roaring steadily. Norman shook his head.

"Maybe a fool's errand after all. No—I'm still sure we're right! But it seems that we don't prove it this time."

"Going down?" asked Hackett.

"We'll have to, in minutes. Even with its own air feed the motor can't stand this height for—"

*   *   *   *   *

Norman never finished the words. There was a sound, a keen rising, rushing sound of immense power that reached their ears over the motor's roar. Then in an instant the universe seemed to go mad about them: they saw the gray ball of Earth and the sun above skyrocketing around them as the plane whirled madly.

The rushing sound was in that moment thunderous, terrible, and as winds smashed and rocked the plane like giant hands, Hackett glimpsed another sphere that was not the sphere of Earth, a greenish globe that expanded with lightning speed in the firmament beside their spinning plane! The winds stilled; the green globe changed abruptly to a landscape of green land and sea toward which the plane was falling! Norman was fighting the controls—land and sea were gyrating up to them with dizzy speed—crash!

With that cracking crash the plane was motionless. Sunlight poured through its windows, and great green growths were all around it. Hackett, despite Norman's warning cry, forced the door open and was bursting outside, Norman after him. They staggered and fell, with curious lightness and slowness, on the ground outside, then clutched the plane for support and gazed stupefiedly around them.

The plane had crashed down into a thicket of giant green reeds that rose a yard over their heads, its pancake landing having apparently not damaged it. The ground beneath their feet was soft and soggy, the air warm and balmy, and the giant reeds hid all the surrounding landscape from view.

In the sky the sun burned near one horizon with unusual brilliance. But it was dwarfed, in size, by the huge gray circle that filled half the heavens overhead. A giant gray sphere it was, screened here and there by floating white mists and clouds, that had yet plain on it the outlines of dark continents and gleaming seas. A quaking realization held the two as they stared up at it.

*   *   *   *   *

"Earth!" Norman was babbling. "It's Earth, Hackett—above us; my God, I can't believe even yet that we've done it!"

"Then we're on—the satellite—the second satellite!—" Hackett fought for reality."Those winds that caught us—"

"They were the atmosphere of this world, of the second satellite! They caught us and carried us on inside this smaller world's atmosphere, Hackett. We're moving with it around Earth at terrific speed now!"

"The second satellite, and we on it!" Hackett whispered, incredulously. "But these reeds—it can't all be like this—"

They stepped together away from the plane. The effort sent each of them sailing upward in a great, slow leap, to float down more than a score of feet from the plane. But unheeding in their eagerness this strange effect of the satellite's lesser gravitational power, they moved on, each step a giant, clumsy leap. Four such steps took them out of the towering reeds onto clear ground.

It was a gentle, grassy slope they were on, stretching away along a gray green sea that extended out to the astoundingly near horizon on their right. To the left it rose into low hills covered with dense masses of green junglelike vegetation. Hackett and Norman, though, gazed neither at sea or hills for the moment, but at the half score grotesque figures who had turned toward them as they emerged from the reeds. A sick sense of the unreal held them as they gazed, frozen with horror. For the great figures returning their gaze a few yards from them were—frog men!

*   *   *   *   *

Frog men! Great mottled green shapes seven to eight feet in height, with bowed, powerful legs and arms that ended in webbed paws. The heads were bulbous ones in which wide, unwinking frog eyes were set at the sides, the mouths white lipped and white lined. Three of the creatures held each a black metal tube and handle oddly like a target pistol.

"Norman!" Hackett's voice was a crescendo of horror. "*Norman!*"

"Back to the plane!" Norman cried thickly. "The plane—"

The two staggered back, but the frog men, recovering from their own first surprise, were running forward with great hopping steps! The two fliers flung themselves back in a floating leap toward the reeds, but the green monsters were quick after them. A croaking cry came from one and as another raised his tube and handle, something flicked from it that burst close beside Norman. There was no sound or light as it burst, but the reeds for a few feet around it vanished!

*   *   *   *   *

A hoarse cry from Hackett—the creatures had reached him, grasped him at the edge of the reeds! Norman swerved in his floating leap to strike the struggling flier and frog men. The scene whirled around him as he fought them, great paws reaching for him. With a sick, frantic rage he felt his clenched fist drive against cold, green, billowy bodies. Croaking cries sounded in his ears; then, Hackett and he were jerked to their feet, held tightly by four of the creatures.

"My God, Norman," panted Hackett, helpless. "What are they—frog things?—"

"Steady, Hackett. They're the people of the second satellite, it seems; wait!"

One of the armed frog men approached and inspected them, and then croaked an order in a deep voice. Then, still holding the two tightly, the party of monsters began to move along the slope, skirting the sea's edge. In a few minutes they reached two curious objects resting on the slope. They seemed long black metal boats, slender and with sharp prow and stern. A compact mechanism and control board filled the prow, while at the stern and sides were long tubes mounted on swivels like machine guns.

The frog men motioned Norman and Hackett into one, fastening the two prisoners and themselves into their seats with metal straps provided for the purpose. Four had entered the one boat, the others that of the captives. One at the prow moved his paws over the control board and with a purring of power the boat, followed by the other, rose smoothly into the air. It headed out over the gray green sea, land dropping quickly from sight behind, the horizons water bounded on all sides. From their nearness Norman guessed that this second satellite of Earth's was small indeed beside its mother planet. He had to look up to earth's great gray sphere overhead to attain a sense of reality.

Hackett was whispering beside him, the frog men watchful. "Norman, it's not real—it can't be real! These things—these boats—intelligent like men—"

The other sought to steady him. "It's a different world, Hackett. Gravitation different, light different, everything different, and evolution here has had a different course. On Earth men evolved to be the most intelligent life forms, but here the frog races, it seems."

"But where are they taking us? Could we ever find the plane again?"

"God knows. If we ever get away from these things we might. And we've got to find Fellows, too; I wonder where he is on this world."

*　　*　　*　　*　　*

For many minutes the two boats raced on at great speed over the endless waters before the watery skyline was broken far ahead by something dark and unmoving. Hackett and Norman peered with intense interest toward it. It seemed at first a giant squat mountain rising from the sea, but as they shot nearer they saw that its outline was too regular, and that colossal as it was in size it was the work of intelligence. They gasped as they came nearer and got a better view of it.

For it was a gigantic dome of black metal rising sheer from the lonely sea, ten miles if anything in diameter, a third that in greatest height. There was no gate or window or opening of any kind in it. Just the colossal, smooth black dome rearing from the watery plain. Yet the two boats were flashing lower toward it.

"They can't be going inside!" Hackett conjectured. "There's no way in and what could be in there? The whole thing's mad—"

"There's some way," Norman said. "They're slowing—"

The flying boats were indeed slowing as they dipped lower. They were very near the dome now, its curving wall a looming, sky high barrier before them. Suddenly the boats dipped sharply downward toward the green sea. Before the two fliers could comprehend their purpose, could do aught more than draw instinctive great breaths in preparation, the two craft had shot down into the waters and were arrowing down through the green depths.

Blinded, flung against his metal strap by the resistance of the waters they ripped through, Norman yet retained enough of consciousness to glimpse beams of light that stabbed ahead from the prows of their rushing boats, to see vaguely strange creatures of the deep blundering in and out of those beams as the boats hurtled forward. The water that forced its way between his lips was fresh, he was vaguely aware, and even as he fought to hold his breath was aware too that the frog men seemed in no way incommoded by the sudden transition into the water, their amphibian nature allowing them to stay under it far longer than any human could do.

The boats ripped through the waters at terrific speed and in a few seconds there loomed before them the giant metal wall of the great dome, going down into the depths here. Norman glimpsed vaguely that the whole colossal dome rested on a vast pedestal like mountain of rock that rose from the sea's floor almost to the surface. Then a great round opening in the wall; the boats flashed into it and were hurtling along a water filled tunnel. Norman felt his lungs near bursting—when the tunnel turned sharply upward and the boats whizzed up and abruptly out of the water tunnel into air!

*   *   *   *   *

But it was not the open air again. They were beneath the gigantic dome! For as Norman and Hackett breathed deep, awe fell on their faces as they took in the scene. Far overhead stretched the dome's colossally curving roof, and far out on all sides. It was lit beneath that roof by a clear light that the two would have sworn was sunlight. The dome was in effect the roof of a gigantic, illuminated building, and upon its floor there stretched a mighty city.

The city of the frog men! Their boats were rising up over it and Norman and Hackett saw it clear. Square mile upon square mile of structures stretched beneath the dome, black buildings often of immense size, varying in shape, but all of square, rectangular proportions. Between them moved countless frog hordes, swirling throngs in streets and squares, and over the roofs darted thick swarms of flying boats. And at the city's center, in a great, circular, clear space, lay a wide, round, green pool—the opening of the water tunnel up through which they had come.

Norman pointed down toward it. "That's your answer!" he cried. "The only entrance to this frog city is from the sea, up through that water tunnel!"

"Good God, an amphibian city!" Hackett was shaken, white faced.

The two boats were driving quickly over the city, through the swarming craft. Norman glimpsed towering buildings that might have been palaces, temples, laboratories. They slowed and dipped toward one block like building not far from the water tunnel's opening. Armed frog guards were on its roof, and other boats rested there. The two came to rest and the two captives were jerked out, the guards seizing them.

Half dragged and half floating they were led toward an opening in the roof from which a stair led downward. They passed down thus into the building's interior, lit by many windows. Norman glimpsed long halls ending in barred doors, guards here and there. Tube lines ran along the walls and somewhere machines were throbbing dully. They came at last to a barred door whose guard opened it at the croaking order of the frog men who held the two, and they were thrust inside, as the door clanged. They turned, and exclaimed in amazement. The room held fully a half hundred men!

They were men such as the two fliers had never seen before, like humans except that their skins were a light green instead of the normal white and pink. They were dressed in dark short tunics, and kept talking to each other in a tongue quite unintelligible to Norman and Hackett. They came closer, flocking curiously around the two men, with a babel of voices quite meaningless to the two. Then one of the men uttered an exclamation, and all turned.

*   *   *   *   *

The barred door had swung open and a half dozen frog guards entered, followed by two frog men carrying a square little mechanism from which tubing led back out through the door.

"Norman—these men—" Hackett was whispering rapidly. "If there are men in this world too, it may be that—"

"Quiet, Hackett—look at what they're doing."

The two frog men had set their mechanism in place and then croaked out a brief word or order. Slowly, reluctantly, one of the green men moved toward them. Quickly they removed a metal disk fastened to his arm, exposing a small orifice like an unhealed wound. Onto this they fastened a suckerlike object from which a transparent tube led back through the mechanism. The machine hummed and at once a red stream pulsed through the tube and back through the mechanism. The man to whom it was attached was growing rapidly pale!

Norman, sick with horror, clutched his companion. "Hackett—these frog men are sucking his blood from him!"

"Good God! And look—they're doing it with another!"

"All of these men—kept prisoners to furnish them with blood. It must be the damned creatures' food! And we here with the others—"

A common horror shook the two. It did not seem to affect the green men in the room, though, who advanced to the mechanism one by one with a reluctant air as of cows unwilling to be milked. Each was attached to the mechanism by the sucking disk on his arm, and out of each the blood poured through the tube. The metal disk was replaced on his arm then and he went back to the others. Norman saw that the frog men took only from each an amount of blood that they could lose and yet live, since, though each came back pale and weak from the mechanism, they were able to walk.

"It must be their food—human blood!" Norman repeated. "They may have thousands on thousands of humans penned up like this, like so many herds of cows, and perhaps they live entirely on the life blood they milk from them. Human cows—God!"

"Norman—look—they're calling to us!"

*   *   *   *   *

The two stiffened. All the others in the room had taken their turn at the blood sucking mechanism and now the frog men croaked their order to the two fliers. They had forgotten their own predicament in the horror of the scene, but now it became real to them. They backed against the room's wall, quivering, dangerous.

The frog guards came forward to drag them to the machine. A webbed paw was outstretched but Hackett with a wild blow drove the frog man back and downward. The frog guards leaped, and Norman and Hackett struck them back with all the greater strength the lesser gravitation gave them. The room was in an uproar, the green men shouting hoarsely and seeming on the point of rushing to their aid.

But the menacing force pistols of the other frog guards held back the shouting men and in moments the two fliers were overpowered by sheer weight of frog bodies. Norman felt himself dragged to the machine.

Pain needled his upper arm as an incision was made. He felt the sucking disk attached; then the machine hummed, and a sickening nausea swept him as the blood drained from his body. Held tightly by the guards he went dizzy, weak, but at last felt the sucker removed and a metal disk fastened over the incision. He was jerked aside and Hackett, his face deathly white, was dragged into his place. In a moment some of the latter's blood had been pumped from him also.

The machine was withdrawn, Norman and Hackett were released, and the frog men, with their black force pistols watchfully raised, withdrew, the door clanging. The room settled back to quietness, the green men stretching in lassitude on the metal bunks around it. The two fliers crouched down near the door, shuddering nausea and weakness still holding them.

Norman found that Hackett was laughing weakly. "To think that twenty four hours ago I was in New York," he half laughed, half sobbed. "On Earth—Earth—"

The other gripped his arm. "It's horrible, Hackett, I know. But it isn't instant death, and we've still a chance to escape. Hell, can damn frog men keep us here? Where's your nerve, man?"

A voice beside them made them turn in amazement. "You are men from Earth?" it asked, in queerly accented English. "From Earth?"

*　　*　　*　　*　　*

Astonishment held them as they saw who spoke. It was one of the green men in the room, who had settled down by their side. A tall figure with superb muscles and frank, clean countenance, his dark eyes afire with eagerness.

"English?" Norman exclaimed. "You know English—you understand me?"

The other showed his teeth in a smile. "I know, yes. I'm Sarja, and I learned to speak it from Fallas, in my city, before the Ralas caught me."

"Fallas—" Norman repeated, puzzled; then suddenly he flamed. "By God, he means Fellows!"

"Fallas, yes," said the other. "From the sky he fell into our city in a strange flying boat that was smashed. He was hurt but we cared for him, and he taught me his speech, which I heard you talking now."

"Then Fellows is in your city now?" asked Hackett eagerly. "Where is that?"

"Across this sea—back in the hills," the other waved. "It is far from the sea but I was rash one day and came too near the water in my flying boat. The Ralas were out raiding and they saw me, caught me, and brought me here. No escape now, until I die."

"The Ralas—you mean these frog men?" Norman asked.

Sarja nodded. "Of course. They are the tyrants and oppressors of this world. Our little world is but a tenth or less the size of your great Earth which it circles, but it has its lands and rivers, and this one great fresh water sea into which the latter empty. In this sea long ago developed the Ralas, the great frog men who acquired such intelligence and arts that they became lords of this world.

"Through the centuries, while on the land our races of green men have been struggling upward, the Ralas have oppressed them. Long ago the Ralas left all their other cities to build this one great amphibian city at the sea's center. Entrance to it is only by the water tunnel from without, and being frog people entrance thus is easy for them since they can move for many minutes under water, though they drown like any other breathing animal if kept under too long. Humans dare not try to enter it thus by the water tunnel, since, before they could find it and make their way up through it, they would have drowned.

*   *   *   *   *

"So the Ralas have ruled from this impregnable amphibian city. Its colossal metal dome is invulnerable to ordinary attack, and though solid and without openings it is always as light beneath the dome here as outside, since the Ralas' scientists contrived light condensers and conductors that catch light outside and bring it in to release inside. So when it is day outside the sunlight is as bright here, and when night comes the Earth light shines here the same as without.

"From this city their raiding parties have gone out endlessly to swoop down on the cities of us green men. Since we learned to make flying boats like theirs, with molecular motors, and to make the guns like theirs that fire shells filled with annihilating force, we have resisted them stoutly but their raids have not ceased. And always they have brought their prisoners back in to this, their city.

"Tens of thousands of green men they have prisoned here like us, for the sole purpose of supplying them with blood. For the Ralas live on this blood alone, changing it chemically to fit their own bodies and then taking it into their bodies. It eliminates all necessity for food here for them. Every few days they drain blood from us, and since we are well fed and cared for to keep us good blood producers, we will be here for a long time before we die."

"But haven't you made any attempt to get out of here—to escape?" Norman asked.

Sarja smiled. "Who could escape the city of the Ralas? In all recorded history it has never been done, for even if by some miracle you got a flying boat, the opening of the water tunnel that leads outward is guarded always."

"Guards or no guards, we're going to try it and not sit here to furnish blood for the Ralas," Norman declared. "Are you willing to help, to try to get to Fellows and your city?"

The green man considered. "It is hopeless," he said, "but as well to die beneath the force shells of the Ralas as live out a lifetime here. Yes, I will help, though I cannot see how you expect to escape even from this room."

"I think we can manage that," Norman told him. "But first—not a word to these others. We can't hope to escape with them all, and there is no knowing what one might not betray us to the frog men."

He went on then to outline to the other two the idea that had come to him. Both exclaimed at the simpleness of the idea, though Sarja remained somewhat doubtful. While Hackett slept, weak still from his loss of blood, Norman had the green man scratch on the metal floor as well as possible a crude map of the satellite's surface, and found that the city, where Fellows was, seemed some hundreds of miles back from the sea.

* * * * *

While they talked, the sunlight, apparently sourceless, that came through the heavily barred windows of the room faded rapidly, and dusk settled over the great amphibian city beneath the giant dome, kept from total darkness by a silvery pervading light that Norman reflected must be the light from Earth's great sphere. With the dusk's coming the activities in the frog city lessened greatly.

With dusk, too, frog guards entered the room bearing long metal troughs filled with a red jellylike substance, that they placed on racks along the wall. As the guards withdrew the men in the room rushed toward the troughs, elbowing each other aside and striking each other to scoop up and eat as much of the red jelly as possible. It was for all the world like the feeding of farm animals, and Hackett and Norman so sickened at the sight that they had no heart to try the food. Sarja, though, had no such scruples and seemed to make a hearty meal at one of the troughs.

After the meal the green men sought the bunks and soon were stretched in sonorous slumber. It was, Norman reflected, exactly the existence of domesticated animals— to eat and sleep and give food to their masters. A deeper horror of the frog men shook him, and a deeper determination to escape them. He waited until all in the room were sleeping before beckoning to Sarja and Hackett.

"Quiet now," he whispered to them. "If these others wake they'll make such a clamor we won't have a chance in the world. Ready, Sarja?"

The green man nodded. "Yes, though I still think such a thing's impossible."

"Probably is," Norman admitted. "But it's the one chance we've got, the immensely greater strength of our Earth muscle that the frog men must have forgotten when they put us in here."

They moved silently to the room's great barred door, outside which a frog guard paced. They waited until he had passed the door and on down the hall, then Norman and Hackett and Sarja grasped together one of the door's vertical bars. It was an inch and a half in thickness, of solid metal, and it seemed ridiculous that any men could bend it by the sheer strength of their muscles.

Norman, though, was relying on the fact that on the second satellite, with its far lesser gravitational influence, their Earth muscles gave them enormous strength. He grasped the bar, Hackett and Sarja gripping it below him, and then at a whispered word they pulled with all their force. The bar resisted and again, with sweat starting on their foreheads, they pulled. It gave a little.

*　　*　　*　　*　　*

They shrank back from it as the guard returned, moving past. Then grasping the bar again they bent all their force once more upon it. Each effort saw it bending more, the opening in the door's bars widening. They gave a final great wrench and the bent bar squealed a little. They shrank back, appalled, but the guard had not heard or noticed. He moved past it on his return along the hall, and no sooner was past it than Norman squeezed through the opening and leaped silently for the great frog man's back.

It went down with a wild flurry of waving webbed paws and croaking cries, stilled almost instantly by Norman's terrific blows. There was silence then as Hackett and Sarja squeezed out after him, the momentary clamor of the battle having aroused no one.

The three leaped together toward the stairs. In two great floating leaps they were on the floor above, Hackett and Norman dragging Sarja between them. They were not seen, were sailing in giant steps up another stair, hopes rising high. The last stair—the roof opening above;

and then from beneath a great croaking cry swelled instantly into chorus of a alarmed shouts.

"They've found the door—the guard!" panted Hackett.

They were bursting out onto the roof. Frog guards were on it who came in a hopping rush toward them, force pistols raised. But a giant leap took Hackett among them, to amaze them for a moment with great flailing blows. Sarja had leaped for the nearest flying boat resting on the roof, and was calling in a frantic voice to Norman and Hackett. Norman was turning toward Hackett, the center of a wild combat, but the latter emerged from it for a brief second to motion him frantically back.

"No use, Norman—get away—get away!" he cried hoarsely, frenziedly.

"Hackett—for God's sake—!" Norman half leaped to the other, but an arm caught him, pulled him desperately onto the boat's surface. It was Sarja, the long craft flying over the roof beneath his control.

"They come!" he panted. "Too late now—" Frog men were pouring up onto the roof from below. Sarja sent the craft rocketing upward, as Hackett gestured them away for a last frantic time before going down beneath the frog men's onslaught.

*   *   *   *   *

The roof and the combat on it dropped back and beneath them like a stone as their craft ripped across the silvery dusk over the mighty frog city. They were shooting toward the city's center, toward the green pool that was the entrance to the water tunnel, while behind and beneath an increasing clamor of alarm spread swiftly. Norman raged futilely.

"Hackett—Hackett! We can't leave him—"

"Too late!" Sarja cried. "We cannot help him but only be captured again. We escape now and come back—come back—"

The truth of it pierced Norman's brain even in the wild moment. Hackett had fought and held back the frog guards only that they might escape. He shouted suddenly.

"Sarja—the water tunnel!" A half dozen boats with frog guards on them were rising round it in answer to the alarm!

"The force gun!" cried the green man. "Beside you—!"

Norman whirled, glimpsed the long tube on its swivel beside him, trained it on the boats rising ahead as they rocketed nearer. He fumbled frantically at a catch at the gun's rear, then felt a stream of shells flicking out of it. Two of the boats ahead vanished as the shells released their annihilating force, another sagged and fell. From the remaining three invisible force shells flicked around them, but in an instant Sarja had whirled the boat through them and down into the water tunnel!

Norman clung desperately to his seat as the boat flashed down through the waters, and then, as Sarja sent it flying out through the great tunnel's waters, glimpsed, close behind, the beams of the three Rala boats as they pursued them through the tunnel, overtaking them. Could the force shells be fired under water? Norman did not know, but desperately he swung the force gun back as they rushed through the waters, and pressed the catch. An instant later beams and boats behind them in the tunnel vanished.

His lungs were afire; it seemed that he must open them to the strangling water. The boat was ripping the waters at such tremendous speed that he felt himself being torn from his hold on it. Pain seemed poured like molten metal through his chest—he could hold out no longer; and then the boat stabbed up from the waters into clear air!

*   *   *   *   *

Norman panted, sobbed. Behind them rose the colossal metal dome of the frog city, gleaming dully in the silvery light that flooded the far stretching seas. That light poured down from a stupendous silver crescent in the night skies. Norman saw dully the dark outlines on it before he remembered. Earth! He laughed a little hysterically. Sarja was driving the flying boat out over the sea and away from the frog city at enormous speed. At last he glanced back. Far behind them lay the great dome and up around it gleaming lights were pouring, lights of pursuing Rala boats.

"We escape," Sarja cried, "the city of the Ralas, from which none ever before escaped!"

Remembrance smote Norman. "Hackett! Held off those frog men so we could get away—we'll come back for him, by God!"

"We come back!" said Sarja. "We come back with all the green men of this world to the Ralas' city, yes! I know what Fallas has planned."

"Can you find your way to him—to your city?" Norman asked.

Sarja nodded, looking upward. "Before the next sun has come and gone we can reach it."

The boat flew onward, and the great dome and the searching lights around it dropped beneath the horizon. Norman felt the warm wind drying his drenched garments as they rushed onward. Crouched on the boat he gazed up toward the silver crescent of Earth sinking toward the horizon ahead. That meant, he told himself, that the satellite turned slowly on its axis as it whirled around Earth. It came to him that its night and day periods must be highly irregular.

When the sun climbed from the waters behind them they were flying still over a boundless waste of waters, but soon they sighted on the horizon ahead the thin green line of land. Sarja slowed as they reached it, took his bearings, and sent the craft flying onward.

They passed over a green coastal plain and then over low hills joined in long chains and mantled by dense and mighty jungles, towering green growths of unfamiliar appearance to Norman. He thought he glimpsed, more than once, huge beastlike forms moving in them. He did see twice in the jungles great clearings where were fair sized cities of bright green buildings, a metal tower rising from each. But when he pointed to them Sarja shook his head.

* * * * *

At last, as they passed over another range of hills and came into sight of a third green city with its looming tower, the other pointed, his face alight.

"My city," he said. "Fallas there."

Fellows! Norman's heart beat faster.

They shot closer and lower and he saw that the buildings were obviously green to lend them a certain protective coloration similar to that of the green jungles around them. The tower with its surmounting cage puzzled him though, but before he could ask Sarja concerning it his answer came in a different way. A long metal tube poked slowly out of the cage on the tower's top and sent a hail of force shells flicking around them.

"They're firing on us!" Norman cried. "This can't be your city!"

"They see our black boat!" Sarja exclaimed. "They think we're Rala raiders and unless we let them know they'll shoot us out of the air! Stand up, wave to them—!"

Both Norman and Sarja sprang to their feet and waved wildly to those in the tower cage, their flying boat drifting slowly forward. Instantly the force shells ceased to hail toward them, and as they moved nearer a sirenlike signal broke from the cage. At once scores of flying boats like their own, but glittering metal instead of black, shot up from the city where they had lain until now, and surrounded them.

As Sarja called in his own tongue to them the green men on the surrounding boats broke into resounding cries. They shot down toward the city, Norman gazing tensely. Great crowds of green men in their dark tunics had swarmed out into its streets with the passing of the alarm, and their craft and the others came to rest in an open square that was the juncture of several streets.

The green men that crowded excitedly about Norman and Sarja gave way to a half dozen hurrying into the square from the greatest of the buildings facing on it. All but one were green men like the others. But that one— the laughing eyed tanned face—the worn brown clothing, the curious huge steps with which he came—Norman's heart leapt.

"Fellows!"

"Great God—Norman!" The other's face was thunderstruck. "Norman—how by all that's holy did you get here?"

*   *   *   *   *

Norman, mind and body strained to the breaking point, was incoherent. "We guessed how you'd gone—the second satellite, Fellows—Hackett and I came after you— taken to that frog city—"

As Norman choked the tale, Fellows' face was a study. And when it was finished he swallowed, and gripped Norman's hand viselike.

"And you and Hackett figured it out and came after me—took that risk? Crazy, both of you. Crazy—"

"Fellows, Hackett's still there, if he's alive! In the Rala city!"

Fellows' voice was grim, quick. "We'll have him out. Norman, if he still lives. And living or dead, the Ralas will pay soon for this and for all they've done upon this world in ages. Their time nears—yes."

He led Norman, excited throngs of the green men about them, into the great building from which he had emerged. There were big rooms inside, workshops and laboratories that Norman but vaguely glimpsed in passing. The room to which the other led him was one with a long metal couch. Norman stretched protestingly upon it at the other's bidding, drifted off almost at once into sleep.

He woke to find the sunlight that had filled the room gone and replaced by the silvery Earth light. From the window he saw that the silver lit city outside now held tremendous activity, immense hordes of green men surging through it with masses of weapons and equipment, flying boats pouring down out of the night from all directions. He turned as the door of the room clicked open behind him. It was his old friend Fellows.

"I thought you'd be awake by now, Norman. Feeling fit?"

"As though I'd slept a week," Norman said, and the other laughed his old care free laugh.

"You almost have, at that. Two days and nights you've slept, but it all adds up to hardly more than a dozen hours."

"This world!" Norman's voice held all his incredulity. "To think that we should be on it—a second satellite of Earth's—it seems almost beyond belief."

*   *   *   *   *

"Sometimes it seems so to me, too," Fellows said thoughtfully. "But it's not a bad world—not the human part of it, at least. When this satellite's atmosphere caught me and pitchforked me down among these green men, smashing the plane and almost myself, they took care of me. You say three others vanished as I did? I never heard of them here; they must have crashed into the sea or jungles. Of course, I'd have got back to Earth on one of these flying boats if I'd been able, but their molecular power won't take them far from this world's surface, so I couldn't.

"As it was, the green men cared for me, and when I found how those frog men have dominated this world for ages, how that city of the Ralas has spread endless terror among the humans here, I resolved to smash those monsters whatever I did. I taught some of the green men like Sarja my own speech, later learning theirs, and in the weeks I've been here I've been working out a way to smash the Ralas.

"You know that amphibian city is almost impregnable because humans can hardly live long enough under the water to get into it, let alone fight under water as the frog men can. To meet them on even terms the green men needed diving helmets with an oxygen supply. They'd never heard of such an idea, too afraid of the sea ever to experiment in it, but I convinced them and they've made enough helmets for all their forces. In them they can meet the Ralas under water on equal terms.

"And there's a chance we can destroy that whole Rala city with their help. It's built on a giant pedestal of rock rising from the sea's floor, as you saw, and I've had some of the green men make huge force shells or force bombs that ought to be powerful enough to split that pedestal beneath the city. If we can get a chance to place those bombs it may smash the frog men forever on this world. But one thing is sure: we're going to get Hackett out if he still lives!"

"Then you're, going to attack the Rala city now?" Norman cried.

Fellows nodded grimly. "While you have slept all the forces of the green men on this world have been gathering. Your coming has only precipitated our plans, Norman—the whole soul of the green races has been set upon this attack for weeks!"

*   *   *   *   *

Norman, half bewildered at the swiftness with which events rushed upon him, found himself striding with

Fellows in great steps out through the building into the great square. It was shadowed now by mass on mass of flying boats, crowded with green men, that hung over it and over the streets. One boat, Sarja at its controls, waited on the ground and as they entered and buckled themselves into the seats the craft drove up to hang with the others.

A shattering cheer greeted them. Norman saw that in the silvery light of Earth's great crescent there stretched over the city and surrounding jungle now a veritable plain of flying boats. On each were green men and each bristled with force guns, and had as many great goggled helmets fastened to it as it had occupants. He glimpsed larger boats loaded with huge metal cylinders—the force bombs Fellows had mentioned.

Fellows rose and spoke briefly in a clear voice to the assembled green men on their craft, and another great shout roared from them, and from these who watched in the city below. Then as he spoke a word, Sarja sent their craft flying out over the city, and the great mass of boats, fully a thousand in number, were hurtling in a compact column after them.

Fellows leaned to Norman as the great column of purring craft shot on over the silver lit jungles. "We'll make straight for the Rala city and try setting into it before they understand what's happening."

"Won't they have guards out?"

"Probably, but we can beat them back into the city before their whole forces can come out on us. That's the only way in which we can get inside and reach Hackett. And while we're attacking the force bombs can be placed, though I don't rely too much on them."

"If the attack only succeeds in getting us inside," Norman said, grim lipped, "we'll have a chance—"

"It's on the knees of the gods. These green men are doing an unprecedented thing in attacking the Ralas, the masters of this world, remember. But they've got ages of oppression to avenge; they'll fight."

The fleet flew on, hills and rivers a silver lit panorama unreeling beneath them. Earth's crescent sank behind them, and by the time they flashed out over the great fresh water sea, the sun was rising like a flaming eye from behind it. Land sank from sight behind and the green men were silent, tense, as they saw stretching beneath only the gray waters that for ages had been the base of the dread frog men. But still the fleet's column raced on.

*   *   *   *   *

At last the column slowed. Far ahead the merest bulge broke the level line where sky and waters met. The amphibian city of the Ralas! At Fellows' order the flying boats sank downward until they moved just above the waters. Another order made the green hosts don the grotesque helmets. Norman found that while cumbersome their oxygen supply was unfailing. They shot on again at highest speed, but as the gigantic black dome of the frog city grew in their vision there darted up from around it suddenly a far flung swarm of black spots.

"Rala boats!"

The muffled exclamation was Fellows'. There needed now no order on his part, though. Like hawks, leaping for prey, the fleet of the green men sprang through the air. Norman, clutching the force gun between his knees, had time only to see that the Rala craft were a few hundred in number and that, contemptuous of the greater odds that favored these humans they had so long oppressed, they were flying straight to meet them. Then the two fleets met—and were spinning side by side above the waters.

Norman saw the thing only as a wild whirl of Rala boats toward and beside them, great green frog men crowding the craft, their force guns hailing shells. Automatically, with the old air fighting instinct, his fingers had pressed the catch of the gun between his knees and as its shells flicked toward the rushing boats he saw areas of nothingness opening suddenly in their mass, shells striking and exploding in annihilating invisibility there and in their own fleet.

The two fleets mingled and merged momentarily, the battle becoming a thing of madness, a huge whirl of black and glittering flying boats together, striking shells exploding nothingness about them. The Ralas were fighting like demons.

The merged, terrific combat lasted but moments; could last but moments. Norman, his gun's magazine empty, seemed to see the mass of struggling ships splittering, diverging; then saw that the black craft were dropping, plummeting downward toward the waves! The Ralas, stunned by that minute of terrific combat, were fleeing. Muffled cries and cheers came from about him as the glittering flying boats of the green men shot after them. They crashed down into the waters and curved deeply into their green depths, toward the gigantic dome.

* * * * *

Ahead the Rala boats were in flight toward their city, and now their pursuers were like sharks striking after them. There in the depths the force guns of black and glittering boats alike were spitting, and giant waves and underwater convulsions rocked pursued and pursuers as the exploding shells annihilated boats and water about them. The tunnel! Its round opening yawned in the looming wall ahead, and Norman saw the Rala craft, reduced to scores in number, hurtling into it, to rouse all the forces of the great amphibian city. Their own boats were flashing into the opening after them. He glimpsed as he glanced back for a moment the larger craft with the great force bombs veering aside behind them.

It was nightmare in the water tunnel. Flashing beams of the craft ahead and waters that rocked and smashed around them as in flight the Ralas still rained back force shells toward them in a chaos of action. Once the frog men turned to hold them back in the tunnel, but by sheer weight the rushing ships of the green men crashed them onward. Boats were going into nothingness all around them. A part of Norman's brain wondered calmly why they survived even while another part kept his gun again working, with refilled magazine. Fellows and Sarja were grotesque shapes beside him. Abruptly the tunnel curved upward and as they flashed up after the remaining Rala craft their boats ripped up into clear air! They were beneath the giant dome!

The frog men chased inward spread out in all directions over their mighty, swarming city and across it a terrific clamor of alarm ran instantly as the green men emerged after them! Norman saw flying boats beginning to rise across all the city and realized that moments would see all the immense force of the Ralas, the thousands of craft they could muster, pouring upon them. He pointed out over the city to a block like building, and shouted madly through his helmet to Fellows and Sarja:

"Hackett!"

But already Sarja had sent their craft whirling across the city toward the structure, half their fleet behind it, with part still emerging from the water tunnel. Rala boats rose before them, but nothing could stop them now, their force shells raining ahead to clear a path for their meteor flight. They shot down toward the block structure, and Norman, half crazed by now, saw that to descend and enter was suicide in the face of the frog forces rising now over all the city. He cried to Fellows, and with two of the guns as they swooped lower they sprayed force shells along the building's side.

*   *   *   *   *

The shells struck and whiffed away the whole side, exposing the level on the building's interior. Out from it rushed swarms of crazed green men, sweeping aside the frog men guards, while far over the city the invading craft

were loosing shells on the block like buildings that held
the prisoners, tens of thousands of them swarming forth.
In the throng below as they raced madly forth Norman
saw one, and shouted wildly. The one brown garbed
figure looked up, saw their boat swooping lower, and
leaped for it in a tremendous forty foot spring that
brought his fingers to its edge. Norman pulled him
frenziedly up.

"Norman!" he babbled. "In God's name—Fellows—!"

"That helmet, Hackett!" Fellows flung at him. "My
God, look at those prisoners—Norman!"

The countless thousands of green men released from
the buildings whose walls had vanished under the shells
of the invaders had poured forth to make the amphibian
city a chaos of madness. Oblivious to all else they were
throwing themselves upon the city's crowding frog men in
a battle whose ferocity was beyond belief, disregarding all
else in this supreme chance to wreak vengeance on the
monstrous beings who had fed upon their blood. In the
incredible insanity of that raging fury the craft of the
green men hanging over the city were all but forgotten.

Suddenly the city and the mighty dome over it
quivered violently, and then again. There came from
beneath a dull, vast, grinding roar.

"The great force bombs!" Fellows screamed. "They've
set them off—the city's sinking—out of here, for the love
of God!"

The boat whirled beneath Sarja's hands toward the
pool of the water tunnel, all their fleet rushing with them.
The grinding roar was louder, terrible; dome and city
were shaking violently now; but in the insensate fury of
their struggle the frog men and their released prisoners
were hardly aware of it. The whole great dome seemed
sinking upon them and the city falling beneath it as
Sarja's craft ripped down into the tunnel's waters, and
then out, at awful speed, as the great tunnel's walls
swayed and sank around them! They shot out into the
green depths from it to hear a dull, colossal crashing

through the waters from behind as the great pedestal of rock on which the city had stood, shattered by the huge force bombs, collapsed. And as their boats flashed up into the open air they saw that the huge dome of the city of the Ralas was gone.

Beneath them was only a titanic whirlpool of foaming waters in which only the curved top of the settling dome was visible for a moment as it sank slowly and ponderously downward, with a roar as of the roar of falling worlds. Buckling, collapsing, sinking, it vanished in the foam wild sea with all the frog men who for ages had ruled the second satellite, and with all those prisoners who had at the last dragged them down with them to death! Ripping off their helmets, with all the green men shouting crazily about them, Norman and Fellows and Hackett stared down at the colossal maelstrom in the waters that was the tomb of the masters of a world.

Then the depression's sides collapsed, the waters rushing together ... and beneath them was but troubled, tossing sea....

*   *   *   *   *

Earth's great gray ball was overhead again and the sun was sinking again to the horizon when the three soared upward in the long, gleaming plane, its motor roaring. Norman, with Hackett and Fellows crowding the narrow cabin beside him, waved with them through its windows. For all around them were rising the flying boats of the green men.

They were waving wildly, shouting their farewells, Sarja's tall figure erect at the prow of one. Insistent they had been that the three should stay, the three through whom the monstrous age old tyranny of the frog men had been lifted, but Earth sickness was on them, and they had flown to where the plane lay still unharmed among the reeds, a hundred willing hands dragging it forth for the take off.

The plane soared higher, motor thundering, and they saw the flying boats sinking back from around them. They caught the wave of Sarja's hand still from the highest, and then that, too, was gone.

Upward they flew toward the great gray sphere, their eyes on the dark outlines of its continents and on one continent. Higher—higher—green land and gray tea receding beneath them; Hackett and Fellows intent and eager as Norman kept the plane rising. The satellite lay, a greenish globe, under them. And as they went higher still a rushing sound came louder to their ears.

"The edge of the satellite's atmosphere?" Fellows asked, as Norman nodded.

"We're almost to it—here we go!"

As he shot the plane higher, great forces smote it, gray Earth and green satellite and yellow sun gyrating round it as it reeled and plunged. Then suddenly it was falling steadily, gray Earth and its dark continent now beneath, while with a dwindling rushing roar its second satellite whirled away above them, passing and vanishing. Passing as though, to Norman it seemed, all their strange sojourn on it were passing; the frog men and their mighty city, Sarja and their mad flight, the green men and the last terrific battle; all whirling away— whirling away.

THE MAN WHO SAW THE FUTURE

ORIGINALLY PUBLISHED IN *AMAZING STORIES*, OCTOBER, 1930

THE MAN WHO SAW THE FUTURE

Jean de Marselait, Inquisitor Extraordinary of the King of France, raised his head from the parchments that littered the crude desk at which he sat. His glance shifted along the long stone-walled, torchlit room to the file of mail-clad soldiers who stood like steel statues by its door. A word from him and two of them sprang forward.

"You may bring in the prisoner," he said.

The two disappeared through the door, and in moments there came a clang of opening bolts and grating of heavy hinges from somewhere in the building. Then the clang of the returning soldiers, and they entered the room with another man between them whose hands were fettered.

He was a straight figure, and was dressed in drab tunic and hose. His dark hair was long and straight, and his face held a dreaming strength, altogether different from the battered visages of the soldiers or the changeless mask of the Inquisitor. The latter regarded the prisoner for a moment, and then lifted one of the parchments from before him and read from it in a smooth, clear voice.

"Henri Lothiere, apothecary's assistant of Paris," he read, "is charged in this year of our lord one thousand four hundred and forty-four with offending against God and the king by committing the crime of sorcery."

The prisoner spoke for the first time, his voice low but steady. "I am no sorcerer, sire."

Jean de Marselait read calmly on from the parchment. "It is stated by many witnesses that for long that part of Paris, called Nanley by some, has been troubled by works of the devil. Ever and anon great claps of thunder have been heard issuing from an open field there without visible cause. They were evidently caused by a sorcerer of power since even exorcists could not halt them.

"It is attested by many that the accused, Henri Lothiere, did in spite of the known diabolical nature of the thing, spend much time at the field in question. It is also attested that the said Henri Lothiere did state that in his opinion the thunderclaps were not of diabolical origin, and that if they were studied, their cause might be discovered.

"It being suspected from this that Henri Lothiere was himself the sorcerer causing the thunderclaps, he was watched and on the third day of June was seen to go in the early morning to the unholy spot with certain instruments. There he was observed going through strange and diabolical conjurations, when there came suddenly another thunderclap and the said Henri Lothiere did vanish entirely from view in that moment. This fact is attested beyond all doubt.

"The news spreading, many hundreds watched around the field during that day. Upon that night before midnight, another thunderclap was heard and the said Henri Lothiere was seen by these hundreds to appear at the field's center as swiftly and as strangely as he had vanished. The fear-stricken hundreds around the field heard him tell them how, by diabolical power, he had gone for hundreds of years into the future, a thing surely possible only to the devil and his minions, and heard him tell other blasphemies before they seized him and brought him to the Inquisitor of the King, praying that he be burned and his work of sorcery thus halted.

"Therefore, Henri Lothiere, since you were seen to vanish and to reappear as only the servants of the evil one might do, and were heard by many to utter the blasphemies mentioned, I must adjudge you a sorcerer with the penalty of death by fire. If anything there be that you can advance in palliation of your black offense, however, you may now do so before final sentence is passed upon you."

Jean de Marselait laid down the parchment, and raised his eyes to the prisoner. The latter looked round him quickly for a moment, a half-glimpsed panic for an instant in his eyes, then seemed to steady.

"Sire, I cannot change the sentence you will pass upon me," he said quietly, "yet do I wish well to relate once, what happened to me and what I saw. Is it permitted me to tell that from first to last?"

The Inquisitor's head bent, and Henri Lothiere spoke, his voice gaining in strength and fervor as he continued.

*　*　*　*　*

"Sire, I, Henri Lothiere, am no sorcerer but a simple apothecary's assistant. It was always my nature, from earliest youth, to desire to delve into matters unknown to men; the secrets of the earth and sea and sky, the knowledge hidden from us. I knew well that this was wicked, that the Church teaches all we need to know and that heaven frowns when we pry into its mysteries, but so strong was my desire to know, that many times I concerned myself with matters forbidden.

"I had sought to know the nature of the lightning, and the manner of flight of the birds, and the way in which fishes are able to live beneath the waters, and the mystery of the stars. So when these thunderclaps began to be heard in the part of Paris in which I lived, I did not fear them so much as my neighbors. I was eager to learn only what was causing them, for it seemed to me that their cause might be learned.

"So I began to go to that field from which they issued, to study them. I waited in it and twice I heard the great thunderclaps myself. I thought they came from near the field's center, and I studied that place. But I could see nothing there that was causing them. I dug in the ground, I looked up for hours into the sky, but there was nothing. And still, at intervals, the thunderclaps sounded.

"I still kept going to the field, though I knew that many of my neighbors whispered that I was engaged in sorcery. Upon that morning of the third day of June, it had occurred to me to take certain instruments, such as loadstones, to the field, to see whether anything might be learned with them. I went, a few superstitious ones following me at a distance. I reached the field's center, and started the examinations I had planned. Then came suddenly another thunderclap and with it I passed from the sight of those who had followed and were watching, vanished from view.

"Sire, I cannot well describe what happened in that moment. I heard the thunderclap come as though from all the air around me, stunning my ears with its terrible burst of sound. And at the same moment that I heard it, I was buffeted as though by awful winds and seemed falling downward through terrific depths. Then through the hellish uproar, I felt myself bumping upon a hard surface, and the sounds quickly ceased from about me.

"I had involuntarily closed my eyes at the great thunderclap, but now, slowly, I opened them. I looked around me, first in stupefaction, and then in growing amazement. For I was not in that familiar field at all, sire, that I had been in a moment before. I was in a room, lying upon its floor, and it was such a room as I had never seen before.

"Its walls were smooth and white and gleaming. There were windows in the walls, and they were closed with sheets of glass so smooth and clear that one seemed looking through a clear opening rather than through glass. The floor was of stone, smooth and seamless as though carven from one great rock, yet seeming not, in some way, to be stone at all. There was a great circle of smooth metal inset in it, and it was on it that I was lying.

"All around the room were many great things the like of which I had never seen. Some seemed of black metal, seemed contrivances or machines of some sort. Black cords of wire connected them to each other and from part of them came a humming sound that did not stop. Others had glass tubes fixed on the front of them, and there were square black plates on which were many shining little handles and buttons.

"There was a sound of voices, and I turned to find that two men were bending over me. They were men like myself, yet they were at the same time like no men I had ever met! One was white-bearded and the other plump and bare of face. Neither of them wore cloak or tunic or hose. Instead they wore loose and straight-hanging garments of cloth.

"They were both greatly excited, it seemed, and were talking to each other as they bent over me. I caught a word or two of their speech in a moment, and found it was French they were talking. But it was not the French I knew, being so strange and with so many new words as to be almost a different language. I could understand the drift, though, of what they were saying.

"'We have succeeded!' the plump one was shouting excitedly. 'We've brought someone through at last!'

"'They will never believe it,' the other replied. 'They'll say it was faked.'

"'Nonsense!' cried the first. 'We can do it again, Rastin; we can show them before their own eyes!'

"They bent toward me, seeing me staring at them.

"'Where are you from?' shouted the plump-faced one. 'What time—what year—what century?'

"'He doesn't understand, Thicourt,' muttered the white-bearded one. 'What year is this now, my friend?' he asked me.

"I found voice to answer. 'Surely, sirs, whoever you be, you know that this is the year fourteen hundred and forty-four,' I said.

"That set them off again into a babble of excited talk, of which I could make out only a word here and there. They lifted me up, seeing how sick and weak I felt, and

seated me in a strange, but very comfortable chair. I felt
dazed. The two were still talking excitedly, but finally the
white-bearded one, Rastin, turned to me. He spoke to me,
very slowly, so that I understood him clearly, and he
asked me my name. I told him.

"'Henri Lothiere,' he repeated. 'Well, Henri, you must
try to understand. You are not now in the year 1444. You
are five hundred years in the future, or what would seem
to you the future. This is the year 1944.'

"'And Rastin and I have jerked you out of your own
time across five solid centuries,' said the other, grinning.

"I looked from one to the other. 'Messieurs,' I pleaded,
and Rastin shook his head.

"'He does not believe,' he said to the other. Then to
me, 'Where were you just before you found yourself here,
Henri?' he asked.

"'In a field at the outskirts of Paris,' I said.

"'Well, look from that window and see if you still
believe yourself in your 15th-century Paris.'

*   *   *   *   *

"I went to the window. I looked out. Mother of God,
what a sight before my eyes! The familiar gray little
houses, the open fields behind them, the saunterers in
the dirt streets—all these were gone and it was a new
and terrible city that lay about me! Its broad streets were
of stone and great buildings of many levels rose on either
side of them. Great numbers of people, dressed like the
two beside me, moved in the streets and also strange
vehicles or carriages, undrawn by horse or ox, that
rushed to and fro at undreamed-of speed! I staggered
back to the chair.

"'You believe now, Henri?' asked the whitebeard,
Rastin, kindly enough, and I nodded weakly. My brain
was whirling.

"He pointed to the circle of metal on the floor and the machines around the room. 'Those are what we used to jerk you from your own time to this one,' he said.

"'But how, sirs?' I asked. 'For the love of God, how is it that you can take me from one time to another? Have ye become gods or devils?'

"'Neither the one nor the other, Henri,' he answered. 'We are simply scientists, physicists—men who want to know as much as man can know and who spend our lives in seeking knowledge.'

"I felt my confidence returning. These were men such as I had dreamed might some day be. 'But what can you do with time?' I asked. 'Is not time a thing unalterable, unchanging?'

"Both shook their heads. 'No, Henri, it is not. But lately have our men of science found that out.'

"They went on to tell me of things that I could not understand. It seemed they were telling that their men of knowledge had found time to be a mere measurement, or dimension, just as length or breadth or thickness. They mentioned names with reverence that I had never heard—Einstein and De Sitter and Lorentz. I was in a maze at their words.

"They said that just as men use force to move or rotate matter from one point along the three known measurements to another, so might matter be rotated from one point in time, the fourth measurement, to another, if the right force were used. They said that their machines produced that force and applied it to the metal circle from five hundred years before to this time of theirs.

"They had tried it many times, they said, but nothing had been on the spot at that time and they had rotated nothing but the air above it from the one time to the other, and the reverse. I told them of the thunderclaps that had been heard at the spot in the field and that had made me curious. They said that they had been caused by the changing of the air above the spot from the one time to the other in their trials. I could not understand these things.

"They said then that I had happened to be on the spot when they had again turned on their force and so had been rotated out of my own time into theirs. They said that they had always hoped to get someone living from a distant time in that way, since such a man would be a proof to all the other men of knowledge of what they had been able to do.

"I could not comprehend, and they saw and told me not to fear. I was not fearful, but excited at the things that I saw around me. I asked of those things and Rastin and Thicourt laughed and explained some of them to me as best they could. Much they said that I did not understand but my eyes saw marvels in that room of which I had never dreamed.

"They showed me a thing like a small glass bottle with wires inside, and then told me to touch a button beneath it. I did so and the bottle shone with a brilliant light exceeding that of scores of candles. I shrank back, but they laughed, and when Rastin touched the button again, the light in the glass thing vanished. I saw that there were many of these things in the ceiling.

"They showed me also a rounded black object of metal with a wheel at the end. A belt ran around the wheel and around smaller wheels connected to many machines. They touched a lever on this object and a sound of humming came from it and the wheel turned very fast, turning all the machines with the belt. It turned faster than any man could ever have turned it, yet when they touched the lever again, its turning ceased. They said that it was the power of the lightning in the skies that they used to make the light and to turn that wheel!

"My brain reeled at the wonders that they showed. One took an instrument from the table that he held to his face, saying that he would summon the other scientists or men of knowledge to see their experiment that night. He spoke into the instrument as though to different men, and let me hear voices from it answering him! They said that the men who answered were leagues separated from him!

"I could not believe—and yet somehow I did believe! I was half-dazed with wonder and yet excited too. The white-bearded man, Rastin, saw that, and encouraged me. Then they brought a small box with an opening and placed a black disk on the box, and set it turning in some way. A woman's voice came from the opening of the box, singing. I shuddered when they told me that the woman was one who had died years before. Could the dead speak thus?

*   *   *   *   *

"How can I describe what I saw there? Another box or cabinet there was, with an opening also. I thought it was like that from which I had heard the dead woman singing, but they said it was different. They touched buttons on it and a voice came from it speaking in a tongue I knew not. They said that the man was speaking thousands of leagues from us, in a strange land across the uncrossed western ocean, yet he seemed speaking by my side!

"They saw how dazed I was by these things, and gave me wine. At that I took heart, for wine, at least, was as it had always been.

"'You will want to see Paris—the Paris of our time, Henri?' asked Rastin.

"'But it is different—terrible—' I said.

"'We'll take you,' Thicourt said, 'but first your clothes—'

"He got a long light coat that they had me put on, that covered my tunic and hose, and a hat of grotesque round shape that they put on my head. They led me then out of the building and into the street.

"I gazed astoundedly along that street. It had a raised walk at either side, on which many hundreds of people moved to and fro, all dressed in as strange a fashion. Many, like Rastin and Thicourt, seemed of gentle blood, yet, in spite of this, they did not wear a sword or even a dagger. There were no knights or squires, or priests or peasants. All seemed dressed much the same.

"Small lads ran to and fro selling what seemed sheets of very thin white parchment, many times folded and covered with lettering. Rastin said that these had written in them all things that had happened through all the world, even but hours before. I said that to write even one of these sheets would take a clerk many days, but they said that the writing was done in some way very quickly by machines.

"In the broad stone street between the two raised walks were rushing back and forth the strange vehicles I had seen from the window. There was no animal pulling or pushing any one of them, yet they never halted their swift rush, and carried many people at unthinkable speed. Sometimes those who walked stepped before the rushing vehicles, and then from them came terrible warning snarls or moans that made the walkers draw back.

"One of the vehicles stood at the walk's edge before us, and we entered it and sat side by side on a soft leather seat. Thicourt sat behind a wheel on a post, with levers beside him. He touched these and a humming sound came from somewhere in the vehicle and then it too began to rush forward. Faster and faster along the street it went, yet neither of them seemed afraid.

"Many thousands of these vehicles were moving swiftly through the streets about us. We passed on, between great buildings and along wider streets, my eyes and ears numbed by what I saw about me. Then the buildings grew smaller, after we had gone for miles through them, and we were passing through the city's outskirts. I could not believe, hardly, that it was Paris in which I was.

"We came to a great flat and open field outside the city and there Thicourt stopped and we got out of the vehicle. There were big buildings at the field's end, and I saw other vehicles rolling out of them across the field, ones different from any I had yet seen, with flat winglike projections on either side. They rolled out over the field very fast and then I cried out as I saw them rising from the ground into the air. Mother of God, they were flying! The men in them were flying!

"Rastin and Thicourt took me forward to the great buildings. They spoke to men there and one brought forward one of the winged cars. Rastin told me to get in, and though I was terribly afraid, there was too terrible a fascination that drew me in. Thicourt and Rastin entered after me, and we sat in seats with the other man. He had before him levers and buttons, while at the car's front was a great thing like a double-oar or paddle. A loud roaring came and that double-blade began to whirl so swiftly that I could not see it. Then the car rolled swiftly forward, bumping on the ground, and then ceased to bump. I looked down, then shuddered. The ground was already far beneath! I too, was flying in the air!

"We swept upward at terrible speed that increased steadily. The thunder of the car was terrific, and, as the man at the levers changed their position, we curved around and over downward and upward as though birds. Rastin tried to explain to me how the car flew, but it was all too wonderful, and I could not understand. I only knew that a wild thrilling excitement held me, and that it were worth life and death to fly thus, if but for once, as I had always dreamed that men might some day do.

"Higher and higher we went. The earth lay far beneath and I saw now that Paris was indeed a mighty city, its vast mass of buildings stretching away almost to the horizons below us. A mighty city of the future that it had been given my eyes to look on!

"There were other winged cars darting to and fro in the air about us, and they said that many of these were starting or finishing journeys of hundreds of leagues in the air. Then I cried out as I saw a great shape coming nearer us in the air. It was many rods in length, tapering to a point at both ends, a vast ship sailing in the air! There were great cabins on its lower part and in them we glimpsed people gazing out, coming and going inside, dancing even! They told me that vast ships of the air like this sailed to and fro for thousands of leagues with hundreds inside them.

"The huge vessel of the air passed us and then our winged car began to descend. It circled smoothly down to the field like a swooping bird, and, when we landed there, Rastin and Thicourt led me back to the ground-vehicle. It was late afternoon by then, the sun sinking westward, and darkness had descended by the time we rolled back into the great city.

"But in that city was not darkness! Lights were everywhere in it, flashing brilliant lights that shone from its mighty buildings and that blinked and burned and ran like water in great symbols upon the buildings above the streets. Their glare was like that of day! We stopped before a great building into which Rastin and Thicourt led me.

"It was vast inside and in it were many people in rows on rows of seats. I thought it a cathedral at first but saw soon that it was not. The wall at one end of it, toward which all in it were gazing, had on it pictures of people, great in size, and those pictures were moving as though themselves alive! And they were talking one to another, too, as though with living voices! I trembled. What magic!

"With Rastin and Thicourt in seats beside me, I watched the pictures enthralled. It was like looking through a great window into strange worlds. I saw the sea, seemingly tossing and roaring there before me, and then saw on it a ship, a vast ship of size incredible, without sails or oars, holding thousands of people. I seemed on that ship as I watched, seemed moving forward with it. They told me it was sailing over the western ocean that never men had crossed. I feared!

"Then another scene, land appearing from the ship. A great statue, upholding a torch, and we on the ship seemed passing beneath it. They said that the ship was approaching a city, the city of New York, but mists hid all before us. Then suddenly the mists before the ship cleared and there before me seemed the city.

*   *   *   *   *

"Mother of God, what a city! Climbing range on range of great mountain-like buildings that aspired up as though to scale heaven itself! Far beneath narrow streets pierced through them and in the picture we seemed to land from the ship, to go through those streets of the city. It was an incredible city of madness! The streets and ways were mere chasms between the sky-toppling buildings! People—people—people—millions on millions of them rushed through the endless streets. Countless ground-vehicles rushed to and fro also, and other different ones that roared above the streets and still others below them!

"Winged flying-cars and great airships were sailing to and fro over the titanic city, and in the waters around it great ships of the sea and smaller ships were coming as man never dreamed of surely, that reached out from the mighty city on all sides. And with the coming of darkness, the city blazed with living light!

"The pictures changed, showed other mighty cities, though none so terrible as that one. It showed great mechanisms that appalled me. Giant metal things that scooped in an instant from the earth as much as a man might dig in days. Vast things that poured molten metal from them like water. Others that lifted loads that hundreds of men and oxen could not have stirred.

"They showed men of knowledge like Rastin and Thicourt beside me. Some were healers, working miraculous cures in a way that I could not understand. Others were gazing through giant tubes at the stars, and the pictures showed what they saw, showed that all of the stars were great suns like our sun, and that our sun was greater than earth, that earth moved around it instead of the reverse! How could such things be, I wondered. Yet they said that it was so, that earth was round like an apple, and that with other earths like it, the planets, moved round the sun. I heard, but could scarce understand.

"At last Rastin and Thicourt led me out of that place of living pictures and to their ground-vehicle. We went again through the streets to their building, where first I had found myself. As we went I saw that none challenged my right to go, nor asked who was my lord. And Rastin said that none now had lords, but that all were lord, king and priest and noble, having no more power than any in the land. Each man was his own master! It was what I had hardly dared to hope for, in my own time, and this, I thought, was greatest of all the marvels they had shown me!

"We entered again their building but Rastin and Thicourt took me first to another room than the one in which I had found myself. They said that their men of knowledge were gathered there to hear of their feat, and to have it proved to them.

"'You would not be afraid to return to your own time, Henri?' asked Rastin, and I shook my head.

"'I want to return to it,' I told them. 'I want to tell my people there what I have seen—what the future is that they must strive for.'

"'But if they should not believe you?' Thicourt asked.

"'Still I must go—must tell them,' I said.

"Rastin grasped my hand. 'You are a man, Henri,' he said. Then, throwing aside the cloak and hat I had worn outside, they went with me down to the big white-walled room where first I had found myself.

"It was lit brightly now by many of the shining glass things on ceiling and walls, and in it were many men. They all stared strangely at me and at my clothes, and talked excitedly so fast that I could not understand. Rastin began to address them.

"He seemed explaining how he had brought me from my own time to his. He used many terms and words that I could not understand, incomprehensible references and phrases, and I could understand but little. I heard again the names of Einstein and De Sitter that I had heard before, repeated frequently by these men as they disputed with Rastin and Thicourt. They seemed disputing about me.

"One big man was saying, 'Impossible! I tell you, Rastin, you have faked this fellow!'

"Rastin smiled. 'You don't believe that Thicourt and I brought him here from his own time across five centuries?'

"A chorus of excited negatives answered him. He had me stand up and speak to them. They asked me many questions, part of which I could not understand. I told them of my life, and of the city of my own time, and of king and priest and noble, and of many simple things that they seemed quite ignorant of. Some appeared to believe me but others did not, and again their dispute broke out.

"'There is a way to settle the argument, gentlemen,' said Rastin finally.

"'How?' all cried.

"'Thicourt and I brought Henri across five centuries by rotating the time-dimensions at this spot,' he said. 'Suppose we reverse that rotation and send him back before your eyes—would that be proof?'

"They all said that it would. Rastin turned to me. 'Stand on the metal circle, Henri,' he said. I did so.

"All were watching very closely. Thicourt did something quickly with the levers and buttons of the mechanisms in the room. They began to hum, and blue light came from the glass tubes on some. All were quiet, watching me as I stood there on the circle of metal. I met Rastin's eyes and something in me made me call goodbye to him. He waved his hand and smiled. Thicourt pressed more buttons and the hum of the mechanisms grew louder. Then he reached toward another lever. All in the room were tense and I was tense.

"Then I saw Thicourt's arm move as he turned one of the many levers.

"A terrific clap of thunder seemed to break around me, and as I closed my eyes before its shock, I felt myself whirling around and falling at the same time as though into a maelstrom, just as I had done before. The awful falling sensation ceased in a moment and the sound subsided. I opened my eyes. I was on the ground at the center of the familiar field from which I had vanished hours before, upon the morning of that day. It was night now, though, for that day I had spent five hundred years in the future.

"There were many people gathered around the field, fearful, and they screamed and some fled when I appeared in the thunderclap. I went toward those who remained. My mind was full of things I had seen and I wanted to tell them of these things. I wanted to tell them how they must work ever toward that future time of wonder.

"But they did not listen. Before I had spoken minutes to them they cried out on me as a sorcerer and a blasphemer, and seized me and brought me here to the Inquisitor, to you, sire. And to you, sire, I have told the truth in all things. I know that in doing so I have set the seal of my own fate, and that only a sorcerer would ever tell such a tale, yet despite that I am glad. Glad that I have told one at least of this time of what I saw five centuries in the future. Glad that I saw! Glad that I saw the things that someday, sometime, must come to be—"

*   *   *   *   *

It was a week later that they burned Henri Lothiere. Jean de Marselait, lifting his gaze from his endless parchment accusation and examens on that afternoon, looked out through the window at a thick curl of black smoke going up from the distant square.

"Strange, that one," he mused. "A sorcerer, of course, but such a one as I had never heard before. I wonder," he half-whispered, "was there any truth in that wild tale of his? The future—who can say—what men might do—?"

There was silence in the room as he brooded for a moment, and then he shook himself as one ridding himself of absurd speculations. "But tush—enough of these crazy fancies. They will have me for a sorcerer if I yield to these wild fancies and visions *of the future.*"

And bending again with his pen to the parchment before him, he went gravely on with his work.

Monsters of Mars

Originally Published in *Astounding Stories*, April 1931

Monsters Of Mars

Three Martian duped Earth men swing open the gates of space that for so long had barred the greedy hordes of the Red Planet.

Allan Randall stared at the man before him. "And that's why you sent for me, Milton?" he finally asked.

The other's face was unsmiling. "That's why I sent for you, Allan," he said quietly. "To go to Mars with us to night!"

There was a moment's silence, in which Randall's eyes moved as though uncomprehendingly from the face of Milton to those of the two men beside him. The four sat together at the end of a roughly furnished and electric lit living room, and in that momentary silence there came in to them from the outside night the distant pounding of the Atlantic upon the beach. It was Randall who first spoke again.

"To Mars!" he repeated. "Have you gone crazy, Milton—or is this some joke you've put up with Lanier and Nelson here?"

Milton shook his head gravely. "It is not a joke, Allan. Lanier and I are actually going to flash out over the gulf to the planet Mars to night. Nelson must stay here, and since we wanted three to go I wired you as the most likely of my friends to make the venture."

"But good God!" Randall exploded, rising. "You, Milton, as a physicist ought to know better. Space ships and projectiles and all that are but fictionists' dreams."

"We are not going in either space ship or projectile," said Milton calmly. And then as he saw his friend's bewilderment he rose and led the way to a door at the room's end, the other three following him into the room beyond.

*   *   *   *   *

It was a long laboratory of unusual size in which Randall found himself, one in which every variety of physical and electrical apparatus seemed represented. Three huge dynamo motor arrangements took up the room's far end, and from them a tangle of wiring led through square black condensers and transformers to a battery of great tubes. Most remarkable, though, was the object at the room's center.

It was like a great double cube of dull metal, being in effect two metal cubes each twelve feet square, supported a few feet above the floor by insulated standards. One side of each cube was open, exposing the hollow interiors of the two cubical chambers. Other wiring led from the big electronic tubes and from the dynamos to the sides of the two cubes.

The four men gazed at the enigmatic thing for a time in silence. Milton's strong, capable face showed only in its steady eyes what feelings were his, but Lanier's younger countenance was alight with excitement; and so too to some degree was that of Nelson. Randall simply stared at the thing, until Milton nodded toward it.

"That," he said, "is what will flash us out to Mars to night."

Randall could only turn his stare upon the other, and Lanier chuckled. "Can't take it in yet, Randall? Well, neither could I when the idea was first sprung on us."

*   *   *   *   *

Milton nodded to seats behind them, and as the half dazed Randall sank into one the physicist faced him earnestly.

"Randall, there isn't much time now, but I am going to tell you what I have been doing in the last two years on this God forsaken Maine coast. I have been for those two years in unbroken communication by radio with beings on the planet Mars!

"It was when I still held my physics professorship back at the university that I got first onto the track of the thing. I was studying the variation of static vibrations, and in so doing caught steady signals—not static—at an unprecedentedly high wave length. They were dots and dashes of varying length in an entirely unintelligible code, the same arrangement of them being sent out apparently every few hours.

"I began to study them and soon ascertained that they could be sent out by no station on earth. The signals seemed to be growing louder each day, and it suddenly occurred to me that Mars was approaching opposition with earth! I was startled, and kept careful watch. On the day that Mars was closest the earth the signals were loudest. Thereafter, as the red planet receded, they grew weaker. The signals were from some being or beings on Mars!

"At first I was going to give the news to the world, but saw in time that I could not. There was not sufficient proof, and a premature statement would only wreck my own scientific reputation. So I decided to study the signals farther until I had irrefutable proof, and to answer them if possible. I came up here and had this place built, and the aerial towers and other equipment I wanted set up. Lanier and Nelson came with me from the university, and we began our work.

*   *   *   *   *

"Our chief object was to answer those signals, but it proved heartbreaking work at first. We could not produce a radio wave of great enough length to pierce out through earth's insulating layer and across the gulf to Mars. We used all the power of our great windmill dynamo hook ups, but for long could not make it. Every few hours like clockwork the Martian signals came through. Then at last we heard them repeating one of our own signals. We had been heard!

"For a time we hardly left our instruments. We began the slow and almost impossible work of establishing intelligent communication with the Martians. It was with numbers we began. Earth is the third planet from the sun and Mars the fourth, so three represented earth and four stood for Mars. Slowly we felt our way to an exchange of ideas, and within months were in steady and intelligent communication with them.

"They asked us first concerning earth, its climates and seas and continents, and concerning ourselves, our races and mechanisms and weapons. Much information we flashed out to them, the language of our communication being English, the elements, of which they had learned, with a mixture of numbers and symbolical dot dash signals.

"We were as eager to learn about them. They were somewhat reticent, we found, concerning their planet and themselves. They admitted that their world was a dying one and that their great canals were to make life possible on it, and also admitted that they were different in bodily form from ourselves.

"They told us finally that communication like this was too ineffective to give us a clear picture of their world, or vice versa. If we could visit Mars, and then they visit earth, both worlds would benefit by the knowledge of the other. It seemed impossible to me, though I was eager enough for it. But the Martians said that while spaceships and the like were impossible, there was a way by which living beings could flash from earth to Mars and back by radio waves, even as our signals flashed!"

*   *   *   *   *

Randall broke in in amazement. "By radio!" he exclaimed, and Milton nodded.

"Yes, so they said, nor did the idea of sending matter by radio seem too insane, after all. We send sound, music by radio waves across half the world from our broadcasting stations. We send light, pictures, across the world from our television stations. We do that by changing the wave length of the light vibrations to make them radio vibrations, flashing them out thus over the world, to receivers which alter their wave lengths again and change them back into light vibrations.

"Why then could not matter be sent in the same way? Matter, it has been long believed, is but another vibration of the ether, like light and radiant heat and radio vibrations and the like, having a lower wave length than any of the others. Suppose we take matter and by applying electrical force to it change its wave length, step it up to the wave length of radio vibrations? Then those vibrations can be flashed forth from the sending station to a special receiver that will step them down again from radio vibrations to matter vibrations. Thus matter, living or non living, could be flashed tremendous distances in a second!

*   *   *   *   *

"This the Martians told us, and said they would set up a matter transmitter and receiver on Mars and would aid and instruct us so that we could set up a similar transmitter and receiver here. Then part of us could be flashed out to Mars as radio vibrations by the transmitter, and in moments would have flashed across the gulf to the red planet and would be transformed back from radio vibrations to matter vibrations by the receiver awaiting us there!

"Naturally we agreed enthusiastically to build such a matter transmitter and receiver, and then, with their instructions signalled to us constantly, started the work.

Weeks it took, but at last, only yesterday, we finished it. The thing's two cubical chambers are one for the transmitting of matter and the other for its reception. At a time agreed on yesterday we tested the thing, placing a guinea pig in the transmitting chamber and turning on the actuating force. Instantly the animal vanished, and in moments came a signal from the Martians saying that they had received it unharmed in their receiving chamber.

"Then we tested it the other way, they sending the same guinea pig to us, and in moments it flashed into being in our receiving chamber. Of course the step down force in the receiving chamber had to be in operation, since had it not been at that moment the radio vibrations of the animal would have simply flashed on endlessly in endless space. And the same would happen to any of us were we flashed forth and no receiving chamber turned on to receive us.

"We signalled the Martians that all tests were satisfactory, and told them that on the next night at exactly midnight by our time we would flash out ourselves on our first visit to them. They have promised to have their receiving chamber operating to receive us at that moment, of course, and it is my plan to stay there twenty four hours, gathering ample proofs of our visit, and then flash back to earth.

"Nelson must stay here, not only to flash us forth to night, but above all to have the receiving chamber operating to receive us at the destined moment twenty four hours later. The force required to operate it is too great to use for more than a few minutes at a time, so it is necessary above all that that force be turned on and the receiving chamber ready for us at the moment we flash back. And since Nelson must stay, and Lanier and I wanted another, we wired you, Randall, in the hope that you would want to go with us on this venture. And do you?"

*   *   *   *   *

As Milton's question hung, Randall drew a long breath. His eyes were on the two great cubical chambers, and his brain seemed whirling at what he had heard. Then he was on his feet with the others.

"Go? Could you keep me from going? Why, man, it's the greatest adventure in history!"

Milton grasped his hand, as did Lanier, and then the physicist shot a glance at the square clock on the wall. "Well, there's little enough time left us," he said, "for we've hardly an hour before midnight, and at midnight we must be in that transmitting chamber for Nelson to send us flashing out!"

Randall could never recall but dimly afterward how that tense hour passed. It was an hour in which Milton and Nelson went with anxious faces and low voiced comments from one to another of the pieces of apparatus in the room, inspecting each carefully, from the great dynamos to the transmitting and receiving chambers, while Lanier quickly got out and made ready the rough khaki suits and equipment they were to take.

It lacked but a quarter hour of midnight when they had finally donned those suits, each making sure that he was in possession of the small personal kit Milton had designated. This included for each a heavy automatic, a small supply of concentrated foods, and a small case of drugs chosen to counteract the rarer atmosphere and lesser gravity which Milton had been warned to expect on the red planet. Each had also a strong wrist watch, the three synchronized exactly with the big laboratory clock.

*   *   *   *   *

When they had finished checking up on this equipment the clock's longer hand pointed almost to the figure twelve, and the physicist gestured expressively toward the transmitting chamber. Lanier, though, strode

for a moment to one of the laboratory's doors and flung it
open. As Randall gazed out with him they could see far
out over the tossing sea, dimly lit by the great canopy of
the summer stars overhead. Right at the zenith among
those stars shone brightest a crimson spark.

"Mars," said Lanier, his voice a half whisper. "And
they're waiting out there for us now—out there where
we'll be in minutes!"

"And if they shouldn't be waiting—their receiving
chamber not ready—"

But Milton's calm voice came across the room to them:
"Zero hour," he said, stepping up into the big
transmitting chamber.

Lanier and Randall slowly followed, and despite
himself a slight shudder shook the latter's body as he
stepped into the mechanism that in moments would send
him flashing out through the great void as impalpable
ether vibrations. Milton and Lanier were standing silent
beside him, their eyes on Nelson, who stood watchfully
now at the big switchboard beside the chambers, his own
gaze on the clock. They saw him touch a stud, and
another, and the hum of the great dynamos at the room's
end grew loud as the swarming of angry bees.

The clock's longer hand was crawling over the last
space to cover the smaller hand. Nelson turned a knob
and the battery of great glass tubes broke into brilliant
white light, a crackling coming from them. Randall saw
the clock's pointer clicking over the last divisions, and as
he saw Nelson grip a great switch there came over him a
wild impulse to bolt from the transmitting chamber. But
then as his thoughts whirled maelstromlike there came a
clang from the clock and Nelson flung down the switch in
his grasp. Blinding light seemed to break from all the
chamber onto the three; Randall felt himself hurled into
nothingness by forces titanic, inconceivable, and then
knew no more.

*   *   *   *   *

Randall came back to consciousness with a humming sound in his ears and with a sharp pain piercing his lungs at every breath. He felt himself lying on a smooth hard surface, and heard the humming stop and be succeeded by a complete silence. He opened his eyes, drawing himself to his feet as Milton and Lanier were doing, and stared about him.

He was standing with his two friends inside a cubical metal chamber almost exactly the same as the one they had occupied in Milton's laboratory a few moments before. But it was not the same, as their first astounded glance out through its open side told them.

For it was not the laboratory that lay around them, but a vast conelike hall that seemed to Randall's dazed eyes of dimensions illimitable. Its dull gleaming metal walls slanted up for a thousand feet over their heads, and through a round aperture at the tip far above and through great doors in the walls came a thin sunlight. At the center of the great hall's circular floor stood the two cubical chambers in one of which the three were, while around the chambers were grouped masses of unfamiliar looking apparatus.

*   *   *   *   *

To Randall's untrained eyes it seemed electrical apparatus of very strange design, but neither he nor Milton nor Lanier paid it but small attention in that first breathless moment. They were gazing in fascinated horror at the scores of creatures who stood silent amid the apparatus and at its switches, gazing back at them. Those creatures were erect and roughly man like in shape, but they were not human men. They were—the thought blasted to Randall's brain in that horror filled moment—crocodile men.

Crocodile men! It was only so that he could think of them in that moment. For they were terribly like great crocodile shapes that had learned in some way to carry themselves erect upon their hinder limbs. The bodies were not covered with skin, but with green bony plates. The limbs, thick and taloned at their paw ends, seemed greater in size and stronger, the upper two great arms and the lower two the legs upon which each walked, while there was but the suggestion of a tail. But the flat head set on the neckless body was most crocodilian of all, with great fanged, hinged jaws projecting forward, and with dark unwinking eyes set back in bony sockets.

Each of the creatures wore on his torso a gleaming garment like a coat of metal scales, with metal belts in which some had shining tubes. They were standing in groups here and there about the mechanisms, the nearest group at a strange big switch panel not a half dozen feet from the three men. Milton and Lanier and Randall returned in a tense silence the unwinking stare of the monstrous beings around them.

"The Martians!" Lanier's horror filled exclamation was echoed in the next instant by Randall's.

"The Martians! God, Milton! They're not like anything we know—they're reptilian!"

*   *   *   *   *

Milton's hand clutched his shoulder. "Steady, Randall," he muttered. "They're terrible enough, God knows—but remember we must seem just as grotesque to them."

The sound of their voices seemed to break the great hall's spell of silence, and they saw the crocodilian Martians before them turning and speaking swiftly to each other in low hissing speech sounds that were quite unintelligible to the three. Then from the small group nearest them one came forward, until he stood just outside the chamber in which they were.

Randall felt dimly the momentousness of the moment, in which beings of earth and Mars were confronting each other for the first time in the solar system's history. The creature before them opened his great jaws and uttered slowly a succession of sounds that for the moment puzzled them, so different were they from the hissing speech of the others, though with the same sibilance of tone. Again the thing repeated the sounds, and this time Milton uttered an exclamation.

"He's speaking to us!" he cried. "Trying to speak the English that I taught them in our communication! I caught a word—listen...."

As the creature repeated the sounds, Randall and Lanier started to hear also vaguely expressed in that hissing voice familiar words: "You—are Milton and—others from—earth?"

Milton spoke very clearly and slowly to the creature: "We are those from earth," he said. "And you are the Martians with whom we have communicated?"

"We are those Martians," said the other's hissing voice slowly. "These"—he waved a taloned paw toward those behind him—"have charge of the matter transmitter and receiver. I am of our ruler's council."

"Ruler?" Milton repeated. "A ruler of all Mars?"

"Of all Mars," the other said. "Our name for him would mean in your words the Martian Master. I am to take you to him."

*   *   *   *   *

Milton turned to the other two with face alight with excitement. "These Martians have some supreme ruler they call the Martian Master," he said quickly; "and we're to go before him. As the first visitors from earth we're of immense importance here."

As he spoke, the Martian official before them had uttered a hissing call, and in answer to it a long shape of shining metal raced into the vast hall and halted beside them. It was like a fifty foot centipede of metal, its scores of supporting short legs actuated by some mechanism inside the cylindrical body. There was a transparent walled control room at the front end of that body, and in it a Martian at the controls who snapped open a door from which a metal ladder automatically descended.

The Martian official gestured with a reptilian arm toward the ladder, and Milton and Lanier and Randall moved carefully out of the cube chamber and across the floor to it, each of their steps being made a short leap forward by the lesser gravity of the smaller planet. They climbed up into the centipede machine's control room, their guide following, and then as the door snapped shut, the operator of the thing pulled and turned the knob in his grasp and the long machine scuttled forward with amazing smoothness and speed.

In a moment it was out of the building and into the feeble sunlight of a broad metal paved street. About them lay a Martian city, seen by their eager eyes for the first time. It was a city whose structures were giant metal cones like that from which they had just come, though none seemed as large as that titanic one. Throngs of the hideous crocodilian Martians were moving busily to and fro in the streets, while among them there scuttled and flashed numbers of the centipede machines.

*   *   *   *   *

As their strange vehicle raced along, Randall saw that the conelike structures were for the most part divided into many levels, and that inside some could be glimpsed ranks of great mechanisms and hurrying Martians tending them. Away to their right across the vast forest of cones that was the city the sun's little disk was shining, and he glimpsed in that direction higher ground covered with a vast tangle of bright crimson jungle that sloped upward from a great, half glimpsed waterway.

The Martian beside them saw the direction of his gaze and leaned toward him. "No Martians live there," he hissed slowly. "Martians live only in cities where canals meet."

"Then there's no life in those crimson jungles?" Randall asked, repeating the question a moment later more slowly.

"No Martians there, but life—living things," the other told him, searching for words. "But not intelligent, like Martians and you."

He turned to gaze ahead, then pointed. "The Martian Master's cone," he hissed.

The three saw that at the end of the broad metal street down which their vehicle was racing there loomed another titanic cone structure, fully as large as the mighty one in which they first found themselves. As the centipede machine swept up to its great door opening and halted, they descended to the metal paving and then followed their reptilian guide through the opening.

*   *   *   *   *

They found themselves in a great hall in which scores of the Martians were coming and going. At the hall's end stood a row of what seemed guards, Martians grasping shining tubes such as they had already glimpsed. These gave way to allow their passage when their conductor uttered a hissing order, and then they were moving down a shorter hall at whose end also were guards. As these sprang aside before them, a great door of massive metal they guarded moved softly upward, disclosing a mighty circular hall or room inside. Their crocodilian guide turned to them.

"The hall of the Martian Master," he hissed.

They passed inside with him. The great hall seemed to extend upward to the giant cone's tip, thin light coming down from an opening there. Upon the dull metal of its looming walls were running friezes of lighter metal, grotesque representations of reptilian shapes that they could but vaguely glimpse. Around the walls stood rank after rank of guards.

At the hall's center was a low dias, and in a semicircle around and behind it stood a half hundred great crocodilian shapes. Randall guessed even at the moment that they were the council of which their conductor had named himself a member. But like Milton and Lanier, he had eyes in that first moment only for the dais itself. For on it was—the Martian Master.

Randall heard Milton and Lanier choke with the horror that shook his own heart and brain as he gazed. It was not simply another great crocodilian shape that sat upon that dais. It was a monstrous thing formed by the joining of three of the great reptilian bodies! Three distinct crocodile like bodies sitting close together upon a metal seat, that had but a single great head. A great, grotesque crocodilian head that bulged backward and to either side, and that rested on the three thick short necks that rose from the triple body! And that head, that triple bodied thing, was living, its unwinking eyes gazing at the three men!

*   *   *   *   *

The Martian Master! Randall felt his brain reel as he gazed at that mind shattering thing. The Martian Master—this great head with three bodies! Reason told Randall, even as he strove for sanity, that the thing was but logical, that even on earth biologists had formed multiple headed creatures by surgery, and that the Martians had done so to combine in one great head, one great brain, the brains of three bodies. Reason told him that the great triple brain inside that bulging head needed the bloodstreams of all three bodies to nourish it, must be a giant intellect indeed, one fitted to be the supreme Martian Master. But reason could not overcome the horror that choked him as he gazed at the awful thing.

A hissing voice sounding before him made him aware that the Martian Master was speaking.

"You are the Earth beings with whom we communicated, and whom we instructed to build a matter transmitter and receiver on earth?" the slow voice asked. "You have come safely to Mars by means of that station?"

"We have come safely." Milton's voice was shaken and he could find no other words.

"That is well. Long had we desired to have such a station built on earth, since with it there to flash back and forth between the two worlds is easy. You have come, then, to learn of this world and to take back what you learn to your races?"

"That is why we came." Milton said, more steadily. "We want to stay only hours on this first visit, and then flash back to earth as we came."

*   *   *   *   *

The head's awful eyes seemed to consider them. "But when do you intend to go back?" its strange voice asked. "Unless the one at your earth station has its receiver operating at the right moment you will simply flash on endlessly as radio waves—will be annihilated."

Milton found the courage to smile. "We started from earth at our midnight exactly, and at midnight exactly twenty four earth hours later, we are to flash back and the receiver will be awaiting us."

There was silence when he had said that, a silence that seemed to Randall's strained mind to have become suddenly tense, sinister. The great triple bodied creature before them considered them again, its eyes moving over them, and when it again spoke the hissing words came very slowly.

"Twenty four earth hours," it said; "and then your receiver on earth will be awaiting you. That time we can measure to the moment, and that is well. For it is not you three Earth beings who will flash back to earth when that moment comes! It will be Martians, the first of our Martian masses who have waited for ages for that moment and who will begin then our conquest of the earth!

"Yes, Earth beings, our great plan comes to its end now at last! At last! Age on age, prisoned on this dying, arid world, we have desired the earth that by right of power shall be ours, have sought for ages to communicate with its beings. You finally heard us, you hearkened to us, you built the matter transmitting and receiving station on earth that was the one thing needed for our plan. For when the matter receiver of that station is turned on in twenty four of your hours, and ready to receive matter flashes from here, it will be the first of our millions who will flash at last to earth!

"I, the Martian Master, say it. Those first to go shall seize that matter receiver on earth when first they appear there, shall build other and larger receivers, and through them within days all our Martian hordes shall have been flashed to earth! Shall have poured out over it and conquered with our weapons your weak races of Earth beings, who cannot stand before us, and whose world you have delivered at last into our hands!"

For a moment, when the great monster's hissing voice had ceased, Milton and Randall and Lanier gazed toward it as though petrified, the whole unearthly scene spinning about them. And then, through the thick silence, the thin sound of Milton's voice:

"Our world—our earth—delivered to the Martians, and by us! God—no!"

With that last cry of agonized comprehension and horror, Milton did what surely had never any in the great hall expected, leaped onto the dais with a single spring toward the Martian Master! Randall heard a hundred wild hissing cries break from about him, saw the crocodilian forms of guards and council rushing forward even as he and Lanier sprang after Milton, and then glimpsed shining tubes levelled from which brilliant shafts of dazzling crimson light or force were stabbing toward them!

*　　*　　*　　*　　*

To Randall the moment that followed was but a split second flash and whirl of action. As his earthly muscles took him forward with Lanier after Milton in a great leap to the dais, he was aware of the brilliant red rays stabbing behind him closely, and knew that only the tremendous size of his leap had taken him past them. In the succeeding instant he was made aware of what he had escaped, for the hastily loosed rays struck squarely a group of three or four Martian guards rushing to the dais from the opposite side, and they vanished from view with a sharp detonation as though clicked out of existence!

Randall was not to know then, that the red rays were ones that annihilated matter by neutralizing or damping the matter vibrations in the ether. But he did know that no more rays were loosed, for by then he and Milton and Lanier were on the dais and were wrapped in a hurricane combat with the guards that had rushed between them and the Martian Master.

Gleaming fangs—great scaled forms—reaching talons—it was all a wild phantasmagoria of grotesque forms spinning around him as he struck with all the power of his earthly muscles and felt crocodilian forms staggering and going down beneath his frenzied blows. He heard the roar of an automatic close beside him in the melee as Milton remembered at last through the red haze of his fury the weapon he carried, but before either Randall or Lanier could reach their own weapons a new wave of crocodilian forms had poured onto them that by sheer pressing weight held them helpless, to be disarmed.

*　　*　　*　　*　　*

Hissing orders sounded, the arms and legs of the three were tightly grasped by great taloned paws, and the masses of Martians about them melted back from the dais. Held each by two great creatures, Milton and Randall and Lanier faced again the triple bodied Martian Master, who in all that wild moment of struggle appeared not to have changed his position. The big monster's black eyes stared unmovedly down at them.

"You Earth beings seem of lower intelligence even than we thought," his hissing voice informed them. "And those weapons—crude, very crude."

Milton, his face set, spoke back: "It may be that you will find human weapons of some power if your hordes reach earth," he said.

"But what compared with the power of ours?" the other asked coldly. "And since our scientists even now devise new weapons to annihilate the earth's races, I think they would be glad of three of those races to experiment with now. The one use we can make of you, certainly."

The creature turned its bulging head a little towards the guards who held the three men, and uttered a brief hissing order. Instantly the six Martians, grasping the three tightly, marched them across the great hall and through a different door than that by which they had entered.

They were taken down a narrow corridor that turned sharply twice as they went on. Randall saw that it was lit by squares inset in the walls that glowed with crimson light. It came to him as they marched on that night must be upon the Martian city without, since the sun had been sinking when they had crossed it in the centipede machine.

*   *   *   *   *

Through what seemed an ante room they were taken, and then into a long hall instantly recognizable as a laboratory. There were many glowing squares illuminating it, and narrow windows high in the wall gave them a glimpse of the city outside, a pattern of crimson lights. Long metal tables and racks filled the big room's farther end, while along the walls were ranged shining mechanisms of unfamiliar and grotesque appearance. Fully a score of the crocodilian Martians were busy in the room, some intent on their work at the racks and tables, others operating some of the strange machines.

The guards conducted the three to an open space by the wall, below one of the high window openings and between two great cylindrical mechanisms. Then, while five of their number held the three men prisoned in that space by the threat of their levelled ray tubes, the other moved toward one of the busy Martian scientists and held with him a brief interchange of hissing speech.

Milton leaned to whisper to the other two: "We've got to get out of this while we're still living," he whispered. "You heard the Martian Master—in constructing that matter receiver on earth, we've opened a door through which all the Martian millions will pour onto our world!"

"It's useless, Milton," said Randall dully. "Even if we got clear of this the Martians will be at their matter transmitter in hordes when the moment comes to flash back to earth."

"I know that, but we've got to try," the other insisted. "If we or some of us could get clear of this, we might in some way hide near the matter transmitter until the moment came and then fight to it."

"But how to get out of the hands of these, even?" asked Lanier, nodding toward the alert guards before them.

*   *   *   *   *

"There's but one way," Milton whispered swiftly. "Our earthly muscles would enable us, I think, to get through this window opening above us in a leap, if we had a moment's chance. Well, whichever of us they take to experiment with or examine first, must make a struggle or disturbance that will turn the guards' attention for a moment and give the other two a chance to make the attempt!"

"One to stay and the other two to get away...." Randall said slowly; but Milton's tense whisper interrupted:

"It's the only way, and even then a thousand to one chance! But it's we who have opened this gate for the Martian invasion of our world and it's we who must—"

Before he could finish, the approach of hissing voices told them that the leader of the six guards and the Martian who seemed the chief of the experimenters in the hall were nearing them. The three men stood silent and tense as the two crocodilian monsters stopped before them. The scientist, who carried in his metal belt, instead of a ray tube a compact case of instruments, surveyed them as though in curiosity.

He came closer, his quick reptilian eyes taking in with evident interest every feature of their bodily appearance. Intuitively the three knew that one of them was to be chosen for a first investigation by the Martian scientists, and that that one would have not even the slender hope of escape open to the other two. A strange lottery of life and death!

*   *   *   *   *

Randall saw the creature's gaze turn from one to another of them, and then heard the hiss of his voice as he pointed a taloned paw toward Milton. Instantly two of the guards had seized Milton and had jerked him out from the wall, the other guards holding back Randall and Lanier with threatening tubes. It was upon Milton that the fatal choice had fallen!

Randall and Lanier made together a half movement forward, but Milton, a tense message in his eyes, forced them back. The guards who held the physicist led him, at the direction of the Martian scientist, toward a great upright frame at the room's far end, upon which were clustered a score of dial indicators. From these flexible cords led; and now the scientists began attaching these by clips to various spots on Milton's body. Some mechanical examination of his bodily characteristics were apparently to be made. Milton shot suddenly a glance at the two by the wall, and his head nodded in an almost imperceptible signal. The muscles of Lanier and Randall tensed.

Then abruptly Milton seemed to go mad. He shouted aloud in a terrible voice, and at the same moment tore from him the cords just attached, his fists striking out then at the amazed Martians around him. As they leaped back from that sudden explosion of activity and sound on Milton's part the guards before Randall and Lanier whirled instinctively for an instant toward it. And in that instant the two had leaped.

*   *   *   *   *

It was upward they leaped, with all the force of their earthly muscles, toward the big window opening a half dozen feet in the wall above them. Like released steel springs they sat up, and Randall heard the thump of their feet as they struck the opening's sill, heard wild cries suddenly coming from beneath them, as the guards turned back toward them. Crimson rays clove up like light toward them, but the instant's surprise had been enough, and in it they had leaped on and through the opening, into the outside night!

As they shot downward and struck the metal paving outside, Randall heard a wild babble of cries from inside. A moment he and Lanier gazed frenziedly around them, then were running with great leaps along the base of the building from which they had just escaped.

In the darkness of night the Martian city stretched away to their right, its massive dark cone structures outlined by points of glowing ruddy light here and there upon them. Beside the city's metal streets were illuminated by the brilliant field of stars overhead and by the soft light of the two moons, one much larger than the other, that moved among those stars.

Along the street crocodilian Martians were coming and going still, though in small numbers, there being but few in sight in the dim lit street's length. Lanier pointed ahead as they leaped onward.

"Straight onward, Randall!" he jerked. "There seem fewer of the Martians this way!"

"But the great cone of the matter station is the other way!" Randall exclaimed.

"We can't risk making for it now!" cried the other. "We've got to keep clear of them until the alarm is over. Hear them now?"

For even as they leaped forward a rising clamor of hissing cries and rush of feet was coming from behind as scores of Martians poured out into the darkness from the great cone building. The two fugitives had passed by then from the shadow of the mighty structure, and as they ran along the broad metal street toward the shadow of the next cone, through the light of the moons above, they heard higher cries and then glimpsed narrow shafts of crimson force cleaving the night around them.

*   *   *   *   *

Randall, as the deadly rays drove past him, heard the low detonating sound made by their destruction of the air in their path, and the inrush of new air. But in the misty and uncertain moonlight the rays could not be loosed accurately, and before they could be swept sidewise to annihilate the two fleeing men they had gained, with a last great leap, the shadow of the next building.

On they ran, the clatter of the Martian pursuit growing more noisy behind them. Randall heard Lanier gasping with each great leap, and felt himself at every breath a knife of pain stabbing through his lungs, the rarified atmosphere of the red planet taking its toll. Again from the darkness behind them the crimson rays clove, but this time were wide of their mark.

With every moment the clamor of pursuit seemed growing louder, the alarm spreading out over the Martian city and arousing it. As they raced past cone after cone, Randall knew even the increased power of their muscles could not long aid them against the exhaustion which the thin air was imposing on them. His thoughts spun for a moment to Milton, in the laboratory behind, and then back to their own desperate plight.

Abruptly shapes loomed in the misty light before them! A group of three great Martians, reptilian shapes that had been coming toward them and had stopped for an instant in amazement at sight of the running pair. There was no time to halt themselves, to evade the three, and with a mutual instinct Lanier and Randall seized together the last expedient open to them. They ran straight forward toward the astounded three, and when a half score feet from them, leaped with all their force upward and toward them, their tensed bodies flying through the air with feet outstretched before them.

Then they had struck the group of three with feet foremost, and with the impetus of that great leap had knocked them sprawling to this side and that, while with a supreme effort the two kept their balance and leaped on. The cries of the three added to the din behind them as they threw themselves forward.

*   *   *   *   *

They flung themselves past a last cone building to halt for an instant in utter amazement despite the nearing pursuit. Before them were no more streets and structures, but a huge smooth flowing waterway! It gleamed in the moonlight and lay at right angles across their path, seeming to flow along the Martian city's edge.

"A canal!" cried Lanier. "It's one of the canals that meet at this city and flow around it! We're trapped—we've reached the city's edge!"

"Not yet!" Randall gasped. "Look!"

As he pointed to the left Lanier shot a glance there; and then both of them were running in that direction, along the smooth metal paving that bordered the mighty canal. They came to what Randall had seen, a mighty metal arch that soared out over the waterway to its opposite side. A bridge!

They were on it, were racing up the smooth incline of it. Randall glanced back as they reached the arch's summit. From that height the city stretched far away behind them, a lace of crimson lights in the night. He glimpsed the gleam of the giant waterway that encircled the city completely, one that was fed by other canals from far away that emptied into it, the great city's vital water supply brought thus from this world's melting polar snows.

There were moving lights behind now, too, pouring out onto the metal paving by the waterway, moving to and fro as though in confusion, with a babel of hissing cries. It was not until Randall and Lanier were running down the descending incline of the great arched bridge, though, that the lights and shouts of their pursuers began to move up on that bridge after them.

*   *   *   *   *

Running off the bridge's smooth way, the two found themselves stumbling on through the darkness over more metal paving, and then over soft ground. There were no lights or buildings or sounds of any sort on this farther side of the great waterway. A tall dark wall seemed suddenly to loom up out of the darkness some distance ahead of the two.

"The crimson jungle!" Randall cried. "The jungles we glimpsed from the city! It's a chance to hide!"

They raced toward the protecting blackness of that wall of vegetation. They reached it, flung themselves inside, just as the pursuing Martians, a mass of running crocodilian shapes and of great racing centipede machines, swept up over the bridge's arch behind. A moment the two halted in the thick vegetation's shelter, gasping for breath, then were moving forward through the jungle's denser darkness.

Thick about them and far above them towered the masses of strange trees and plant life through which they made their way. Randall could see but dimly the nature of these plant forms, but could make out that they were grotesque and unearthly in appearance, all leafless, and with masses of thin tendrils branching from them instead of leaves. He realized that it was only beside the arid planet's great canals that this profusion of plant life had sufficient moisture for existence, and that it was the broad bands of jungle bordering the canals that had made the latter visible to earth's astronomers.

* * * * *

Lanier and he halted for a moment to listen. The thick jungle about them seemed quite silent. But from behind there came through it a vague tumult of hissing calls; and then, as they glimpsed red flashes far behind, they heard the crashing of great masses of the leafless trees.

"The rays!" whispered Lanier. "They're beating through the jungle with them and the centipede machines after us!"

They paused no more, but pushed on through the thick growths with renewed urgency. Now and then, as they passed through small clearings, Randall glimpsed overhead the fast moving nearer moon and slower sailing farther moon of Mars, moving across the steady stars. In some of these clearings they saw, too, strange great openings burrowed in the ground as though by some strange animal.

The crashing clamor of the Martians beating the jungle behind was coming close, ever closer, and as they came to still another misty lit clearing, Lanier paused, with face white and tense.

"They're closing in on us!" he said. "They're hunting us down by beating the jungle with those centipede machines, and even if we escape them we're getting farther from the city and the matter station each moment!"

Randall's eyes roved desperately around the clearing; and then, as they fell on a group of the great burrowed openings that seemed present everywhere about them, he uttered an exclamation.

"These holes! We can hide in one until they've passed over us, and then steal back to the city!"

Lanier's eyes lit. "It's a chance!"

*   *   *   *   *

They sprang toward the openings. They were each of some four feet diameter, extending indefinitely downward as though the mouths of tunnels. In a moment Randall was lowering himself into one, Lanier after him. The tunnel in which they were, they found, curved to one side a few feet below the surface. They crawled down this curve until they were out of sight of the opening above. They crouched silent, then, listening.

There came down to them the dull, distant clamor of the centipede machines crashing through the jungle, cutting a way with rays, their clamor growing ever louder. Then Randall, who was lowest in the tunnel, turned suddenly as there came to him a strange rustling sound from *beneath* him. It was as though some crawling or creeping thing was moving in the tunnel below them!

He grasped the arm of Lanier, beside and a little above him, to warn him, but the words he was about to whisper never were uttered. For at this moment a big shapeless living thing seemed to flash up toward them through the darkness from beneath, cold ropelike tentacles gripped both tightly; and then in an instant they were being dragged irresistibly down into the lightless tunnel's depths!

*　*　*　*　*

As they were pulled swiftly downward into the tunnel by the tentacles that grasped them an involuntary cry of horror came from Randall and Lanier alike. They twisted frantically in the cold grip that held them, but found it of the quality of steel. And as Randall twisted in it to strike frantically down through the darkness at whatever thing of horror held them, his clenched fist met but the cold smooth skin of some big, soft bodied creature!

Down—down—remorselessly they were being drawn farther into the black depths of the tunnel by the great thing crawling down below them. Again and again the two twisted and struck, but could not shake its hold. In sheer exhaustion they ceased to struggle, dragged helplessly farther down.

Was it minutes or hours, Randall wondered afterward, of that horrible progress downward, that passed before they glimpsed light beneath? A feeble glow, hardly discernible, it was, and as they went lower still he saw that it was caused by the tunnel passing through a strata of radio active rock that gave off the faint light. In that light they glimpsed for the first time the horror dragging them downward.

It was a huge worm creature! A thing like a giant angleworm, three feet or more in thickness and thrice that in length, its great body soft and cold and worm like. From the end nearest them projected two long tentacles with which it had gripped the two men and was dragging them down the tunnel after it! Randall glimpsed a mouth aperture in the tentacled end of the worm body also, and two scarlike marks above it, placed like eyes, although eyes the monstrous thing had not.

*   *   *   *   *

But a moment they glimpsed it and then were in darkness again as the tunnel passed through the radio active strata and lower. The horror of that moment's glimpse, though, made them strike out in blind repulsion, but relentlessly the creature dragged them after it.

"God!" It was Lanier's panting cry as they were dragged on. "This worm monster—we're hundreds of feet below the surface!"

Randall sought to reply, but his voice choked. The air about them was close and damp, with an overpowering earthy smell. He felt consciousness leaving him.

A gleam of soft light—they were passing more radio active patches. He felt the wild convulsive struggles of Lanier against the thing; and then suddenly the tunnel ended, debouched into a far stretching, low ceilinged cavity. It was feebly illuminated by radio active patches here and there in walls and ceiling, and as the monster that held them halted on entering the cavity, Randall and Lanier lay in its grip and stared across the weird place with intensified horror.

For it was swarming with countless worm monsters! All were like the one who held them, thick long worm bodies with projecting tentacles and with black eyeless faces. They were crawling to and fro in this cavern far beneath the surface, swarming in hordes around and over each other, pouring in and out of the awful place from countless tunnels that led upward and downward from it!

*   *   *   *   *

A world of worm monsters, beneath the surface of the Martian jungles! As Randall stared across that swarming, dim lit cave of horror, physically sick at sight of it, he remembered the countless tunnel openings they had glimpsed in their flight through the jungle, and remembered the remark of the Martian who had first guided them across the city, that in the jungles were living things, of a sort. These were the things, worm monsters whose unthinkable networks of tunnels and burrows formed beneath the surface a veritable worm world!

"Randall!" It was Lanier's thick exclamation. "Randall—those scar marks on their—faces—you see—?"

"See?"

"Those marks! These creatures had eyes once but must have been forced down here by the Martians. These may once have been—ages ago—human!"

At that thought Randall felt horror overcoming his senses. He was aware that the great worm monster holding them was dragging them forward through the cavern, that others of the swarms there were crowding around them, feeling them blindly with their tentacles, helping to drag them forward.

Half carried and half dragged they went, scores of tentacles now holding them, great worm shapes crawling forward on all sides of them and accompanying them along the cavern's length. He glimpsed worm monsters here and there emerging from the upward tunnels with masses of strange plant stuff in their grasp that others blindly devoured. His senses reeled from the suffocating air, the great cavity being but a half score feet in height, burrowed from the damp earth by these numberless things.

*   *   *   *   *

The faint, strange light of the radio active patches showed him that they were approaching the cavern's end. Tunnels opened from its end as from all its walls and floor, and into one Randall was dragged by the creatures, one before and one behind, grasping him, and Lanier being brought behind him in the same way. In the close tunnel the heavy air was deadly, and he was but partly conscious when again, after moments of crawling along it, he felt himself dragged out into another cavern.

This earth walled cavity, though, seemed to extend farther than the first, though of the same height as the first and with a few radio active illuminating patches. In it seethed and swarmed literally hundreds on hundreds of the worm monsters, a sea of great crawling bodies. Randall and Lanier saw that they were being carried and dragged now toward the farther end of this larger cavity.

As they approached it, pushing through the swarming creatures who felt them with inquisitive tentacles as their captors took them forward, the two men saw that a great shape was looming up in the faint light at the cave's far end. In moments they were close enough to discern its nature, and a horror and awe filled them at sight of it more intense than they had yet felt.

For the looming shape was a huge earthen image or statue of a worm! It was shaped with a childish crudeness from the solid earth, a giant earthen worm shape whose body looped across the cave's end, and whose tentacled head or front end was reared upward to the cavity's roof. Before this awful earthen shape was a section of the cave's floor higher than the rest, and on it a great crudely shaped rectangular earthen block.

"Lanier—that shape!" whispered Randall in his horror. "That earthen image, made by these creatures—it's the worm god they've made for themselves!"

"A worm god!" Lanier repeated, staring toward it as they were dragged nearer. "Then that block...."

"Its altar!" Randall exclaimed. "These things have some dim spark of intelligence or memory! They're brought us here to—"

*   *   *   *   *

Before he could finish, the clutching tentacles of the worm monsters about them had dragged them up onto the raised floor beside the block, beneath the looming earthen worm shape. There they glimpsed for the first time in the faint light another who stood there held tightly by the tentacles of two worm monsters. It was a Martian!

The big crocodilian shape was apparently a prisoner like themselves, captured and brought down from above. His reptilian eyes surveyed Lanier and Randall quickly as they were dragged up and held beside him, but he took no other interest. To the two men, at the moment, it seemed that his great crocodilian shape was human, almost, so much more man like was it than the grotesque worm monsters before them.

With a half dozen of the creatures holding the two men and the Martian tightly, another great worm monster crawled to the edge of the raised earth floor in front of the giant worm god's image, and then reared up the first third of his thick body into the air. By then the great, faint lit cavity stretching before them was filled with countless numbers of the monsters, pouring into it from all the tunnels that opened into it from above and below, packing it thick with their grotesque bodies as far as the eye could reach in the dim light.

They were seething and crawling in that great mass; but as the worm monster on the elevation upreared, all in the cavity seemed suddenly to quiet. Then the upreared eyeless thing began to move his long tentacles. Very slowly at first he waved them back and forth, and slowly the masses of monsters in the cavity, all turned by some sense toward him, did likewise, the cavity becoming a forest of upraised tentacles waving rhythmically back and forth in unison with those of the leader.

*   *   *   *   *

Back and forth—back and forth—Randall felt caught in some torturing nightmare as he watched the countless tentacle feelers waving thus from one side to the other. It was a ceremony, he knew—some strange rite springing perhaps from dim memory alone, that these worm monsters carried out thus before the looming shape of their worm god. Only the six that held the three captives never relaxed their grip.

Still on and on went the strange and senseless rite. By then the close, damp air of that cavity far beneath Mars' surface was sinking Randall and Lanier deeper into a half consciousness. The Martian beside them never moved or spoke. The upstretched tentacles of the leader and of the great worm horde before him never ceased swaying rhythmically from side to side.

Randall, half hypnotized by those swaying tentacles and but semi conscious by then, could only estimate afterward how long that grotesque rite went on. Hours it must have endured, he knew, hours in which each opening of his eyes revealed only the dimly illuminated cavern, the worm monsters that filled it, the forest of tentacles waving in unison. It was only toward the end of those hours that he noticed vaguely that the tentacles were waving faster and faster.

And as the tentacles of leader and worm horde waved alike ever more swiftly an atmosphere of growing excitement and expectation seemed to hold the horde. At last the upstretched feelers were whipping back and forth almost too swiftly for the eye to follow. Then abruptly the worm leader ceased the motion himself, and while the horde before him continued it, turned and crawled to the three captives.

*   *   *   *   *

In an instant, at though in answer to a second command, the two worm monsters who held the Martian dragged him forward toward the great earthen block before the worm god's image. Two others of the creatures came from the side, and the four swiftly stretched the Martian flat on the block's top, each of the four grasping with their tentacles one of his four taloned limbs. They seemed to hesitate then, the worm leader beside them, the tentacles of the horde waving swiftly still.

Abruptly the tentacles of the leader flashed up as though in a signal. There was a dull ripping sound, and in that moment Randall and Lanier saw the Martian on the block torn literally limb from limb by the four great worm monsters who had held his four limbs!

The tentacles of the horde waved suddenly with increased, excited swiftness at that. Randall shrank in horror.

"They've brought us here for that!" he cried. "To sacrifice us on that altar that way to their worm god!"

But Lanier too had cried out, appalled, as he saw that awful sacrifice, and both strained madly against the grip of the worm creatures. Their struggles were in vain, and then in answer to another unspoken command the two monsters that held Randall were dragging him also to the earthen altar!

He felt himself gripped by the four great creatures around the block, felt as he struggled with his last strength that he was being stretched out on the block, each of the four at one of its corners grasping one of his limbs. He heard Lanier's mad cries as though from a great distance, glimpsed as he was held thus on his back the great shape of the earthen worm god reared over him, and then glimpsed the leader of the monsters rearing beside him.

* * * * *

The dull sound of the swift waving tentacles of the horde came to him, there was a tense moment of agony of waiting, and then the tentacles of the leader flashed up in the signal!

But at the same moment Randall felt his limbs released by the four monsters that had held them! There seemed sudden wild confusion in the great cave. The strange rite broke off; the horde of worm monsters crawled frantically this way and that in it. Randall slipped off the block; staggered to his feet.

The worm monsters in the cave were swarming toward the downward tunnel openings! The two captives forgotten, the creatures were pouring in crawling, fighting swarms toward those openings. And then, as Randall and Lanier stared stupefied, there came a red flash from one of the upward tunnels and a brilliant crimson ray stabbed down and mowed a path of annihilation in the cave's earthen side!

The two heard great thumping sounds from above, saw the tunnels leading from above becoming suddenly many times greater in size as red rays flashed down along them to gouge the tunnel's walls. Then down from those enlarged tunnels there were bursting long shining shapes, great centipede machines crawling down the tunnels which their rays made larger before them! And as the centipede machines burst down into the cavern their crimson rays stabbed right and left to cut paths of annihilation among the worms.

"The Martians!" Lanier cried. "They didn't find us above—they knew we must have been taken by these things—and they've come down after us!"

*   *   *   *   *

"Back, Lanier!" Randall shouted. "Quick, before they see us, behind this—"

As he spoke he was jerking Lanier with him behind the looming earthen statue of the great worm god. Crouched there between the statue and the cave's wall they were hidden precariously from the view of those in the cavern. And now that cavern had become a scene of horror unthinkable as the centipede machines pouring down into it blasted the frantically crawling worm monsters with their rays.

The worm monsters attempted no resistance, but sought only to escape into their downward tunnels, and in moments those not caught by the rays had vanished in the openings. But the centipede machines, after racing swiftly around the cavity, were following them, were going down into those downward tunnels also, their rays blasting down ahead of each to make the tunnel large enough for them to follow.

In a moment all but one had vanished down into the openings, the remaining one having its front or head jammed in one of the openings from the failure of its operator to blast a large enough opening before him. As Lanier and Randall watched tensely they saw the machine's control room door open and a Martian descend. He inspected the tunnel opening in which his vehicle was jammed, then with a hand ray tube began to disintegrate the earth around that opening to free his machine.

Randall clutched his companion's arm. "That machine!" he whispered. "If we could capture it, it would give us a chance to get back to the city—to Milton and the matter transmitter!"

Lanier started, then nodded swiftly. "We'll chance it," he whispered. "For our twenty four hours here must be almost up."

* * * * *

They hesitated a moment, then crept forward from behind the great earthen statue. The Martian had his back to them, his attention on the freeing of his mechanism. Across the dim lit cavern they crept softly, and were within a dozen feet of the Martian when some sound made him wheel quickly to confront them with the deadly tube. But even as he whirled the two had leaped.

The force of their leap sent them flying through that dozen feet of space to strike the Martian at the moment his tube levelled. One hissing call he uttered as they struck him, and then with all his strength Lanier had grasped the crocodilian body and bent it backward. Something in it snapped, and the Martian collapsed limply. The two looked wildly around.

Nothing showed that the Martian's call had been heard, and after a moment's glance that showed the head of the centipede machine already freed, they were clambering up into its control room, closing the door. Randall seized the knob with which he had seen the machines operated. As he pulled it toward him the machine moved across the tunnel opening and raced smoothly over the cavern's floor. As he turned the knob the machine turned swiftly in the same direction.

He headed the long mechanism toward one of the upward curving tunnels which the Martians had blasted larger in descending. They were almost to it when there flashed up into the cavity from one of the downward tunnel openings a centipede machine, and then another, and another. The Martians in their transparent windowed control rooms took in at a glance the dead crocodilian on the floor, and then the three great machines were darting toward that of Randall and Lanier.

"The Martian we killed!" Randall cried. "They heard his call and are coming after us!"

"Turn to the wall!" Lanier shouted to him. "I have the rays—"

*   *   *   *   *

At that moment there was a clicking beside Randall and he glimpsed Lanier pulling forth two small grips he had found, then saw that two crimson rays were stabbing from tubes in their machine's front toward the others even as their own rays darted back. The beams that had been loosed toward them grazed past them as Randall whirled their machine to the wall, and he saw one of the three attacking mechanisms vanish as Lanier's beams struck it.

Around—back—with instinctive, lightninglike motions he whirled their centipede machine in the great dim lit cave as the two remaining ones leapt again to the attack. Their rays shot right and left to catch the two men's vehicle in a trap of death, and as Randall swung their own mechanism straight ahead he glimpsed at the cavern's far end the great earthen worm god still upreared.

On either side of them the red beams burned as they leapt forward, but as though running a gauntlet of death Randall kept the machine racing forward in the succeeding second until the two others loomed on either side of it. Then Lanier's beams were driving in turn to right and left of them and the two vanished as though by magic as they were struck.

"Up to the surface!" Lanier cried, his eyes on the glowing dial of his wrist watch. "We've been held hours here—we've but a half hour or more before earth midnight!"

*   *   *   *   *

Randall sent their machine racing again toward one of the upward tunnels, and as the long mechanism began to climb smoothly up the darkness he heard Lanier agonizing beside him.

"God, if we have only enough time to get to that matter transmitter before the Martians start flashing to earth through it!"

"But Milton?" Randall cried. "We don't know whether he's alive or dead! We can't leave him!"

"We must!" said Lanier solemnly. "Our duty's to the earth now, man, to the world that we alone can save from the Martian invasion and conquest! At the hour of twelve Nelson will have the matter receiver turned on and at that hour the Martian will start flashing to earth—unless we prevent!"

Suddenly Randall grasped the knob in his hands more tightly as light showed above them. They had been climbing upward through the enlarged tunnel at their machine's highest speed, and now as the tunnel curved the light grew stronger. Suddenly they were emerging into the thin sunlight of the Martian day.

In the crimson jungle about them were many Martians, milling excitedly to and fro, and other centipede machines that were blasting their way down through tunnels to the worm world beneath.

Randall and Lanier, breathless, crouched low in the transparent windowed control room as they sent their mechanism racing through this scene of swarming activity. Both gasped as one of the centipede machines clashed against their own in passing, its Martian driver turning to stare after them. But there came no alarm, and in a moment they had passed out of the swarm of Martians and machines and were heading through the jungle in the direction of the city.

* * * * *

Through the weird red vegetation their mechanism raced with them, Randall holding it at its highest speed, and in minutes they came out of the jungle and were racing over the clear space between it and the great canal. Beyond that canal loomed into the thin sunlight the clustering cones of the mighty Martian city, two towering above all the others—the cone of the Martian Master and the other cone in which the matter transmitter and receiver.

It was toward the latter that Lanier pointed. "Head straight toward that cone, Randall—we've but minutes left!"

They were racing now up over the great arch of the canal's metal bridge, and then scuttling smoothly off it and along the broad metal street through which they had fled in darkness hours before. In it Martians and centipede machines were coming and going in great numbers, but none noticed the human forms of the two crouched low in their mechanism's control room.

They were rushing then toward the looming cone of the Martian Master. As they flashed past it Randall saw Lanier's face working, knew the desire that tore at him even as at himself to burst inside and ascertain whether or not Milton still lived in the laboratories from which they had fled. But they were past it, faces white and grim, were rushing on through the Martian city at reckless speed toward the other mighty cone.

*   *   *   *   *

It seemed that all in the great city were heading toward the same goal, streams of crocodilian Martians and masses of shining centipede machines filling the streets as they moved toward it. As they came closer to the mighty structure, hearts pounding, they saw that around it surged a mighty mass of Martians and machines. The hordes waiting to be released through the matter transmitter inside upon the unsuspecting earth!

"Try to get the machine inside!" Lanier whispered tensely. "If we can smash that transmitter yet...."

Randall nodded grimly. "Keep ready at the ray tubes," he told the other.

As unobtrusively as possible he sent their long mechanism worming forward through the vast throng of machines and Martians, toward the great cone's door. Crouching low, the hands of their watches closing fast toward the twelfth figure, they edged forward in the long machine. At last they were moving through the mighty door, into the cone's interior.

They moved slowly on through the mass of machines and crocodile forms inside, then halted. For at the great crowd's center was a clear circle hundreds of feet across, and as Randall gazed across it his heart seemed to leap once and then stop.

At the center of that clear circle rose the two cubical metal chambers of the matter transmitter and receiver. The transmitting chamber, they saw, was flooded with humming force, with white light pouring from its inner walls. It was already in operation, and the masses of Martians in the great cone were only waiting for the moment to sound when the receiver on earth would be operating also. Then they would pour into the chamber to be flashed in masses across the gulf to earth! The eyes of all in the cone seemed turned toward an erect dial mechanism beside the chambers which was clocklike in appearance, and that would mark the moment when the first Martian could enter the transmitting chamber and flash out.

*　　*　　*　　*　　*

A little distance from the two metal chambers stood a low dais on which there sat the hideous triple bodied form of the Martian Master. Around him were the massed members of his council, waiting like him for the start of their age planned invasion of earth. And beside the dais was a figure between two crocodilian guards at sight of whom Randall forgot all else.

"Milton! My God, Lanier, it's Milton!"

"Milton! They've brought him here to torture or kill him if they find he's lied about the moment they could flash to earth!"

Milton! And at sight of him something snapped in Randall's brain.

With a single motion of the knob he sent their centipede machine crashing out into the clear circle at the mighty cone's center. A wild uproar of hissing cries broke from all the thousands in it as he sent the mechanism whirling toward the dais of the Martian Master. He saw the crocodilian forms there scattering blindly before him, and then as his rays drove out and spun and stabbed in mad figures of crimson death through the astounded Martian masses he saw Milton looking up toward them, crying out crazily to them as his two guards loosed him for the moment.

A high call from the Martian Master ripped across the hall and was answered by a shattering roar of hissing voices as Martians and machines surged madly toward them. Randall and Lanier in a single leap were out of the centipede machine, and in an instant had half dragged Milton with them in a great leap up to the edge of the humming transmitting chamber.

*   *   *   *   *

Milton was shouting hoarsely to them over the wild uproar. To enter that transmitting chamber before the destined moment was annihilation, to be flashed out with no receiver on earth awaiting them. They turned, struck with all their strength at the first Martians rushing up to them. No rays flashed, for a ray loosed would destroy the chamber behind them that was the one gate for the Martians to the world they would invade. But as the Martian Master's high call hissed again all the countless crocodilian forms in the great cone were rushing toward them.

Braced at the very edge of the humming, light filled chamber, Randall and Lanier and Milton struck madly at the Martians surging up toward them. Randall seemed in a dream. A score of taloned paws clutched him from beneath; scaled forms collapsed under his insane blows.

The whole vast cone and surging reptilian hordes seemed spinning at increasing speed around him. As his clenched fists flashed with waning strength he glimpsed crocodilian forms swarming up on either side of them, glimpsed Lanier down, talons reaching toward him, Milton fighting over him like a madman. Another moment would see it ended—reptilian arms reaching in scores to drag him down—Milton jerking Lanier half to his feet. The Martian Master's call sounded—and then came a great clanging sound at which the Martian hordes seemed to freeze for an instant motionless, at which Milton's voice reached him in a supreme cry.

"Randall—the transmitter!"

For in that instant Milton was leaping back with Lanier, and as Randall with his last strength threw himself backward with them into the humming transmitting chamber's brilliant light, he heard a last frenzied roar of hissing cries from the Martian hordes about them. Then as the brilliant light and force from the chamber's walls smote them, Randall felt himself hurled into blackness inconceivable, that smashed like a descending curtain across his brain.

The curtain of blackness lifted for a moment. He was lying with Milton and Lanier in another chamber whose force beat upon them. He saw a yellow lit room instead of the great cone—saw the tense, anxious face of Nelson at the switch beside them. He strove to move, made to Nelson a gesture with his arm that seemed to drain all strength and life from him; and then, as in answer to it Nelson drove up the switch and turned off the force of the matter receiver in which they lay, the black curtain descended on Randall's brain once more.

*   *   *   *   *

Two hours later it was when Milton and Randall and Lanier and Nelson turned to the laboratory's door. They paused to glance behind them. Of the great matter transmitter and receiver, of the apparatus that had crowded the laboratory, there remained now but wreckage.

For that had been their first thought, their first task, when the astounded Nelson had brought the three back to consciousness and had heard their amazing tale. They had wrecked so completely the matter station and its actuating apparatus that none could ever have guessed what a mechanism of wonder the laboratory a short time before had held.

The cubical chambers had been smashed beyond all recognition, the dynamos were masses of split metal and fused wiring, the batteries of tubes were shattered, the condensers and transformers and wiring demolished. And it had only been when the last written plans and blue prints of the mechanism had been burned that Milton and Randall and Lanier had stopped to allow their exhausted bodies a moment of rest.

*   *   *   *   *

Now as they paused at the laboratory's door, Lanier reached and swung it open. Together, silent, they gazed out.

It all seemed to Randall exactly as upon the night before. The shadowy masses in the darkness, the heaving, dim lit sea stretching far away before them, the curtain of summer stars stretched across the heavens. And, sinking westward amid those stars, the red spark of Mars toward which as though toward a magnet all their eyes had turned.

Milton was speaking. "Up there it has shone for centuries—ages—a crimson spot of light. And up there the Martians have been watching, watching—until at last we opened to them the gate."

Randall's hand was on his shoulder. "But we closed that gate, too, in the end."

Milton nodded slowly. "We—or the fate that rules our worlds. But the gate is closed, and God grant, shall never again be opened by any on this world."

"God grant it," the other echoed.

And they were all gazing still toward the thing. Gazing up toward the crimson spot of light that burned there among the stars, toward the planet that shone red,

menacing, terrible, but whose menace and whose terror
had been thrust back even as they had crouched to spring
at last upon the earth.

THE SARGASSO OF SPACE

ORIGINALLY PUBLISHED IN *ASTOUNDING STORIES*, SEPTEMBER 1931

THE SARGASSO OF SPACE

Captain Crain faced his crew calmly. "We may as well face the facts, men," he said. "The ship's fuel-tanks are empty and we are drifting through space toward the dead-area."

The twenty-odd officers and men gathered on the middle-deck of the freighter *Pallas* made no answer, and Crain continued:

"We left Jupiter with full tanks, more than enough fuel to take us to Neptune. But the leaks in the starboard tanks lost us half our supply, and we had used the other half before discovering that. Since the ship's rocket-tubes cannot operate without fuel, we are simply drifting. We would drift on to Neptune if the attraction of Uranus were not pulling us to the right. That attraction alters our course so that in three ship-days we shall drift into the dead-area."

Rance Kent, first-officer of the *Pallas*, asked a question: "Couldn't we, raise Neptune with the radio, sir, and have them send out a fuel-ship in time to reach us?"

"It's impossible, Mr. Kent," Crain answered. "Our main radio is dead without fuel to run its dynamotors, and our auxiliary set hasn't the power to reach Neptune."

"Why not abandon ship in the space-suits," asked Liggett, the second-officer, "and trust to the chance of some ship picking us up?"

The captain shook his head. "It would be quite useless, for we'd simply drift on through space with the ship into the dead-area."

The score of members of the crew, bronzed space-sailors out of every port in the solar system, had listened mutely. Now, one of them, a tall tube-man, stepped forward a little.

"Just what is this dead-area, sir?" he asked. "I've heard of it, but as this is my first outer-planet voyage, I know nothing about it."

"I'll admit I know little more," said Liggett, "save that a good many disabled ships have drifted into it and have never come out."

*   *   *   *   *

"The dead area," Crain told them, "is a region of space ninety thousand miles across within Neptune's orbit, in which the ordinary gravitational attractions of the solar system are dead. This is because in that region the pulls of the sun and the outer planets exactly balance each other. Because of that, anything in the dead-area, will stay in there until time ends, unless it has power of its own. Many wrecked space-ships have drifted into it at one time or another, none ever emerging; and it's believed that there is a great mass of wrecks somewhere in the area, drawn and held together by mutual attraction."

"And we're drifting in to join them," Kent said. "Some prospect!"

"Then there's really no chance for us?" asked Liggett keenly.

Captain Crain thought. "As I see it, very little," he admitted. "If our auxiliary radio can reach some nearby ship before the *Pallas* enters the dead-area, we'll have a chance. But it seems a remote one."

He addressed himself to the men: "I have laid the situation frankly before you because I consider you entitled to the truth. You must remember, however, that while there is life there is hope.

"There will be no change in ship routine, and the customary watches will be kept. Half-rations of food and water will be the rule from now on, though. That is all."

As the men moved silently off, the captain looked after them with something of pride.

"They're taking it like men," he told Kent and Liggett. "It's a pity there's no way out for them and us."

"If the *Pallas* does enter the dead-area and join the wreck-pack," Liggett said, "how long will we be able to live?"

"Probably for some months on our present condensed air and food supplies," Crain answered. "I would prefer, myself, a quicker end."

"So would I," said Kent. "Well, there's nothing left but to pray for some kind of ship to cross our path in the next day or two."

*   *   *   *   *

Kent's prayers were not answered in the next ship-day, nor in the next. For, though one of the *Pallas'* radio-operators was constantly at the instruments under Captain Crain's orders, the weak calls of the auxiliary set raised no response.

Had they been on the Venus or Mars run, Kent told himself, there would be some chance, but out here in the vast spaces, between the outer planets, ships were fewer and farther between. The big, cigar-shaped freighter drifted helplessly on in a broad curve toward the dreaded area, the green light-speck of Neptune swinging to their left.

On the third ship-day Kent and Captain Crain stood in the pilot-house behind Liggett, who sat at the now useless rocket-tube controls. Their eyes were on the big glass screen of the gravograph. The black dot on it that represented their ship was crawling steadily toward the bright red circle that stood for the dead-area....

They watched silently until the dot had crawled over the circle's red line, heading toward its center.

"Well, we're in at last," Kent commented. "There seems to be no change in anything, either."

Crain pointed to the instrument-panel. "Look at the gravitometers."

Kent did. "All dead! No gravitational pull from any direction—no, that one shows a slight attraction from ahead!"

"Then gravitational attraction of some sort does exist in the dead-area after all!" Liggett exclaimed.

"You don't understand," said Crain. "That attraction from ahead is the pull of the wreck-pack at the dead-area's center."

"And it's pulling the *Pallas* toward it?" Kent exclaimed.

Crain nodded. "We'll probably reach the wreck-pack in two more ship-days."

*   *   *   *   *

The next two ship-days seemed to Kent drawn out endlessly. A moody silence had grown upon the officers and men of the ship. All seemed oppressed by the strange forces of fate that had seized the ship and were carrying it, smoothly and soundlessly, into this region of irrevocable doom.

The radio-operators' vain calls had ceased. The *Pallas* drifted on into the dreaded area like some dumb ship laden with damned souls. It drifted on, Kent told himself, as many a wrecked and disabled ship had done before it, with the ordinary activities and life of the solar system forever behind it, and mystery and death ahead.

It was toward the end of the second of those two ship-days that Liggett's voice came down from the pilot-house:

"Wreck-pack in sight ahead!"

"We've arrived, anyway!" Kent cried, as he and Crain hastened up into the pilot house. The crew was running to the deck-windows.

"Right ahead there, about fifteen degrees left," Liggett told Kent and Crain, pointing. "Do you see it?"

Kent stared; nodded. The wreck-pack was a distant, disk-like mass against the star-flecked heavens, a mass that glinted here and there in the feeble sunlight of space. It did not seem large, but, as they drifted steadily closer in the next hours, they saw that in reality the wreck-pack was tremendous, measuring at least fifty miles across.

Its huge mass was a heterogeneous heap, composed mostly of countless cigar-like space-ships in all stages of wreckage. Some appeared smashed almost out of all recognizable shape, while others were, to all appearances unharmed. They floated together in this dense mass in space, crowded against one another by their mutual attraction.

There seemed to be among them every type of ship known in the solar system, from small, swift mail-boats to big freighters. And, as they drifted nearer, the three in the pilot-house could see that around and between the ships of the wreck-pack floated much other matter— fragments of wreckage, meteors, small and large, and space-debris of every sort.

The *Pallas* was drifting, not straight toward the wreck-pack, but in a course that promised to take the ship past it.

"We're not heading into the wreck-pack!" Liggett exclaimed. "Maybe we'll drift past it, and on out the dead-area's other side!"

*   *   *   *   *

Captain Crain smiled mirthlessly. "You're forgetting your space-mechanics, Liggett. We will drift along the wreck-pack's edge, and then will curve in and go round it in a closing spiral until we reach its edge."

"Lord, who'd have thought there were so many wrecks here!" Kent marvelled. "There must be thousands of them!"

"They've been collecting here ever since the first interplanetary rocket-ships went forth," Crain reminded him. "Not only meteor-wrecked ships, but ships whose mechanisms went wrong—or that ran out of fuel like ours—or that were captured and sacked, and then set adrift by space-pirates."

The *Pallas* by then was drifting along the wreck-pack's rim at a half-mile distance, and Kent's eyes were running over the mass.

"Some of those ships look entirely undamaged. Why couldn't we find one that has fuel in its tanks, transfer it to our own tanks, and get away?" he asked.

Crain's eyes lit. "Kent, that's a real chance! There must be some ships in that pack with fuel in them, and we can use the space-suits to explore for them!"

"Look, we're beginning to curve in around the pack now!" Liggett exclaimed.

The *Pallas*, as though loath to pass the wreck-pack, was curving inward to follow its rim. In the next hours it continued to sail slowly around the great pack, approaching closer and closer to its edge.

In those hours Kent and Crain and all in the ship watched with a fascinated interest that even knowledge of their own peril could not kill. They could see swift-lined passenger-ships of the Pluto and Neptune runs shouldering against small space-yachts with the insignia of Mars or Venus on their bows. Wrecked freighters from Saturn or Earth floated beside rotund grain-boats from Jupiter.

The debris among the pack's wrecks was just as varied, holding fragments of metal, dark meteors of differing size—and many human bodies. Among these were some clad in the insulated space-suits, with their transparent glassite helmets. Kent wondered what wreck they had abandoned hastily in those suits, only to be swept with it into the dead-area, to die in their suits.

By the end of that ship-day, the *Pallas*, having floated almost completely around the wreck-pack, finally struck the wrecks at its edge with a jarring shock; then bobbed for a while and lay still. From pilot-house and deck windows the men looked eagerly forth.

*   *   *   *   *

Their ship floated at the wreck-pack's edge. Directly to its right floated a sleek, shining Uranus-Jupiter passenger-ship whose bows had been smashed in by a meteor. On their left bobbed an unmarked freighter of the old type with projecting rocket-tubes, apparently intact. Beyond them in the wreck-pack lay another Uranus craft, a freighter, and, beyond it, stretched the countless other wrecks.

Captain Crain summoned the crew together again on the middle-deck.

"Men, we've reached the wreck-pack at the dead-area's center, and here we'll stay until the end of time unless we get out under our own power. Mr. Kent has suggested a possible way of doing so, which I consider highly feasible.

"He has suggested that in some of the ships in the wreck-pack may be found enough fuel to enable us to escape from the dead-area, once it is transferred to this ship. I am going to permit him to explore the wreck-pack with a party in space suits, and I am asking for volunteers for this service."

The entire crew stepped quickly forward. Crain smiled. "Twelve of you will be enough," he told them. "The eight tube-men and four of the cargo-men will go, therefore, with Mr. Kent and Mr. Liggett as leaders. Mr. Kent, you may address the men if you wish."

"Get down to the lower airlock and into your space-suits at once, then," Kent told them. "Mr. Liggett, will you supervise that?"

As Liggett and the men trooped down to the airlock, Kent turned back toward his superior.

"There's a very real chance of your becoming lost in this huge wreck-pack, Kent," Crain told him: "so be very careful to keep your bearings at all times. I know I can depend on you."

"I'll do my best," Kent was saying, when Liggett's excited face reappeared suddenly at the stair.

"There are men coming toward the *Pallas* along the wreck-pack's edge!" he reported—"a half-dozen men in space-suits!"

"You must be mistaken, Liggett!" exclaimed Crain. "They must be some of the bodies in space-suits we saw in the pack."

"No, they're living men!" Liggett cried. "They're coming straight toward us—come down and see!"

*　　*　　*　　*　　*

Crain and Kent followed Liggett quickly down to the airlock room, where the men who had started donning their space-suits were now peering excitedly from the windows. Crain and Kent looked where Liggett pointed, along the wreck-pack's edge to the ship's right.

Six floating shapes, men in space-suits, were approaching along the pack's border. They floated smoothly through space, reaching the wrecked passenger-ship beside the *Pallas*. They braced their feet against its side and propelled themselves on through the void like swimmers under water, toward the *Pallas*.

"They must be survivors from some wreck that drifted in here as we did!" Kent exclaimed. "Maybe they've lived here for months!"

"It's evident that they saw the *Pallas* drift into the pack, and have come to investigate," Crain estimated. "Open the airlock for them, men, for they'll want to come inside."

Two of the men spun the wheels that slid aside the airlock's outer door. In a moment the half-dozen men outside had reached the ship's side, and had pulled themselves down inside the airlock.

When all were in, the outer door was closed, and air hissed in to fill the lock. The airlock's inner door then slid open and the newcomers stepped into the ship's interior, unscrewing their transparent helmets as they did so. For a few moments the visitors silently surveyed their new surroundings.

Their leader was a swarthy individual with sardonic black eyes who, on noticing Crain's captain-insignia, came toward him with outstretched hand. His followers seemed to be cargo-men or deck-men, looking hardly intelligent enough to Kent's eyes to be tube-men.

*   *   *   *   *

"Welcome to our city!" their leader exclaimed as he shook Crain's hand. "We saw your ship drift in, but hardly expected to find anyone living in it."

"I'll confess that we're surprised ourselves to find any life here," Crain told him. "You're living on one of the wrecks?"

The other nodded. "Yes, on the *Martian Queen*, a quarter-mile along the pack's edge. It was a Saturn-Neptune passenger ship, and about a month ago we were at this cursed dead-area's edge, when half our rocket-tubes exploded. Eighteen of us escaped the explosion, the ship's walls still being tight; and we drifted into the pack here, and have been living here ever since."

"My name's Krell," he added, "and I was a tube-man on the ship. I and another of the tube-men, named Jandron, were the highest in rank left, all the officers and other tube-men having been killed, so we took charge and have been keeping order."

"What about your passengers?" Liggett asked.

"All killed but one," Krell answered. "When the tubes let go they smashed up the whole lower two decks."

Crain briefly explained to him the *Pallas'* predicament. "Mr. Kent and Mr. Liggett were on the point of starting a search of the wreck-pack for fuel when you arrived," he said, "With enough fuel we can get clear of the dead-area."

Krell's eyes lit up. "That would mean a getaway for all of us! It surely ought to be possible!"

"Do you know whether there are any ships in the pack with fuel in their tanks?" Kent asked. Krell shook his head.

"We've searched through the wreck-pack a good bit, but never bothered about fuel, it being no good to us. But there ought to be some, at least: there's enough wrecks in this cursed place to make it possible to find almost anything.

"You'd better not start exploring, though," he added, "without some of us along as guides, for I'm here to tell you that you can lose yourself in this wreck-pack without knowing it. If you wait until to-morrow, I'll come over myself and go with you."

"I think that would be wise," Crain said to Kent. "There is plenty of time."

"Time is the one thing there's plenty of in this damned place," Krell agreed. "We'll be getting back to the *Martian Queen* now and give the good news to Jandron and the rest."

"Wouldn't mind if Liggett and I came along, would you?" Kent asked. "I'd like to see how your ship's fixed— that is, if it's all right with you, sir," he added to his superior.

Crain nodded. "All right if you don't stay long," he said. But, to Kent's surprise Krell seemed reluctant to endorse his proposal.

"I guess it'll be all right," he said slowly, "though there's nothing much on the *Martian Queen* to see."

*   *   *   *   *

Krell and his followers replaced their helmets and returned into the airlock. Liggett followed them, and, as

Kent struggled hastily into a space-suit, he found Captain Crain at his side.

"Kent, look sharp when you get over on that ship," Crain told him. "I don't like the look of this Krell, and his story about all the officers being killed in the explosion sounds fishy to me."

"To me, too," Kent agreed. "But Liggett and I will have the suit-phones in our space-suits and can call you from there in case of need."

Crain nodded, and Kent with space-suit on and transparent helmet screwed tight, stepped into the airlock with the rest. The airlock's inner door closed, the outer one opened, and as the air puffed out into space, Kent and Krell and Liggett leapt out into the void, the others following.

It was no novelty to Kent to float in a space-suit in the empty void. He and the others now floated as smoothly as though under water toward a wrecked liner at the *Pallas'* right. They reached it, pulled themselves around it, and, with feet braced against its side, propelled themselves on through space along the border of the wreck-pack.

They passed a half-dozen wrecks thus, before coming to the *Martian Queen*. It was a silvery, glistening ship whose stern and lower walls were bulging and strained, but not cracked. Kent told himself that Krell had spoken truth about the exploding rocket-tubes, at least.

They struck the *Martian Queen's* side and entered the upper-airlock open for them. Once through the airlock they found themselves on the ship's upper-deck. And when Kent and Liggett removed their helmets with the others they found a full dozen men confronting them, a brutal-faced group who exhibited some surprise at sight of them.

*   *   *   *   *

Foremost among them stood a tall, heavy individual who regarded Kent and Liggett with the cold, suspicious eyes of an animal.

"My comrade and fellow-ruler here, Wald Jandron," said Krell. To Jandron he explained rapidly. "The whole crew of the *Pallas* is alive, and they say if they can find fuel in the wreck-pack their ship can get out of here."

"Good," grunted Jandron. "The sooner they can do it, the better it will be for us."

Kent saw Liggett flush angrily, but he ignored Jandron and spoke to Krell. "You said one of your passengers had escaped the explosion?"

To Kent's amazement a girl stepped from behind the group of men, a slim girl with pale face and steady, dark eyes. "I'm the passenger," she told him. "My name's Marta Mallen."

Kent and Liggett stared, astounded. "Good Lord!" Kent exclaimed. "A girl like you on this ship!"

"Miss Mallen happened to be on the upper-deck at the time of the explosion and, so, escaped when the other passengers were killed," Krell explained smoothly. "Isn't that so, Miss Mallen?"

The girl's eyes had not left Kent's, but at Krell's words she nodded. "Yes, that is so," she said mechanically.

Kent collected his whirling thoughts. "But wouldn't you rather go back to the *Pallas* with us?" he asked. "I'm sure you'd be more comfortable there."

"She doesn't go," grunted Jandron. Kent turned in quick wrath toward him, but Krell intervened.

"Jandron only means that Miss Mallen is much more comfortable on this passenger-ship than she'd be in your freighter." He shot a glance at the girl as he spoke, and Kent saw her wince.

"I'm afraid that's so," she said; "but I thank you for the offer, Mr. Kent."

Kent could have sworn that there was an appeal in her eyes, and he stood for a moment, indecisive,

Jandron's stare upon him. After a moment's thought he turned to Krell.

"You were going to show me the damage the exploding tubes did," he said, and Krell nodded quickly.

"Of course; you can see from the head of the stair back in the after-deck."

He led the way along a corridor, Jandron and the girl and two of the men coming with them. Kent's thoughts were still chaotic as he walked between Krell and Liggett. What was this girl doing amid the men of the *Martian Queen*? What had her eyes tried to tell him?

Liggett nudged his side in the dim corridor, and Kent, looking down, saw dark splotches on its metal floor. Blood-stains! His suspicions strengthened. They might be from the bleeding of those wounded in the tube-explosions. But were they?

*   *   *   *   *

They reached the after-deck whose stair's head gave a view of the wrecked tube-rooms beneath. The lower decks had been smashed by terrific forces. Kent's practiced eyes ran rapidly over the shattered rocket-tubes.

"They've back-blasted from being fired too fast," he said. "Who was controlling the ship when this happened?"

"Galling, our second-officer," answered Krell. "He had found us routed too close to the dead-area's edge and was trying to get away from it in a hurry, when he used the tubes too fast, and half of them back-blasted."

"If Galling was at the controls in the pilot-house, how did the explosion kill him?" asked Liggett skeptically. Krell turned quickly.

"The shock threw him against the pilot-house wall and fractured his skull—he died in an hour," he said. Liggett was silent.

"Well, this ship will never move again," Kent said. "It's too bad that the explosion blew out your tanks, but we ought to find fuel somewhere in the wreck-pack for the *Pallas*. And now we'd best get back."

As they returned up the dim corridor Kent managed to walk beside Marta Mallen, and, without being seen, he contrived to detach his suit-phone—the compact little radiophone case inside his space-suit's neck—and slip it into the girl's grasp. He dared utter no word of explanation, but apparently she understood, for she had concealed the suit-phone by the time they reached the upper-deck.

Kent and Liggett prepared to don their space-helmets, and before entering the airlock, Kent turned to Krell.

"We'll expect you at the *Pallas* first hour to-morrow, and we'll start searching the wreck-pack with a dozen of our men," he said.

He then extended his hand to the girl. "Good-by, Miss Mallen. I hope we can have a talk soon."

He had said the words with double meaning, and saw understanding in her eyes. "I hope we can, too," she said.

Kent's nod to Jandron went unanswered, and he and Liggett adjusted their helmets and entered the airlock.

Once out of it, they kicked rapidly away from the *Martian Queen*, floating along with the wreck-pack's huge mass to their right, and only the star-flecked emptiness of infinity to their left. In a few minutes they reached the airlock of the *Pallas*.

*   *   *   *   *

They found Captain Crain awaiting them anxiously. Briefly Kent reported everything.

"I'm certain there has been foul play aboard the *Martian Queen*," he said. "Krell you saw for yourself, Jandron is pure brute, and their men seem capable of anything.

"I gave the suit-phone to the girl, however, and if she can call us with it, we can get the truth from her. She dared not tell me anything there in the presence of Krell and Jandron."

Crain nodded, his face grave. "We'll see whether or not she calls," he said.

Kent took a suit-phone from one of their space-suits and rapidly, tuned it to match the one he had left with Marta Mallen. Almost at once they heard her voice from it, and Kent answered rapidly.

"I'm so glad I got you!" she exclaimed. "Mr. Kent, I dared not tell you the truth about this ship when you were here, or Krell and the rest would have killed you at once."

"I thought that was it, and that's why I left the suit-phone for you," Kent said. "Just what is the truth?"

"Krell and Jandron and these men of theirs are the ones who killed the officers and passengers of the *Martian Queen*! What they told you about the explosion was true enough, for the explosion did happen that way, and because of it, the ship drifted into the dead-area. But the only ones killed by it were some of the tube-men and three passengers.

"Then, while the ship was drifting into the dead-area, Krell told the men that the fewer aboard, the longer they could live on the ship's food and air. Krell and Jandron led the men in a surprise attack and killed all the officers and passengers, and threw their bodies out into space. I was the only passenger they spared, because both Krell and Jandron—want me!"

*   *   *   *   *

There was a silence, and Kent felt a red anger rising in him. "Have they dared harm you?" he asked after a moment.

"No, for Krell and Jandron are too jealous of each other to permit the other to touch me. But it's been terrible living with them in this awful place."

"Ask her if she knows what their plans are in regard to us," Crain told Kent.

Marta had apparently overheard the question. "I don't know that, for they shut me in my cabin as soon as you left," she said. "I've heard them talking and arguing excitedly, though. I know that if you do find fuel, they'll try to kill you all and escape from here in your ship."

"Pleasant prospect," Kent commented. "Do you think they plan an attack on us now?"

"No; I think that they'll wait until you've refueled your ship, if you are able to do that, and then try treachery."

"Well, they'll find us ready. Miss Mallen, you have the suit-phone: keep it hidden in your cabin and I'll call you first thing to-morrow. We're going to get you out of there, but we don't want to break with Krell until we're ready. Will you be all right until then?"

"Of course I will," she answered. "There's another thing, though. My name isn't Miss Mallen—it's Marta."

"Mine's Rance," said Kent, smiling. "Good-by until to-morrow, then, Marta."

"Good-by, Rance."

Kent rose from the instrument with the smile still in his eyes, but with his lips compressed. "Damn it, there's the bravest and finest girl in the solar system!" he exclaimed. "Over there with those brutes!"

"We'll have her out, never fear," Crain reassured him. "The main thing is to determine our course toward Krell and Jandron."

Kent thought. "As I see it, Krell can help us immeasurably in our search through the wreck-pack for fuel," he said. "I think it would be best to keep on good terms with him until we've found fuel and have it in our tanks. Then we can turn the tables on them before they can do anything."

Crain nodded thoughtfully. "I think you're right. Then you and Liggett and Krell can head our search-party to-morrow."

Crain established watches on a new schedule, and Kent and Liggett and the dozen men chosen for the exploring party of the next day ate a scanty meal and turned in for some sleep.

*   *   *   *   *

When Kent woke and glimpsed the massed wrecks through the window he was for the moment amazed, but rapidly remembered. He and Liggett were finishing their morning ration when Crain pointed to a window.

"There comes Krell now," he said, indicating the single space-suited figure approaching along the wreck-pack's edge.

"I'll call Marta before he gets here," said Kent hastily.

The girl answered on the suit-phone immediately, and it occurred to Kent that she must have spent the night without sleeping. "Krell left a few minutes ago," she said.

"Yes, he's coming now. You heard nothing of their plans?"

"No; they've kept me shut in my cabin. However, I did hear Krell giving Jandron and the rest directions. I'm sure they're plotting something."

"We're prepared for them," Kent assured her. "If all goes well, before you realize it, you'll be sailing out of here with us in the *Pallas*."

"I hope so," she said. "Rance, be careful with Krell in the wreck-pack. He's dangerous."

"I'll be watching him," he promised. "Good-by, Marta."

Kent reached the lower-deck just as Krell entered from the airlock, his swarthy face smiling as he removed his helmet. He carried a pointed steel bar. Liggett and the others were donning their suits.

"All ready to go, Kent?" Krell asked.

Kent nodded. "All ready," he said shortly. Since hearing Marta's story he found it hard to dissimulate with Krell.

"You'll want bars like mine," Krell continued, "for they're damned handy when you get jammed between wreckage masses. Exploring this wreck-pack is no soft job: I can tell you from experience."

Liggett and the rest had their suits adjusted, and with bars in their grasp, followed Krell into the airlock. Kent hung back for a last word with Crain, who, with his half-dozen remaining men, was watching.

"Marta just told me that Krell and Jandron have been plotting something," he told the captain; "so I'd keep a close watch outside."

"Don't worry, Kent. We'll let no one inside the *Pallas* until you and Liggett and the men get back."

*   *   *   *   *

In a few minutes they were out of the ship, with Krell and Kent and Liggett leading, and the twelve members of the *Pallas'* crew following closely.

The three leaders climbed up on the Uranus-Jupiter passenger-ship that lay beside the *Pallas*, the others moving on and exploring the neighboring wrecks in parties of two and three. From the top of the passenger-ship, when they gained it, Kent and his two companions could look far out over the wreck-pack. It was an extraordinary spectacle, this stupendous mass of dead ships floating motionless in the depths of space, with the burning stars above and below them.

His companions and the other men clambering over the neighboring wrecks seemed weird figures in their bulky suits and transparent helmets. Kent looked back at the *Pallas*, and then along the wreck-pack's edge to where he could glimpse the silvery side of the *Martian Queen*. But now Krell and Liggett were descending into the ship's interior through the great opening smashed in its bows, and Kent followed.

They found themselves in the liner's upper navigation-rooms. Officers and men lay about, frozen to death at the instant the meteor-struck vessel's air had rushed out, and the cold of space had entered. Krell led the way on, down into the ship's lower decks, where they found the bodies of the crew and passengers lying in the same silent death.

The salons held beautifully-dressed women, distinguished-looking men, lying about as the meteor's shock had hurled them. One group lay around a card-table, their game interrupted. A woman still held a small child, both seemingly asleep. Kent tried to shake off the oppression he felt as he and Krell and Liggett continued down to the tank-rooms.

They found their quest there useless, for the tanks had been strained by the meteor's shock, and were empty. Kent felt Liggett grasp his hand and heard him speak, the sound-vibrations coming through their contacting suits.

"Nothing here; and we'll find it much the same through all these wrecks, if I'm not wrong. Tanks always give at a shock."

"There must be some ships with fuel still in them among all these," Kent answered.

*　*　*　*　*

They climbed back, up to the ship's top, and leapt off it toward a Jupiter freighter lying a little farther inside the pack. As they floated toward it, Kent saw their men moving on with them from ship to ship, progressing inward into the pack. Both Kent and Liggett kept Krell always ahead of them, knowing that a blow from his bar, shattering their glassite helmets, meant instant death. But Krell seemed quite intent on the search for fuel.

The big Jupiter freighter seemed intact from above, but, when they penetrated into it, they found its whole under-side blown away, apparently by an explosion of its tanks. They moved on to the next ship, a private space-yacht, small in size, but luxurious in fittings. It had been abandoned in space, its rocket-tubes burst and tanks strained.

They went on, working deeper into the wreck-pack. Kent almost forgot the paramount importance of their search in the fascination of it. They explored almost every known type of ship—freighters, liners, cold-storage boats, and grain-boats. Once Kent's hopes ran high at sight of a fuel-ship, but it proved to be in ballast, its cargo-tanks empty and its own tanks and tubes apparently blown simultaneously.

Kent's muscles ached from the arduous work of climbing over and exploring the wrecks. He and Liggett had become accustomed to the sight of frozen, motionless bodies.

As they worked deeper into the pack, they noticed that the ships were of increasingly older types, and at last Krell signalled a halt. "We're almost a mile in," he told them, gripping their hands. "We'd better work back out, taking a different section of the pack as we do."

Kent nodded. "It may change our luck," he said.

It did; for when they had gone not more than a half-mile back, they glimpsed one of their men waving excitedly from the top of a Pluto liner.

They hastened at once toward him, the other men gathering also; and when Kent grasped the man's hand he heard his excited voice.

"Fuel-tanks here are more than half-full, sir!"

*   *   *   *   *

They descended quickly into the liner, finding that though its whole stern had been sheared away by a meteor, its tanks had remained miraculously unstrained.

"Enough fuel here to take the *Pallas* to Neptune!" Kent exclaimed.

"How will you get it over to your ship?" Krell asked. Kent pointed to great reels of flexible metal tubing hanging near the tanks.

"We'll pump it over. The *Pallas* has tubing like this ship's, for taking on fuel in space, and, by joining its tubing to this, we'll have a tube-line between the two ships. It's hardly more than a quarter-mile."

"Let's get back and let them know about it," Liggett urged, and they climbed back out of the liner.

They worked their way out of the wreck-pack with much greater speed than that with which they had entered, needing only an occasional brace against a ship's side to send them floating over the wrecks. They came to the wreck-pack's edge at a little distance from the *Pallas*, and hastened toward it.

They found the outer door of the *Pallas'* airlock open, and entered, Krell remaining with them. As the outer door closed and air hissed into the lock, Kent and the rest removed their helmets. The inner door slid open as they were doing this, and from inside almost a score of men leapt upon them!

Kent, stunned for a moment, saw Jandron among their attackers, bellowing orders to them, and even as he struck out furiously he comprehended. Jandron and the men of the *Martian Queen* had somehow captured the *Pallas* from Crain and had been awaiting their return!

*   *   *   *   *

The struggle was almost instantly over, for, outnumbered and hampered as they were by their heavy space-suits, Kent and Liggett and their followers had no chance. Their hands, still in the suits, were bound quickly behind them at Jandron's orders.

Kent heard an exclamation, and saw Marta starting toward him from behind Jandron's men. But a sweep of Jandron's arm brushed her rudely back. Kent strained madly at his bonds. Krell's face had a triumphant look.

"Did it all work as I told you it would, Jandron?" he asked.

"It worked," Jandron answered impassively. "When they saw fifteen of us coming from the wreck-pack in space-suits, they opened right up to us."

Kent understood, and cursed Krell's cunning. Crain, seeing the fifteen figures approaching from the wreck-pack, had naturally thought they were Kent's party, and had let them enter to overwhelm his half-dozen men.

"We put Crain and his men over in the *Martian Queen*," Jandron continued, "and took all their helmets so they can't escape. The girl we brought over here. Did you find a wreck with fuel?"

Krell nodded. "A Pluto liner a quarter-mile back, and we can pump the fuel over here by connecting tube-lines. What the devil—"

Jandron had made a signal at which three of his men had leapt forward on Krell, securing his hands like those of the others.

"Have you gone crazy, Jandron?" cried Krell, his face red with anger and surprise.

"No," Jandron replied impassively; "but the men are as tired as I am of your bossing ways, and have chosen me as their sole leader."

"You dirty double-crosser!" Krell raged. "Are you men going to let him get away with this?"

The men paid no attention, and Jandron motioned to the airlock. "Take them over to the *Martian Queen* too," he ordered, "and make sure there's no space-helmet left there. Then get back at once, for we've got to get the fuel into this ship and make a getaway."

*   *   *   *   *

The helmets of Kent and Krell and the other helpless prisoners were put upon them, and, with hands still bound, they were herded into the airlock by eight of Jandron's men attired in space-suits also. The prisoners were then joined one to another by a strand of metal cable.

Kent, glancing back into the ship as the airlock's inner door closed, saw Jandron giving rapid orders to his followers, and noticed Marta held back from the airlock by one of them. Krell's eyes glittered venomously through his helmet. The outer door opened, and their guards jerked them forth into space by the connecting cable.

They were towed helplessly along the wreck-pack's rim toward the *Martian Queen*. Once inside its airlock, Jandron's men removed the prisoners' space-helmets and then used the duplicate-control inside the airlock itself to open the inner door. Through this opening they thrust the captives, those inside the ship not daring to enter the airlock. Jandron's men then closed the inner door, re-opened the outer one, and started back toward the *Pallas* with the helmets of Kent and his companions.

Kent and the others soon found Crain and his half-dozen men who rapidly undid their bonds. Crain's men still wore their space-suits, but, like Kent's companions, were without space-helmets.

"Kent, I was afraid they'd get you and your men too!" Crain exclaimed. "It's all my fault, for when I saw Jandron and his men coming from the wreck-pack I never doubted but that it was you."

"It's no one's fault," Kent told him. "It's just something that we couldn't foresee."

*   *   *   *   *

Crain's eyes fell on Krell. "But what's he doing here?" he exclaimed. Kent briefly explained Jandron's treachery toward Krell, and Crain's brows drew ominously together.

"So Jandron put you here with us! Krell, I am a commissioned captain of a space-ship, and as such can legally try you and sentence you to death here without further formalities."

Krell did not answer, but Kent intervened. "There's hardly time for that now, sir," he said. "I'm as anxious to settle with Krell as anyone, but right now our main enemy is Jandron, and Krell hates Jandron worse than we do, if I'm not mistaken."

"You're not," said Krell grimly. "All I want right now is to get within reach of Jandron."

"There's small chance of any of us doing that," Crain told them. "There's not a single space-helmet on the *Martian Queen*."

"You've searched?" Liggett asked.

"Every cubic inch of the ship," Crain told him. "No, Jandron's men made sure there were no helmets left here, and without helmets this ship is an inescapable prison."

"Damn it, there must be some way out!" Kent exclaimed. "Why, Jandron and his men must be starting to pump that fuel into the *Pallas* by now! They'll be sailing off as soon as they do it!"

Crain's face was sad. "I'm afraid this is the end, Kent. Without helmets, the space between the *Martian Queen* and the *Pallas* is a greater barrier to us than a mile-thick wall of steel. In this ship we'll stay, until the air and food give out, and death releases us."

"Damn it, I'm not thinking of myself!" Kent cried. "I'm thinking of Marta! The *Pallas* will sail out of here with her in Jandron's power!"

"The girl!" Liggett exclaimed. "If she could bring us over space-helmets from the *Pallas* we could get out of here!"

Kent was thoughtful. "If we could talk to her—she must still have that suit-phone I gave her. Where's another?"

*   *   *   *   *

Crain quickly detached the compact suit-phone from inside the neck of his own space-suit, and Kent rapidly tuned it to the one he had given Marta Mallen. His heart leapt as her voice came instantly from it:

"Rance! Rance Kent—"

"Marta—this is Rance!" he cried.

He heard a sob of relief. "I've been calling you for minutes! I was hoping that you'd remember to listen!

"Jandron and ten of the others have gone to that wreck in which you found the fuel," she added swiftly. "They unreeled a tube-line behind them as they went, and I can hear them pumping in the fuel now."

"Are the others guarding you?" Kent asked quickly.

"They're down in the lower deck at the tanks and airlocks. They won't allow me down on that deck. I'm up here in the middle-deck, absolutely alone.

"Jandron told me that we'd start out of here as soon as the fuel was in," she added, "and he and the men were laughing about Krell."

"Marta, could you in any way get space-helmets and get out to bring them over here to us?" Kent asked eagerly.

"There's a lot of space-suits and helmets here," she answered, "but I couldn't get out with them, Rance! I couldn't get to the airlocks with Jandron's seven or eight men down there guarding them!"

Kent felt despair; then as an idea suddenly flamed in him, he almost shouted into the instrument:

"Marta, unless you can get over here with helmets for us, we're all lost. I want you to put on a space-suit and helmet at once!"

*　*　*　*　*

There was a short silence, and then her voice came, a little muffled. "I've got the suit and helmet on, Rance. I'm wearing the suit-phone inside it."

"Good! Now, can you get up to the pilot-house? There's no one guarding it or the upper-deck? Hurry up there, then, at once."

Crain and the rest were staring at Kent. "Kent, what are you going to have her do?" Crain exclaimed. "It'll do no good for her to start the *Pallas*: those guards will be up there in a minute!"

"I'm not going to have her start the *Pallas*," said Kent grimly. "Marta, you're in the pilot-house? Do you see the heavy little steel door in the wall beside the instrument-panel?"

"I'm at it, but it's locked with a combination-lock," she said.

"The combination is 6-34-77-81," Kent told her swiftly. "Open it as quickly as you can."

"Good God, Kent!" cried Crain. "You're going to have her—?"

"Get out of there the only way she can!" Kent finished fiercely. "You have the door open, Marta?"

"Yes; there are six or seven control-wheels inside."

"Those wheels control the *Pallas*' exhaust-valves," Kent told her. "Each wheel opens the valves of one of the ship's decks or compartments and allows its air to escape into space. They're used for testing leaks in the different deck and compartment divisions. Marta, you must turn all those wheels as far as you can to the right."

"But all the ship's air will rush out; the guards below have no suits on, and they'll be—" she was exclaiming. Kent interrupted.

"It's the only chance for you, for all of us. Turn them!"

There was a moment of silence, and Kent was going to repeat the order when her voice came, lower in tone, a little strange:

"I understand, Rance. I'm going to turn them."

*   *   *   *   *

There was silence again, and Kent and the men grouped round him were tense. All were envisioning the same thing—the air rushing out of the *Pallas*' valves, and the unsuspecting guards in its lower deck smitten suddenly by an instantaneous death.

Then Marta's voice, almost a sob: "I turned them, Rance. The air puffed out all around me."

"Your space-suit is working all right?"

"Perfectly," she said.

"Then go down and tie together as many space-helmets as you can manage, get out of the airlock, and try to get over here to the *Martian Queen* with them. Do you think you can do that, Marta?"

"I'm going to try," she said steadily. "But I'll have to pass those men in the lower-deck I just—killed. Don't be anxious if I don't talk for a little."

Yet her voice came again almost immediately. "Rance, the pumping has stopped! They must have pumped all the fuel into the *Pallas*!"

"Then Jandron and the rest will be coming back to the *Pallas* at once!" Kent cried. "Hurry, Marta!"

The suit-phone was silent; and Kent and the rest, their faces closely pressed against the deck-windows, peered intently along the wreck-pack's edge. The *Pallas* was hidden from their view by the wrecks between, and there was no sign as yet of the girl.

Kent felt his heart beating rapidly. Crain and Liggett pressed beside him, the men around them; Krell's face was a mask as he too gazed. Kent was rapidly becoming convinced that some mischance had overtaken the girl when an exclamation came from Liggett. He pointed excitedly.

*　　*　　*　　*　　*

She was in sight, unrecognizable in space-suit and helmet, floating along the wreck-pack's edge toward them. A mass of the glassite space-helmets tied together was in her grasp. She climbed bravely over the stern of a projecting wreck and shot on toward the *Martian Queen*.

The airlock's door was open for her, and, when she was inside it, the outer door closed and air hissed into the lock. In a moment she was in among them, still clinging to the helmets. Kent grasped her swaying figure and removed her helmet.

"Marta, you're all right?" he cried. She nodded a little weakly.

"I'm all right. It was just that I had to go over those guards that were all frozen.... Terrible!"

"Get these helmets on!" Crain was crying. "There's a dozen of them, and twelve of us can stop Jandron's men if we get back in time!"

Kent and Liggett and the nearer of their men were swiftly donning the helmets. Krell grasped one and Crain sought to snatch it.

"Let that go! We'll not have you with us when we haven't enough helmets for our own men!"

"You'll have me or kill me here!" Krell cried, his eyes hate-mad. "I've got my own account to settle with Jandron!"

"Let him have it!" Liggett cried. "We've no time now to argue!"

Kent reached toward the girl. "Marta, give one of the men your helmet," he ordered; but she shook her head.

"I'm going with you!" Before Kent could dispute she had the helmet on again, and Crain was pushing them into the airlock. The nine or ten left inside without helmets hastily thrust steel bars into the men's hands before the inner door closed. The outer one opened and they leapt forth into space, floating smoothly along the wreck-pack's border with bars in their grasp, thirteen strong.

Kent found the slowness with which they floated forward torturing. He glimpsed Crain and Liggett ahead, Marta beside him, Krell floating behind him to the left. They reached the projecting freighters, climbed over and around them, braced against them and shot on. They sighted the *Pallas* ahead now. Suddenly they discerned another group of eleven figures in space-suits approaching it from the wreck-pack's interior, rolling up the tube-line that led from the *Pallas* as they did so. Jandron's party!

* * * * *

Jandron and his men had seen them and were suddenly making greater efforts to reach the *Pallas*. Kent and his companions, propelling themselves frenziedly on from another wreck, reached the ship's side at the same time as Jandron's men. The two groups mixed and mingled, twisted and turned in a mad space-combat.

Kent had been grasped by one of Jandron's men and raised his bar to crack the other's glassite helmet. His opponent caught the bar, and they struggled, twisting and turning over and over far up in space amid a half-score similar struggles. Kent wrenched his bar free at last from the other's grasp and brought it down on his helmet. The glassite cracked, and he caught a glimpse of the man's hate-distorted face frozen instantly in death.

Kent released him and propelled himself toward a struggling trio nearby. As he floated toward them, he saw Jandron beyond them making wild gestures of command and saw Krell approaching Jandron with upraised bar. Kent, on reaching the three combatants, found them to be two of Jandron's men overcoming Crain. He shattered one's helmet as he reached them, but saw the other's bar go up for a blow.

Kent twisted frantically, uselessly, to escape it, but before the blow could descend a bar shattered his opponent's helmet from behind. As the man froze in instant death Kent saw that it was Marta who had struck him from behind. He jerked her to his side. The struggles in space around them seemed to be ending.

Six of Jandron's party had been slain, and three of Kent's companions. Jandron's four other followers were giving up the combat, floating off into the wreck-pack in clumsy, hasty flight. Someone grasped Kent's arm, and he turned to find it was Liggett.

"They're beaten!" Liggett's voice came to him! "They're all killed but those four!"

"What about Jandron himself?" Kent cried. Liggett pointed to two space-suited bodies twisting together in space, with bars still in their lifeless grasp.

Kent saw through their shattered helmets the stiffened faces of Jandron and Krell, their helmets having apparently been broken by each other's simultaneous blows.

Crain had gripped Kent's arm also. "Kent, it's over!" he was exclaiming. "Liggett and I will close the *Pallas'* exhaust-valves and release new air in it. You take over helmets for the rest of our men in the *Martian Queen*."

*   *   *   *   *

In several minutes Kent was back with the men from the *Martian Queen*. The *Pallas* was ready, with Liggett in its pilot-house, the men taking their stations, and Crain and Marta awaiting Kent.

"We've enough fuel to take us out of the dead-area and to Neptune without trouble!" Crain declared. "But what about those four of Jandron's men that got away?"

"The best we can do is leave them here," Kent told him. "Best for them, too, for at Neptune they'd be executed, while they can live indefinitely in the wreck-pack."

"I've seen so many men killed on the *Martian Queen* and here," pleaded Marta. "Please don't take them to Neptune."

"All right, we'll leave them," Crain agreed, "though the scoundrels ought to meet justice." He hastened up to the pilot-house after Liggett.

In a moment came the familiar blast of the rocket-tubes, and the *Pallas* shot out cleanly from the wreck-pack's edge. A scattered cheer came from the crew. With gathering speed the ship arrowed out, its rocket-tubes blasting now in steady succession.

Kent, with his arm across Marta's shoulders, watched the wreck-pack grow smaller behind. It lay as when he first had seen it, a strange great mass, floating forever motionless among the brilliant stars. He felt the girl beside him shiver, and swung her quickly around.

"Let's not look back or remember now, Marta!" he said. "Let's look ahead."

She nestled closer inside his arm. "Yes, Rance. Let's look ahead."

The Door Into Infinity

Originally Published In *Weird Tales*,
August-September 1936

The Door Into Infinity

The Brotherhood of the Door

"Where leads the Door?"

"It leads outside our world."

"Who taught our forefathers to open the Door?"

"They Beyond the Door taught them."

"To whom do we bring these sacrifices?"

"We bring them to Those Beyond the Door."

"Shall the Door be opened that They may take them?"

"Let the Door be opened!"

Paul Ennis had listened thus far, his haggard face uncomprehending in expression, but now he interrupted the speaker.

"But what does it all mean, inspector? Why are you repeating this to me?"

"Did you ever hear anyone speak words like that?" asked Inspector Pierce Campbell, leaning tautly forward for the answer.

"Of course not—it just sounds like gibberish to me," Ennis exclaimed. "What connection can it have with my wife?"

He had risen to his feet, a tall, blond young American whose good-looking face was drawn and worn by inward agony, whose crisp yellow hair was brushed back from his forehead in disorder, and whose blue eyes were haunted with an anguished dread.

He kicked back his chair and strode across the gloomy little office, whose single window looked out on the thickening, foggy twilight of London. He bent across the dingy desk, gripping its edges with his hands as he spoke tensely to the man sitting behind it.

"Why are we wasting time talking here?" Ennis cried. "Sitting here talking, when anything may be happening to Ruth!

"It's been hours since she was kidnapped. They may have taken her anywhere, even outside of London by now. And instead of searching for her, you sit here and talk gibberish about Doors!"

Inspector Campbell seemed unmoved by Ennis' passion. A bulky, almost bald man, he looked up with his colorless, sagging face, in which his eyes gleamed like two crumbs of bright brown glass.

"You're not helping me much by giving way to your emotions, Mr. Ennis," he said in his flat voice.

"Give way? Who wouldn't give way?" cried Ennis. "Don't you understand, man, it's Ruth that's gone—my wife! Why, we were married only last week in New York. And on our second day here in London, I see her whisked into a limousine and carried away before my eyes! I thought you men at Scotland Yard here would surely act, do something. Instead you talk crazy gibberish to me!"

"Those words are *not* gibberish," said Pierce Campbell quietly. "And I think they're related to the abduction of your wife."

"What do you mean? How could they be related?"

The inspector's bright little brown eyes held Ennis'. "Did you ever hear of an organization called the Brotherhood of the Door?"

Ennis shook his head, and Campbell continued, "Well, I am certain your wife was kidnapped by members of the Brotherhood."

"What kind of an organization is it?" the young American demanded. "A band of criminals?"

"No, it is no ordinary criminal organization," the detective said. His sagging face set strangely. "Unless I am mistaken, the Brotherhood of the Door is the most unholy and blackly evil organization that has ever existed on this earth. Almost nothing is known of it outside its circle. I myself in twenty years have learned little except its existence and name. That ritual I just repeated to you, I heard from the lips of a dying member of the Brotherhood, who repeated the words in his delirium."

Campbell leaned forward. "But I know that every year about this time the Brotherhood come from all over the world and gather at some secret center here in England. And every year, before that gathering, scores of people are kidnapped and never heard of again. I believe that all those people are kidnapped by this mysterious Brotherhood."

"But what becomes of the people they kidnap?" cried the pale young American. "What do they do with them?"

*   *   *   *   *

Inspector Campbell's bright brown eyes showed a hint of hooded horror, yet he shook his head. "I know no more than you. But whatever they do to the victims, they are never heard of again."

"But you must know something more!" Ennis protested. "What is this Door?"

Campbell again shook his head. "That too I don't know, but whatever it is, the Door is utterly sacred to the members of the Brotherhood, and whomever they mean by They Beyond the Door, they dread and venerate to the utmost."

"Where leads the Door? *It leads outside our world,*" repeated Ennis. "What can that mean?"

"It might have a symbolic meaning, referring to some secluded fastness of the order which is away from the rest of the world," the inspector said. "Or it might——"

He stopped. "Or it might what?" pressed Ennis, his pale face thrust forward.

"It might mean, literally, that the Door leads outside our world and universe," finished the inspector.

Ennis' haunted eyes stared. "You mean that this Door might somehow lead into another universe? But that's impossible!"

"Perhaps unlikely," Campbell said quietly, "but not impossible. Modern science has taught us that there are other universes than the one we live in, universes congruent and coincident with our own in space and time, yet separated from our own by the impassable barrier of totally different dimensions. It is not entirely impossible that a greater science than ours might find a way to pierce that barrier between our universe and one of those outside ones, that a Door should be opened from ours into one of those others in the infinite outside."

"A door into the infinite outside," repeated Ennis broodingly, looking past the inspector. Then he made a sudden movement of wild impatience, the dread leaping back strong in his eyes again.

"Oh, what good is all this talk about Doors and infinite universes doing in finding Ruth? I want to *do* something! If you think this mysterious Brotherhood has taken her, you must surely have some idea of how we can get her back from them? You must know something more about them than you've told."

"I don't know anything more certainly, but I've certain suspicions that amount to convictions," Inspector Campbell said. "I've been working on this Brotherhood for many years, and block after block I've narrowed down to the place I think the order's local center, the London headquarters of the Brotherhood of the Door."

"Where is the place?" asked Ennis tensely.

"It is the waterfront cafe of one Chandra Dass, a Hindoo, down by East India Docks," said the detective officer. "I've been there in disguise more than once, watching the place. This Chandra Dass I've found to be immensely feared by everyone in the quarter, which strengthens my belief that he's one of the high officers of the Brotherhood. He's too exceptional a man to be really running such a place."

"Then if the Brotherhood took Ruth, she may be at that place now!" cried the young American, electrified.

Campbell nodded his bald head. "She may very likely be. Tonight I'm going there again in disguise, and have men ready to raid the place. If Chandra Dass has your wife there, we'll get her before he can get her away. Whatever way it turns out, we'll let you know at once."

"Like hell you will!" exploded the pale young Ennis. "Do you think I'm going to twiddle my thumbs while you're down there? I'm going with you. And if you refuse to let me, by heaven I'll go there myself!"

Inspector Pierce Campbell gave the haggard, fiercely determined face of the young man a long look, and then his own colorless countenance seemed to soften a little.

"All right," he said quietly. "I can disguise you so you'll not be recognized. But you'll have to follow my orders exactly, or death will result for both of us."

That strange, hooded dread flickered again in his eyes, as though he saw through shrouding mists the outline of dim horror.

"It may be," he added slowly, "that something worse even than death awaits those who try to oppose the Brotherhood of the Door—something that would explain the unearthly, superhuman dread that enwraps the secret mysteries of the order. We're taking more than our lives in our hands, I think, in trying to unveil those mysteries, to regain your wife. But we've got to act quickly, at all costs. We've got to find her before the great gathering of the Brotherhood takes place, or we'll never find her."

*   *   *   *   *

Two hours before midnight found Campbell and Ennis passing along a cobble-paved waterfront street north of the great East India Docks. Big warehouses towered black and silent in the darkness on one side, and on the other were old, rotting docks beyond which Ennis glimpsed the black water and gliding lights of the river.

As they straggled beneath the infrequent lights of the ill-lit street, they were utterly changed in appearance. Inspector Campbell, dressed in a shabby suit and rusty bowler, his dirty white shirt innocent of tie, had acquired a new face, a bright red, oily, eager one, and a high, squeaky voice. Ennis wore a rough blue seaman's jacket and a vizored cap pulled down over his head. His unshaven-looking face and subtly altered features made him seem a half-intoxicated seaman off his ship, as he stumbled unsteadily along. Campbell clung to him in true land-shark fashion, plucking his arm and talking wheedlingly to him.

They came into a more populous section of the evil old waterfront street, and passed fried-fish shops giving off the strong smell of hot fat, and the dirty, lighted windows of a half-dozen waterfront saloons, loud with sordid argument or merriment.

Campbell led past them until they reached one built upon an abandoned, moldering pier, a ramshackle frame structure extending some distance back out on the pier. Its window was curtained, but dull red light glowed through the glass window of the door.

A few shabby men were lounging in front of the place but Campbell paid them no attention, tugging Ennis inside by the arm.

"Carm on in!" he wheedled shrilly. "The night ain't 'alf over yet—we'll 'ave just one more."

"Don't want any more," muttered Ennis drunkenly, swaying on his feet inside. "Get away, you damned old shark."

Yet he suffered himself to be led by Campbell to a table, where he slumped heavily into a chair. His stare swung vacantly.

The cafe of Chandra Dass was a red-lit, smoke-filled cave with cheap black curtains on the walls and windows, and other curtains cutting off the back part of the building from view. The dim room was jammed with tables crowded with patrons whose babel of tongues made an unceasing din, to which a three-string guitar somewhere added a wailing undertone. The waiters were dark-skinned and tiger-footed Malays, while the patrons seemed drawn from every nation east and west.

Ennis' glazed eyes saw dandified Chinese from Limehouse and Pennyfields, dark little Levantins from Soho, rough-looking Cockneys in shabby caps, a few crazily laughing blacks. From sly white faces, taut brown ones and impassive yellow ones came a dozen different languages. The air was thick with queer food-smells and the acrid smoke.

Campbell had selected a table near the back curtain, and now stridently ordered one of the Malay waiters to bring gin. He leaned forward with an oily smile to the drunken-looking Ennis, and spoke to him in a wheedling undertone.

"Don't look for a minute, but that's Chandra Dass over in the corner, and he's watching us," he said.

Ennis shook his clutching hand away. "Damned old shark!" he muttered again.

He turned his swaying head slowly, letting his eyes rest a moment on the man in the corner. That man was looking straight at him.

Chandra Dass was tall, dressed in spotless white from his shoes to the turban on his head. The white made his dark, impassive, aquiline face stand out in chiseled relief. His eyes were coal-black, large, coldly searching, as they met Ennis' bleared gaze.

Ennis felt a strange chill as he met those eyes. There was something alien and unhuman, something uncannily disturbing, behind the Hindoo's stare. He turned his gaze vacantly from Chandra Dass to the black curtains at the rear, and then back to his companion.

The silent Malay waiter had brought the liquor, and Campbell pressed a glass toward his companion. "'Ere, matey, take this."

"Don't want it," muttered Ennis, pushing it away. Still in the same mutter, he added, "If Ruth's here, she's somewhere in the back there. I'm going back and find out."

"Don't try it that way, for God's sake!" said Campbell in the wheedling undertone. "Chandra Dass is still watching, and those Malays would be on you in a minute. Wait until I give the word.

"All right, then," Campbell added in a louder, injured tone. "If you don't want it, I'll drink it myself."

He tossed off the glass of gin and set the glass down on the table, looking at his drunken companion with righteous indignation.

"Think I'm tryin' to bilk yer, eh?" he added. "That's a fine way to treat a pal!"

He added in the coaxing lower tone, "All right, I'm going to try it. Be ready to move when I light my cigarette."

He fished a soiled package of Gold Flakes from his pocket and put one in his mouth. Ennis waited, every muscle taut.

The inspector, his red, oily face still injured in expression, struck a match to his cigarette. Almost at once there was a loud oath from one of the shabby loungers outside the front of the building, and the sound of angry voices and blows.

The patrons of Chandra Dass looked toward the door, and one of the Malay waiters went hastily out to quiet the fight. But it grew swiftly, sounded in a moment like a small riot. *Crash*—someone was pushed through the front window. The excited patrons pressed toward the front. Chandra Dass pushed through them, issuing quick orders to his servants.

For the time being the back of the cafe was deserted and unnoticed. Campbell sprang to his feet, and with Ennis close behind him, darted through the black curtains. They found themselves in a black corridor at the end of which a red bulb burned dimly. They could still hear the uproar.

Campbell's gun was in his hand, and the American's in his.

"We dare only stay here a few moments," the inspector cried. "Look in those rooms along the corridor here."

Ennis frantically tore open a door and peered into a dark room smelling of drugs. "Ruth!" he cried softly. "Ruth!"

Death Trap

There was no answer. The light in the corridor behind him suddenly went out, plunging him into pitch-black darkness. He jumped back into the dark corridor, and as he did so, heard a sudden scuffle further along it.

"Campbell!" he exclaimed, lunging forward in the black passageway. There was no answer.

He pitched forward through stygian obscurity, his hands searching ahead of him for the inspector. In the dark something whipped smoothly around his throat, tightened there like a slender, contracting tentacle.

Ennis tore frenziedly at the thing, which he felt to be a slender silken cord, but he could not loosen it. It was choking him. He tried to cry out again to Campbell, but his throat could not emit the sounds. He thrashed, twisted helplessly, hearing a loud roaring in his ears, consciousness receding. Then, dimly as though in a dream, Ennis was aware of being lowered to the floor, of being half carried and half dragged along. The constriction around his throat was gone and rapidly his brain began to clear. He opened his eyes.

He found himself lying on the floor of a room illuminated by a great hanging brass lamp of ornate design. The walls of the room were hung with rich, grotesquely worked red silk Indian draperies. His hands and feet were bound behind him, and beside him, tied in the same manner, lay Inspector Campbell. Over them stood Chandra Dass and two of the Malay servants. The faces of the servants were tigerish in their menace, but Chandra Dass' face was one of dark, impassive scorn.

"So you misguided fools thought you could deceive me so easily as that?" he said in a strong, vibrant voice. "Why, we knew hours ago that you, Inspector Campbell, and you, Mr. Ennis, were coming here tonight. We let you get this far only because it was evident that somehow you had learned too much about us, and that it would be best to let you come here and meet your deaths."

"Chandra Dass, I've men outside," rasped Campbell. "If we don't come out, they'll come in after us."

The Hindoo's proud, dark face did not change its scorn. "They will not come in for a little while, inspector. By that time you two will be dead and we shall be gone with our captives. Yes, Mr. Ennis, your wife is one of those captives," he added to the prostrate young American. "It is too bad we cannot take you and the inspector to share her glorious destiny, but then our accommodations of transport are limited."

"Ruth here?" Ennis' face flamed at the words, and he raised himself a little from the floor on his elbows.

"Then you'll let her go if I pay you? I'll raise any amount, I'll do anything you ask, if you'll set her free."

"No amount of money in the world could buy her from the Brotherhood of the Door," answered Chandra Dass steadily. "For she belongs now, not to us, but to They Beyond the Door. Within a few hours she and many others shall stand before the Door, and They Beyond the Door shall take them."

"What are you going to do to her?" cried Ennis. "What is this damned Door and who are They Beyond it?"

"I do not think that even if I told you, your little mind would be able to accept the mighty truth," Chandra Dass said calmly. His coal-black eyes suddenly flashed with fanatic, frenetic light. "How could your poor, earth-bound little intelligences conceive the true nature of the Door and of those who dwell beyond it? Your puny brains would be stricken senseless by mere apprehension of them, They who are mighty and crafty and dreadful beyond anything on earth."

A cold wind from the alien unknown seemed to sweep the lamplit room with the Hindoo's passionate words. Then that rapt, fanatic exaltation dropped from him as suddenly as it had come, and he spoke in his ordinary vibrant tones.

"But enough of this parley with blind worms of the dust. Bring the weights!"

The last words were addressed to the Malay servants, who sprang to a closet in the corner of the room.

Inspector Campbell said steadily, "If my men find us dead when they come in here, they'll leave none of you living."

*   *   *   *   *

Chandra Dass did not even listen to him, but ordered the dark servants sharply, "Attach the weights!"

The Malays had brought from the closet two fifty-pound lead balls, and now they proceeded quickly to tie these to the feet of the two men. Then one of them rolled back the brilliant red Indian rug from the rough pine floor. A square trap-door was disclosed, and at Chandra Dass' order, it was swung upward and open.

Up through the open square came the sound of waves slap-slapping against the piles of the old pier, and the heavy odors of salt water and of rotting wood invaded the room.

"The water under this pier is twenty feet deep," Chandra Dass told the two prisoners. "I regret to give you so easy a death, but there is no opportunity to take you to the fate you deserve."

Ennis, his skin crawling on his flesh, nevertheless spoke rapidly and as steadily as possible to the Hindoo.

"Listen, I don't ask you to let me go, but I'll do anything you want, let you kill me any way you want, if you'll let Ruth——"

Sheer horror cut short his words. The Malay servants had dragged Campbell's bound body to the door in the floor. They shoved him over the edge. Ennis had one glimpse of the inspector's taut, strange face falling out of sight. Then a dull splash sounded instantly below, and then silence.

He felt hands upon himself, dragging him across the floor. He fought, crazily, hopelessly, twisting his body in its bonds, thrashing his bound limbs wildly.

He saw the dark, unmoved face of Chandra Dass, the brass lamp over his head, the red hangings. Then his head dangled over the opening, a shove sent his body scraping over the edge, and he plunged downward through dank darkness. With a splash he hit the icy water and went under. The heavy weight at his ankles dragged him irresistibly downward. Instinctively he held his breath as the water rushed upward around him.

His feet struck oozy bottom. His body swayed there, chained by the lead weight to the bottom. His lungs already were bursting to draw in air, slow fires seeming to creep through his breast as he held his breath.

Ennis knew that in a moment or two more he would inhale the strangling waters and die. The thought-picture of Ruth flashed across his despairing mind, wild with hopeless regret. He could no longer hold his breath, felt his muscles relaxing against his will, tasted the stinging salt water at the back of his nose.

Then it was a bursting confusion of swift sensations, the choking water in his nose and throat, the roaring in his ears. A scroll of flame unrolled slowly in his brain and a voice shouted there, "You're dying!" He felt dimly a plucking at his ankles.

Abruptly Ennis' dimming mind was aware that he now was shooting upward through the water. His head burst into open air and he choked, strangled and gasped, his tortured lungs gulping the damp, heavy air. He opened his eyes, and shook the water from them.

He was floating in the darkness at the surface of the water. Someone was floating beside him, supporting him. Ennis' chin bumped the other's shoulder, and he heard a familiar voice.

"Easy, now," said Inspector Campbell. "Wait till I cut your hands loose."

"Campbell!" Ennis choked. "How did you get loose?"

"Never mind that now," the inspector answered. "Don't make any noise, or they may hear us up there."

Ennis felt a knife-blade slashing the bonds at his wrists. Then, the inspector's arm helping him, he and his companion paddled weakly through the darkness under the rotting pier. They bumped against the slimy, moldering piles, threaded through them toward the side of the pier. The waves of the flooding tide washed them up and down as Campbell led the way.

They passed out from under the old pier into the comparative illumination of the stars. Looking back up, Ennis saw the long, black mass of the house of Chandra Dass, resting on the black pier, ruddy light glowing from window-cracks. He collided with something and found that Campbell had led toward a little floating dock where some skiffs were moored. They scrambled up onto it from the water, and lay panting for a few moments.

Campbell had something in his hand, a thin, razor-edged steel blade several inches long. Its hilt was an ordinary leather shoe-heel.

The inspector turned up one of his feet and Ennis saw that the heel was missing from that shoe. Carefully Campbell slid the steel blade beneath the shoe-sole, the heel-hilt sliding into place and seeming merely the innocent heel of the shoe.

"So that's how you got loose down in the water!" Ennis exclaimed, and the inspector nodded briefly.

"That trick's done me good service before—even with your hands tied behind your back you can get out that knife and use it. It was touch and go, though, whether I could get it out and cut myself loose in the water in time enough to free you."

Ennis gripped the inspector's shoulder. "Campbell, Ruth is in there! By heaven, we've found her and now we can get her out!"

"Right!" said the officer grimly. "We'll go around to the front and in two minutes we'll be in there with my men."

*   *   *   *   *

They climbed dripping to their feet, and hastened from the little floating dock up onto the shore, through the darkness to the cobbled street.

The shabbily disguised men of Inspector Campbell were not now in front of Chandra Dass' cafe, but lurking in the shadows across the street. They came running toward Campbell and Ennis.

"All right, we're going in there," Campbell exclaimed in steely tones. "Get Chandra Dass, whatever you do, but see that his prisoners are not harmed."

He snapped a word and one of the men handed pistols to him and to Ennis. Then they leaped toward the door of the Hindoo's cafe, from which still streamed ruddy light and the babel of many voices.

A kick from Inspector Campbell sent the door flying inward, and they burst in with guns gleaming wickedly in the ruddy light. Ennis' face was a quivering mask of desperate resolve.

The motley patrons jumped up with yells of alarm at their entrance. The hand of a Malay waiter jerked and a thrown knife thudded into the wall beside them. Ennis yelled as he saw Chandra Dass, his dark face startled, leaping back with his servants through the black curtains.

He and Campbell drove through the squealing patrons toward the back. The Malay who had thrown the knife rushed to bar the way, another dagger uplifted. Campbell's gun coughed and the Malay reeled and stumbled. The inspector and Ennis threw themselves at the black curtains—and were dashed back.

They tore aside the black folds. A dull steel door had been lowered behind them, barring the way to the back rooms. Ennis beat crazily upon it with his pistol-butt, but it remained immovable.

"No use—we can't break that down!" yelled Campbell, over the uproar. "Outside, and around to the other end of the building!"

They burst back out through that mad-house, into the dark of the street. They started along the side of the pier toward the river-end, edging forward on a narrow ledge but inches wide. As they reached the back of the building, Ennis shouted and pointed to dark figures at the end of the pier. There were two of them, lowering shapeless, wrapped forms over the end of the pier.

"There they are!" he cried. "They've got their prisoners out there with them."

Campbell's pistol leveled, but Ennis swiftly struck it up. "No, you might hit Ruth."

He and the inspector bounded forward along the pier. Fire streaked from the dark ahead and bullets thumped the rotting boards around them.

Suddenly the loud roar of an accelerated motor drowned out all other sounds. It came from the river at the pier's end.

Campbell and Ennis reached the end in time to see a long, powerful, gray motor-boat dash out into the black obscurity of the river, and roar eastward with gathering speed.

"There they go—they're getting away!" cried the agonized young American.

Inspector Campbell cupped his hands and shouted out into the darkness, "River police, ahoy! Ahoy there!"

He rasped to Ennis. "The river police were to have a cutter here tonight. We can still catch them."

With swiftly rising roar of speeded motors, a big cutter drove in from the darkness. Its searchlight snapped on, bathing the two men on the pier in a blinding glare.

"Ahoy, there!" called a stentorian voice over the roar of the motors. "Is that Inspector Campbell?"

"Yes. Come alongside," yelled the inspector, and as the big cutter shot close to the end of the pier, its reversing propellers churning the dark water to foam, Ennis and Campbell leaped.

They landed amid unseen men in the cockpit, and as he scrambled to his feet the inspector cried, "Follow that boat that just went down-river. But no shooting!"

*   *   *   *   *

With thunderous drumfire from its exhausts, the cutter jerked forward so rapidly that it almost threw them from their feet again. It shot out onto the bosom of the dark river that flowed like a black sea between the banks of scattered lights that were London.

The moving lights of yachts and barges coming up-river could be seen gliding in that darkness. The captain of the cutter barked an order and one of his three men, the one crouched at the searchlight, switched its powerful beam out over the waters ahead.

In a moment it picked up a distant gray spot racing eastward on the black river, leaving a white trail of foam.

"There she is!" bawled the man at the searchlight. "She's running without lights!"

"Keep her in the searchlight," ordered the captain. "Sound our siren, and give the cutter her head."

Swaying, rocking, the cutter roared on through the darkness on the trail of that distant fleeing speck. As they raced down Blackwall Reach, the distance between the two craft had already begun to lessen.

"We're overtaking him!" cried Campbell, clutching a stanchion and peering ahead against the rush of wind and spray. "He must be making for whatever spot it is in

England that is the center of the Brotherhood of the Door—but he'll never reach it."

"He said that within a few hours Ruth would go with the others through the Door!" cried Ennis, clinging beside him. "Campbell, we mustn't let them get away now!"

Pursuers and pursued flashed on down the dark, broadening river, through mazes of shipping, the cutter hanging doggedly to the motor-boat's trail. The lights of London had dropped behind and those of Tilbury now gleamed away on their left.

Bigger, stronger waves now tossed and pounded the cutter as it raced out of the river mouth toward the heaving black expanse of the sea. The Kent coast was a black blur on their right; the gray motor-boat followed it closely, grazing almost beneath the Sheerness lights.

"He's heading to round North Foreland and follow the coast south to Ramsgate or Dover," the cutter captain cried to Campbell. "But we'll catch him before he passes Margate."

The quarry was now but a quarter-mile ahead. Steadily as they roared onward the gap narrowed, until in the glare of the searchlight they could make out every detail of the powerful gray motor-boat plunging through the tossing black waves.

They saw Chandra Dass' dark face turn and look back at them, and the cutter captain raised his speaking-trumpet to his lips and shouted over the roar of motors and dash of waves.

"Stand by or we'll fire at you!"

"He won't obey," muttered Campbell between his teeth. "He knows we daren't fire with the girl in the boat."

"Yes, blast him!" exclaimed the captain. "But we'll have him in a few minutes, anyway."

The thundering chase had brought them into sight of the lights of Margate on the dark coast to their right. Now only a few hundred feet of black water separated them from the fleeing craft.

Ennis and the inspector, gripping the stanchions of the rushing cutter, saw a white figure suddenly stand erect in the boat ahead and wave its arms to them. The gray motor-boat slowed.

"It's Chandra Dass and he's signaling that he's giving up!" Ennis cried. "He's stopping!"

"By heavens, he is!" Campbell explained. "Drive alongside him, and we'll soon have the irons on him."

The cutter, its own motors hastily throttled down, shot through the water toward the slowing gray craft. Ennis saw Chandra Dass standing erect, awaiting their coming, he and the two Malays beside him holding their hands in the air. He saw a half-dozen or more white-wrapped forms in the bottom of the boat, lying motionless.

"There are their prisoners!" he cried. "Bring the boat closer so we can jump in!"

He and Campbell, their pistols out, hunched to jump as the cutter drove closer to the gray motor-boat. The sides of the two craft bumped, the motors of both idling noisily. Then before Ennis and Campbell could jump into the motor-boat, things happened with cinema-like rapidity. Two of the still white forms at the bottom of the motor-boat leaped up and like suddenly uncoiled springs shot through the air into the cutter. They were two other Malays, their dark faces flaming with fanatic light, keen daggers glinting in their upraised hands.

"'Ware a trick!" yelled Campbell. His gun barked, but the bullet missed and a dagger slit his sleeve.

The Malays, with wild, screeching yells, were laying about them with their daggers in the cutter, insanely.

"God in heaven, they're running amok!" choked the cutter captain.

His slashed neck spurting blood and his face livid, he fell. One of his men slumped coughing beside him, another victim of the crazy daggers.

Up the Water-Tunnel

The man at the searchlight sprang for the maddened Malays, tugging at his pistol as he jumped. Before he got the weapon out, a dagger slashed his jugular and he went down gurgling in death. One of the Malays meanwhile had knocked Inspector Campbell from his feet, his knife-hand swooping down, his eyes blazing.

Ennis' gun roared and the bullet hit the Malay between the eyes. But as he slumped limply, the other fanatic was upon Ennis from the side. Before Ennis could whirl to meet him, the attacker's knife grazed down past his cheek like a brand of living fire. He was borne backward by the rush, felt the hot breath of the crazed Malay in his face, the dagger-point at his throat.

Shots roared quickly, one after another, and with each shot the Malay pressing Ennis back jerked convulsively. With the light of murderous madness fading from his eyes, he still strove to drive the dagger home into the American's throat. But a hand jerked him back and he lay prostrate and still.

Ennis scrambled up to find Inspector Campbell, pale and determined, over him. The detective had shot the attacker from behind.

The captain of the cutter and two of his men lay dead in the cockpit beside the two Malays. The remaining seaman, the helmsman, held his shoulder and groaned.

Ennis whirled. The motor-boat of Chandra Dass was no longer beside the cutter, and there was no sight of it anywhere on the black sea ahead. The Hindoo had taken advantage of the fight to make good his escape with his two other servants and their prisoners.

"Campbell, he's gone!" cried the young American frantically. "He's got away!"

The inspector's eyes were bright with cold flame of anger. "Yes, Chandra Dass sacrificed these two Malays to hold us up long enough for him to escape."

Campbell whirled to the helmsman. "You're not badly hurt?"

"Only a scratch, but I nearly broke my shoulder when I fell," answered the man.

"Then head on around North Foreland!" Campbell cried. "We may still be able to catch up to them."

"But Captain Wilson and the others are killed," protested the helmsman. "I've got to report——"

"You can report later," rasped the inspector. "Do as I say—I'll be responsible."

"Very well, sir," said the helmsman, and jumped back to the wheel.

In a minute the big cutter was roaring ahead over the heaving black waves, its searchlight clawing the darkness ahead. There was no sign now of the craft of Chandra Dass ahead. They raced abreast of the lights of Margate, started rounding the North Foreland, pounded by bigger seas.

Inspector Campbell had dragged the bodies of the dead policemen and their two slayers down into the cabin of the cutter. He came up and crouched down with Ennis beside Sturt, the helmsman.

"I found these on the two Malays," Campbell shouted to the American, holding out two little objects in his spray-wet hand.

Each was a flat star of gray metal in which was set a large oval, cabochon-cut jewel. The jewels flashed and dazzled with deep color, but it was a color wholly unfamiliar and alien to their eyes.

"They're not any color we know on earth," Campbell shouted. "I believe these jewels came from somewhere beyond the Door, and that these are badges of the Brotherhood of the Door."

Sturt, the helmsman, leaned toward the inspector. "We've rounded North Foreland, sir," he cried. "Head straight south along the coast," Campbell ordered. "Chandra Dass must have gone this way. No doubt he thinks he's shaken us off, and is making for the gathering-place of the Brotherhood, wherever that may be."

"The cutter isn't built for seas like this," Sturt said, shaking his head. "But I'll do it."

They were now following the coast southward, the lights of Ramsgate dropping back on their right. The waters out here in the Channel were wilder, great black waves tossing the cutter to the sky one moment, and then dropping it sickeningly the next. Frequently its screws raced loudly as they encountered no resistance but air.

Ennis, clinging precariously on the foredeck, turned the searchlight's stabbing white beam back and forth on the heaving dark sea ahead, but without any sign of their quarry disclosed.

White foam of breaking waves began to show around them like bared teeth, and there was a humming in the air.

"Storm coming up the Channel," Sturt exclaimed. "It'll do for us if it catches us out here."

"We've got to keep on," Ennis told him desperately. "We must come up with them soon!"

The coast on their right was now one of black, rocky cliffs, towering all along the shore in a jagged, frowning wall against which the waves dashed foamy white. The cutter crept southward over the wild waters, tossed like a chip upon the great waves. Sturt was having a hard time holding the craft out from the rocks, and had its prow pointed obliquely away from them.

The humming in the air changed to a shrill whistling as the outrider winds of the storm came upon them. The cutter tossed still more wildly and black masses of water smashed in upon them from the darkness, dazing and drenching them.

Suddenly Ennis yelled, "There's the lights of a boat ahead! There, moving in toward the cliffs!"

He pointed ahead, and Campbell and the helmsman peered through the blinding spray and darkness. A pair of low lights were moving at high speed on the waters there, straight toward the towering black cliffs. Then they vanished suddenly from sight.

"There must be a hidden opening or harbor of some kind in the cliffs!" Inspector Campbell exclaimed. "But that can't be Chandra Dass' boat, for it carried no lights."

"It might be others of the Brotherhood going to the meeting-place!" Ennis exclaimed. "We can follow and see."

*   *   *   *   *

Sturt thrust his head through the flying spray and shouted, "There are openings and water-caverns in plenty along these cliffs, but there's nothing in any of them."

"We'll find out," Campbell said. "Head straight toward the cliffs in there where that boat vanished."

"If we can't find the opening we'll be smashed to flinders on those cliffs," Sturt warned.

"I'm gambling that we'll find the opening," Campbell told him. "Go ahead."

Sturt's face set stolidly and he said, "Yes, sir."

He turned the prow of the cutter toward the cliffs. Instantly they dashed forward toward the rock walls with greatly increased speed, wild waves bearing them onward like charging stallions of the sea.

Hunched beside the helmsman, the searchlight stabbing the dark wildly as the cutter was flung forward by the waves, Ennis and the inspector watched as the cliffs loomed closer ahead. The brilliant white beam struck across the rushing, mountainous waves and showed only the towering barriers of rock, battered and smitten by the raving waters that frothed white. They could hear the booming thunder of the raging ocean striking the rock.

Like a projectile hurled by a giant hand, the cutter fairly flew now toward the cliffs. They now could see even the little streams that ran off the rough rock wall as each giant wave broke against it. They were almost upon it.

Sturt's face was deathly. "I don't see any opening!" he yelled. "And we're going to hit in a moment!"

"To your left!" screamed Inspector Campbell over the booming thunder. "There's an arched opening there."

Now Ennis saw it also, a huge arch-like opening in the cliff that had been concealed by an angle of the wall. Sturt tried frantically to head the cutter toward it, but the wheel was useless as the great waves bore the craft along. Ennis saw they would strike a little to the side of the opening. The cliff loomed ahead, and he closed his eyes to the impact.

There was no impact. And as he heard a hoarse cry from Inspector Campbell, he opened his eyes.

The cutter was flying in through the mighty opening, snatched into it by powerful currents. They were whirled irresistibly forward under the huge rock arch, which loomed forty feet over their heads. Before them stretched a winding water-tunnel inside the cliff.

And now they were out of the wild uproar of the storming waters outside, and in an almost stupefying silence. Smoothly, resistlessly, the current bore them on in the tunnel, whose winding turns ahead were lit up by their searchlight.

"God, that was close!" exclaimed Inspector Campbell.

His eyes flashed. "Ennis, I believe that we have found the gathering-place of the Brotherhood. That boat we sighted is somewhere ahead in here, and so must be Chandra Dass, and your wife."

Ennis' hand tightened on his gun-butt. "If that's so—if we can just find them——"

"Blind action won't help if we do," said the inspector swiftly. "There must be all the number of the Brotherhood's members assembled here, and we can't fight them all."

His eyes suddenly lit and he took the blazing jeweled stars from his pocket. "These badges! With them we can pose as members of the Brotherhood, perhaps long enough to find your wife."

"But Chandra Dass will be there, and if he sees us—
—"

Campbell shrugged. "We'll have to take that chance.
It's the only course open to us."

The current of the inflowing tide was still bearing
them smoothly onward through the winding water-
tunnel, around bends and angles where they scraped the
rock, down long straight stretches. Sturt used the motors
to guide them around the turns. Meanwhile, Inspector
Campbell and Ennis quickly ripped from the cutter its
police-insignia and covered all evidences of its being a
police craft.

Sturt suddenly snicked off the searchlight. "Light
ahead there!" he exclaimed.

Around the next turn of the water-tunnel showed a
gleam of strange, soft light.

"Careful, now!" cautioned the inspector. "Sturt,
whatever we do, you stay in the cutter. And try to have it
ready for a quick getaway, if we leave it."

Sturt nodded silently. The helmsman's stolid face had
become a little pale, but he showed no sign of losing his
courage.

$$*\quad*\quad*\quad*\quad*$$

The cutter sped around the next turn of the tunnel
and emerged into a huge, softly lit cavern. Sturt's eyes
bulged and Campbell uttered an exclamation of
amazement. For in this mighty water-cavern there
floated in a great mass, scores of sea-going craft, large
and small.

All of them were capable of breasting storm and wind,
and some were so large they could barely have entered.
There were small yachts, big motor-cruisers, sea-going
launches, cutters larger than their own, and among them
the gray motor-launch of Chandra Dass.

They were massed together here, those with masts
having lowered them to enter, floating and rubbing sides,

quite unoccupied. Around the edges of the water-cavern ran a wide rock ledge. But no living person was visible and there was no visible source for the soft, strange white light that filled the astounding place.

"These craft must have come here from all over earth!" Campbell muttered. "The Brotherhood of the Door has assembled here—we've found their gathering-place all right."

"But where are they?" exclaimed Ennis. "I don't see anyone."

"We'll soon find out," the inspector said. "Sturt, run close to the ledge there and we'll get out on it."

Sturt obeyed, and as the cutter bumped the ledge, Campbell and Ennis leaped out onto it. They looked this way and that along it, but no one was in sight. The weirdness of it was unnerving, the strangely lit, mighty cavern, the assembled boats, the utter silence.

"Follow me," Campbell said in a low voice. "They must all be somewhere near."

He and Ennis walked a few steps along the ledge, when the American stopped. "Campbell, listen!" he whispered.

Dimly there whispered to them, as though from a distance and through great walls, a swelling sound of chanting. As they listened, hearts beating rapidly, a square of the rock wall of the cavern abruptly flew open beside them, as though hinged like a door. Inside it was the mouth of a soft-lit, man-high tunnel, and in its opening stood two men. They wore over their clothing shroud-like, loose-hanging robes of gray, asbestos-like material. They wore hoods of the same gray stuff over their heads, pierced with slits at the eyes and mouth. And each wore on his breast the blazing star-badge.

Through the eye-slits the eyes of the two surveyed Campbell and Ennis as they halted, transfixed by the sudden apparition. Then one of the hooded men spoke measuredly in a hissing, Mongolian voice.

"Are you who come here of the Brotherhood of the Door?" he asked, apparently repeating a customary challenge.

Campbell answered, his flat voice tremorless. "We are of the Brotherhood."

"Why do you not wear the badge of the Brotherhood, then?"

For answer, the inspector reached in his pocket for the strange emblem and fastened it to his lapel. Ennis did the same.

"Enter, brothers," said the hissing, hooded shape, standing aside to let them pass.

As they stepped into the tunnel, the hooded guard added in slightly more natural tones, "Brothers, you two are late. You must hurry to get your protective robes, for the ceremony soon begins."

Campbell inclined his head without speaking, and he and Ennis started along the tunnel. Its light, as sourceless as that of the great water-cavern, revealed that it was chiseled from solid rock and that it wound downward.

When they were out of sight of the two hooded guards, Ennis clutched the detective's arm convulsively.

"Campbell," he said, "the ceremony begins soon! We've got to find Ruth first!"

"We'll try," the inspector answered swiftly. "Those hooded robes are apparently issued to all the members to be worn during the ceremony as protection, for some reason, and once we get robes and get them on, Chandra Dass won't be able to spot us.

"Look out!" he added an instant later. "Here's the place where the robes are issued!"

The tunnel had debouched suddenly into a wider space in which were a group of men. Several were wearing the concealing hoods and robes, and one of these hooded figures was handing out, from a large rack of the robes, three of the garments to three dark Easterners who had apparently entered in the boat just ahead of the cutter.

The three dark Orientals, their faces gleaming with strange fanaticism, quickly donned the robes and hoods and passed hurriedly on down the tunnel. At once Campbell and Ennis stepped calmly up to the hooded custodians of the robes, and extended their hands.

One of the hooded figures took down two robes and handed them to them. But suddenly one of the other hooded men spoke sharply.

Instantly all the hooded men but the one who had spoken, with loud cries, threw themselves forward on Campbell and Paul Ennis.

Taken utterly by surprize, the two had no chance to draw their guns. They were smothered by gray-robed men, held helpless before they could move, a half-dozen pistols jammed into their bodies.

Stupefied by the sudden dashing of their hopes, the detective and the young American saw the hooded man who had spoken slowly lift the concealing gray cowl from his face. It was the dark, coldly contemptuous face of Chandra Dass.

The Cavern of the Door

Chandra Dass spoke, and his strong, vibrant voice held a scorn that was almost pitying.

"It occurred to me that your enterprise might enable you to escape the daggers of my followers, and that you might trail us here," he said. "That is why I waited here to see if you came.

"Search them," he told the other hooded figures. "Take anything that looks like a weapon from them."

Ennis stared, stupefied, as the gray-hooded men obeyed. He was unable to believe entirely in the abrupt reversal of all their hopes, of their desperate attempt.

The hooded men took their pistols from Ennis and Campbell, and even the small gold knife attached to the chain of the inspector's big, old-fashioned gold watch. Then they stepped back, the pistols of two of them leveled at the hearts of the captives.

Chandra Dass had watched impassively. Ennis, staring dazedly, noted that the Hindoo wore on his breast a different jewel-emblem from the others, a double star instead of a single one.

Ennis' dazed eyes lifted from the blazing badge to the Hindoo's dark face. "Where's Ruth?" he asked a little shrilly, and then his voice cracked and he cried, "You damned fiend, where's my wife?"

"Be comforted, Mr. Ennis," came Chandra Dass' chill voice. "You are going now to join your wife, and to share her fate. You two are going with her and the other sacrifices through the Door when it opens. It is not usual," he added in cold mockery, "for our sacrificial victims to walk directly into our hands. We ordinarily have a more difficult time securing them."

He made a gesture to the two hooded men with pistols, and they ranged themselves close behind Campbell and Ennis.

"We are going to the Cavern of the Door," said the Hindoo. "Inspector Campbell, I know and respect your resourcefulness. Be warned that your slightest attempt to escape means a bullet in your back. You two will march ahead of us," he said, and added mockingly, "Remember, while you live you can cling to the shadow of hope, but if these guns speak, it ends even that shadow."

Ennis and Inspector Campbell, keeping their hands elevated, started at the Hindoo's command down the softly lit rock tunnel. Chandra Dass and the two hooded men with pistols followed.

Ennis saw that the inspector's sagging face was expressionless, and knew that behind that colorless mask, Campbell's brain was racing in an attempt to find a method of escape. For himself, the young American had almost forgotten all else in his eagerness to reach his wife. Whatever happened to Ruth, whatever mysterious horror lay in wait for her and the other victims, he would be there beside her, sharing it!

The tunnel wound a little further downward, then straightened out and ran straight for a considerable length. In this straight section of the rock passage, Ennis and Campbell for the first time perceived that the walls of the tunnel bore crowding, deeply chiseled inscriptions. They had not time to read them in passing, but Ennis saw that they were in many different languages, and that some of the characters were wholly unfamiliar.

"God, some of those inscriptions are in Egyptian hieroglyphics!" muttered Inspector Campbell.

The cool voice of Chandra Dass said, behind them, "There are pre-Egyptian inscriptions on these walls, inspector, could you but recognize them, carven in languages that perished from the face of earth before Egypt was born. Yes, back through time, back through mediaeval and Roman and Egyptian and pre-Egyptian ages, the Brotherhood of the Door has existed and has each year gathered in this place to open the Door and worship with sacrifices They Beyond it."

The fanatic note of unearthly devotion was in his voice now, and Ennis shuddered with a cold not of the tunnel.

As they proceeded, they heard a muffled, hoarse booming somewhere over their heads, a dull, rhythmic thunder that echoed along the long passageway. The walls of the tunnel now were damp and glistening in the sourceless soft light, tiny trickles running down them.

"You hear the ocean over us," came Chandra Dass' voice. "The Cavern of the Door lies several hundred yards out from shore, beneath the rock floor of the sea."

They passed the dark mouths of unlit tunnels branching ahead from this illuminated one. Then over the booming of the raging sea above them, there came to Ennis' ears the distant, swelling chant they had heard in the water-cavern above. But now it was louder, nearer. At the sound of it, Chandra Dass quickened their pace.

Suddenly Inspector Campbell stumbled on the slippery rock floor and went down in a heap. Instantly Chandra Dass and his two followers recoiled from them, the two pistols trained on the detective as he scrambled up.

"Do not do that again, inspector," warned the Hindoo in a deadly voice. "All tricks are useless now."

"I couldn't help slipping on this wet floor," complained Inspector Campbell.

"The next time you make a wrong step of any kind, a bullet will smash your spine," Chandra Dass told him. "Quick—march!"

*   *   *   *   *

The tunnel turned sharply, turned again. As they rounded the turns, Ennis saw with a sudden electric thrill of hope that Campbell held clutched in his hand, concealed by his sleeve, the heel-hilted knife from his shoe. He had drawn it when he stumbled.

Campbell edged a little closer to the young American as they were hastening onward, and whispered to him, a word at a time.

"Be—ready—to jump—them——"

"But they'll shoot, your first move——" whispered Ennis agonizedly.

Campbell did not answer. But Ennis sensed the detective's body tautening.

They came to another turn, the strong, swelling chant coming loud from ahead. They started around that turn.

Then Inspector Campbell acted. He whirled as though on a pivot, the heel-knife flashing toward the men behind them.

Shots coughed from the pistols that were pressed almost against his stomach. His body jerked as the bullets struck it, yet he remained erect, his knife stabbing with lightning rapidity.

One of the hooded men slumped down with a pierced throat, and as Campbell sprang at the other, Ennis desperately launched himself at Chandra Dass. He bore the Hindoo from his feet, but it was as though he was fighting a demon. Inside his gray robe, Chandra Dass writhed with fiendish strength.

Ennis could not hold him, the Hindoo's body seeming of spring-steel. He rolled over, dashed the young American to the floor, and leaped up, his dark face and great black eyes blazing.

Then, half-way erect, he suddenly crumpled, the fire in his eyes dulling, a call for help smothered on his lips. He fell on his face, and Ennis saw that the heel-knife was stuck in his back. Inspector Campbell jerked it out, and put it back into his shoe. And now Ennis, staggering up, saw that Campbell had knifed the two hooded guards and that they lay in a dead heap.

"Campbell!" cried the American, gripping the detective's arm. "They've wounded you—I saw them shoot you."

Campbell's bruised face grinned briefly. "Nothing of the kind," he said, and tapped the soiled gray vest he wore beneath his coat. "Chandra Dass didn't know this vest is bullet-proof."

He darted an alert glance up and down the lighted tunnel. "We can't stay here or let these bodies lie here. They may be discovered at any moment."

"Listen!" said Ennis, turning.

The chanting from ahead swelled down the tunnel, louder than at any time yet, waxing and waxing, reaching a triumphant crescendo, then again dying away.

"Campbell, they're going on with the ceremony now!" Ennis cried. "Ruth!"

The detective's desperate glance fastened on the dark mouth of one of the branching tunnels, a little ahead.

"That side tunnel—we'll pull the bodies in there!" he exclaimed.

Taking the pistols of the dead men for themselves, they rapidly dragged the three bodies into the darkness of the unlit branching tunnel.

"Quick, on with two of these robes," rasped Inspector Campbell. "They'll give us a little better chance."

Hastily Ennis jerked the gray robe and hood from Chandra Dass' dead body and donned it, while Campbell struggled into one of the others. In the robes and concealing hoods, they could not be told from any other two members of the Brotherhood, except that the badge on Ennis' breast was the double star instead of the single one.

Ennis then spun toward the main, lighted tunnel, Campbell close behind him. They recoiled suddenly into the darkness of the branching way, as they heard hurrying steps out in the lighted passage. Flattened in the darkness against the wall, they saw several of the gray-hooded members of the Brotherhood hasten past them from above, hurrying toward the gathering-place.

"The guards and robe-issuers we saw above!" Campbell said quickly when they were passed. "Come on, now."

He and Ennis slipped out into the lighted tunnel and hastened along it after the others.

Boom of thundering ocean over their heads and rising and falling of the tremendous chanting ahead filled their ears as they hurried around the last turns of the tunnel. The passage widened, and ahead they saw a massive rock portal through whose opening they glimpsed an immense, lighted space.

Campbell and Ennis, two comparatively tiny gray-hooded figures, hastened through the mighty portal. Then they stopped. Ennis felt frozen with the dazing shock of it. He heard the detective whisper fiercely beside him.

"It's the Cavern, all right—the Cavern of the Door!"

*   *   *   *   *

re ranged at the back of the dais, just
eaming black oval facet. The guards
them, and they remained standing
dged a little toward Ruth, who stood
line of stiff figures. As he moved
to her, he saw the two priests beside
reaching toward knurled knobs of
side, beneath the spherical web of

at the front of the dais, raised his
rolled out, heavy, commanding,
through all the cavern.

The Door Opens

Door?" rolled the chief priest's voice.
came the reply of hundreds of voices,
ds but loud, echoing to the roof of the
ous response.
our world!"
t waited until the echoes died before
d on in the ritual.
r forefathers to open the Door?"
esperately closer and closer to the line
mighty response reverberate about

he Door taught them!"
s apart from the other priests on the
yards of the captives, of the small

bring these sacrifices?"
iest uttered the words, and before the
ame, a hand grasped Ennis and pulled
line of victims. He spun round to find
the other priests who had jerked him

to Those Beyond the Door!"

They looked across a colossal rock chamber hollowed out beneath the floor of ocean. It was elliptical in shape, three hundred feet by its longer axis. Its black basalt sides, towering, rough-hewn walls, rose sheer and supported the rock ceiling which was the ocean floor, a hundred feet over their heads.

This mighty cathedral hewn from inside the rock of earth was lit by a soft, white, sourceless light like that in the main tunnel. Upon the floor of the cavern, in regular rows across it, stood hundreds on hundreds of human figures, all gray-robed and gray-hooded, all with their backs to Campbell and Ennis, looking across the cavern to its farther end. At that farther end was a flat dais of black basalt upon which stood five hooded men, four wearing the blazing double-star on their breasts, the fifth, a triple-star. Two of them stood beside a cubical, weird-looking gray metal mechanism from which upreared a spherical web of countless fine wires, unthinkably intricate in their network, many of them pulsing with glowing force. The sourceless light of the cavern and the tunnel seemed to pulse from that weird mechanism.

Up from that machine, if machine it was, soared the black basalt wall of that end of the cavern. But there above the gray mechanism the rough wall had been carved with a great, smooth facet, a giant, gleaming black oval face as smooth as though planed and polished. Only, at the middle of the glistening black oval face, were carven deeply four large and wholly unfamiliar characters. As Ennis and Campbell stared frozenly across the awe-inspiring place, sound swelled from the hundreds of throats. A slow, rising chant, it climbed and climbed until the basalt roof above seemed to quiver to it, crashing out with stupendous effect, a weird litany in an unknown tongue. Then it began to fall.

Ennis clutched the inspector's gray-robed arm. "Where's Ruth?" he whispered frantically. "I don't see any prisoners."

"They must be somewhere here," Campbell said swiftly. "Listen——"

As the chant died to silence, on the dais at the farther end of the cavern the hooded man who wore the triple-jeweled star stepped forward and spoke. His deep, heavy voice rolled out and echoed across the cavern, flung back and forth from wall to rocky wall.

"Brothers of the Door," he said, "we meet again here in the Cavern of the Door this year, as for ten thousand years past our forefathers have met here to worship They Beyond the Door, and bring them the sacrifices They love.

"A hundred centuries have gone by since first They Beyond the Door sent their wisdom through the barrier between their universe and ours, a barrier which even They could not open from their side, but which their wisdom taught our fathers how to open.

"Each year since then have we opened the Door which They taught us how to build. Each year we have brought them sacrifices. And in return They have given us of their wisdom and power. They have taught us things that lie hidden from other men, and They have given us powers that other men have not.

"Now again comes the time appointed for the opening of the Door. In their universe on the other side of it, They are waiting now to take the sacrifices which we have procured for them. The hour strikes, so let the sacrifices be brought."

As though at a signal, from a small opening at one side of the cavern a triple file of marchers entered. A file of hooded gray members of the Brotherhood flanked on either side a line of men and women who did not wear the hoods or robes. They were thirty or forty in number. These men and women were of almost all races and classes, but all of them walked stiffly, mechanically, staring ahead with unseeing, distended eyes, like living corpses.

"Drugged!" came Campbell's shaken voice. "They're all drugged, and don't know what is going on."

Enni
chestnut
a straigl
those of t

"Ther
muffled b

He pl
back.

"No!"
simply get

"I can
go!"

Inspect
Ennis!" sai
That robe
star badge
That mean
up there wi
though you
can't tell th
out of which
with the tur
fire my pist
get to that
chance to get

Ennis w
further reply
the main aisl
the dais. He
chief priest, h
as of annoyar
gray figure sli

The gray-h
attention to ei
eagerly, fixed
marched up on
white face an u

The prisoners we
beneath the great, g
stepped back from
stiffly there. Ennis
at the end of that
imperceptibly closer
the gray mechanisr
ebonite affixed to it
pulsing wires.

The chief priest
hands. His voice
reverberating again

"Where leads tl
Back up to him
muffled by the hoo
cavern in a thunde

"*It leads outside*

The chief pries
his deep voice rolle

"Who taught ou

Ennis, edging
of victims, felt th
him.

"*They Beyond t*

Now Ennis wa
dais, within a fe
figure of Ruth.

"To whom do w

As the high p
booming answer
him back from th
that it was one o
back.

"*We bring the*

As the colossal response thundered, the priest who had jerked Ennis back whispered urgently to him. "You go too close to the victims, Chandra Dass! Do you wish to be taken with them?"

The fellow had a tight grip on Ennis' arm. Desperate, tensed, Ennis heard the chief priest roll forth the last of the ritual.

"Shall the Door be opened that They may take the sacrifices?"

Stunning, mighty, a tremendous shout that mingled in it worshipping awe and superhuman dread, the answer crashed back.

"Let the Door be opened!"

The chief priest turned and his up-flung arms whirled in a signal. Ennis, tensing to spring toward Ruth, saw the two priests at the gray mechanism swiftly turn the knurled black knobs. Then Ennis, like all else in the vast cavern, was held frozen and spellbound by what followed.

The spherical web of wires pulsed up madly with shining force. And up at the center of the gleaming black oval facet on the wall, there appeared a spark of unearthly green light. It blossomed outward, expanded, an awful viridescent flower blooming quickly outward farther and farther. And as it expanded, Ennis saw that he could look *through* that green light! He looked through into another universe, a universe lying infinitely far across alien dimensions from our own, yet one that could be reached through this door between dimensions. It was a green universe, flooded with an awful green light that was somehow more akin to darkness than to light, a throbbing, baleful luminescence.

Ennis saw dimly through green-lit spaces a city in the near distance, an unholy city of emerald hue whose unsymmetrical, twisted towers and minarets aspired into heavens of hellish viridity. The towers of that city swayed to and fro and writhed in the air. And Ennis saw that here and there in the soft green substance of that restless city were circles of lurid light that were like yellow eyes.

In ghastly, soul-shaking apprehension of the utterly
alien, Ennis knew that the yellow circles were *eyes*—that
that hell-spawned city of another universe was *living*—
that its unfamiliar life was single yet multiple, that its
lurid eyes looked now through the Door!

Out from the insane living metropolis glided
pseudopods of its green substance, glided toward the
Door. Ennis saw that in the end of each pseudopod was
one of the lurid eyes. He saw those eyed pseudopods come
questing through the Door, onto the dais.

The yellow eyes of light seemed fixed on the row of
stiff victims, and the pseudopods glided toward them.
Through the open door was beating wave on wave of
unfamiliar, tingling forces that Ennis felt even through
the protective robe.

The hooded multitude bent in awe as the green
pseudopods glided toward the victims faster, with avid
eagerness. Ennis saw them reaching for the prisoners, for
Ruth, and he made a tremendous mental effort to break
the spell that froze him. In that moment pistol-shots
crashed across the cavern and a stream of bullets
smashed the pulsing web of wires!

The Door began instantly to close. Darkness crept
back around the edges of the mighty oval. As though
alarmed, the lurid-eyed pseudopods of that hell-city
recoiled from the victims, back through the dwindling
Door. And as the Door dwindled, the light in the cavern
was failing.

"Ruth!" yelled Ennis madly, and sprang forward and
grasped her, his pistol leaping into his other hand.

"Ennis—quick!" shouted Campbell's voice across the
cavern.

The Door dwindled away altogether; the great oval
facet was completely black. The light was fast dying too.

The chief priest sprang madly toward Ennis, and as
he did so, the hooded hordes of the Brotherhood recovered
from their paralysis of horror and surged madly toward
the dais.

"The Door is closed! Death to the blasphemers!" cried the chief priest as he plunged forward.

"Death to the blasphemers!" shrieked the crazed horde below.

Ennis' pistol roared and the chief priest went down. The light in the cavern died completely at that moment.

In the dark a torrent of bodies catapulted against Ennis, screaming vengeance. He struck out with his pistol-barrel in the mad melee, holding Ruth's stiff form close with his other hand. He heard the other drugged, helpless victims crushed down and trampled under foot by the surging horde of vengeance-mad members.

* * * * *

Clinging to the girl, Ennis fought like a madman through a darkness in which none could distinguish friend or foe, toward the door at the side from which Campbell had fired. He smashed down the pistol-barrel on all before him, as hands sought to grab him in the dark. He knew sickeningly that he was lost in the combat, with no sense of the direction of the door.

Then a voice roared loud across the wild din, "Ennis, this way! This way, Ennis!" yelled Inspector Campbell, again and again.

Ennis plunged through the whirl of unseen bodies in the direction of the detective's shouting voice. He smashed through, half dragging and half carrying the girl, until Campbell's voice was close ahead in the dark. He fumbled at the rock wall, found the door opening, and then Campbell's hands grasped him to pull him inside.

Hands grabbed him from behind, striving to tear Ruth from him, to jerk him back. Voices shrieked for help.

Campbell's pistol blazed in the dark and the hands released their grip. Ennis stumbled with the girl through the door into a dark tunnel. He heard Campbell slam a door shut, and heard a bar fall with a clang.

"Quick, for God's sake!" panted Campbell in the dark. "They'll follow us—we've got to get up through the tunnels to the water-cavern!"

They raced along the pitch-dark tunnel, Campbell now carrying the girl, Ennis reeling drunkenly along.

They heard a mounting roar behind them, and as they burst into the main tunnel, no longer lighted but dark like the others, they looked back and saw a flickering of light coming up the passage.

"They're after us and they've got lights!" Campbell cried. "Hurry!"

It was nightmare, this mad flight on stumbling feet up through the dark tunnels where they could hear the sea booming close overhead, and could hear the wild pursuit behind.

Their feet slipped on the damp floor and they crashed into the walls of the tunnel at the turns. The pursuit was closer behind—as they started climbing the last passages to the water-cavern, the torchlight behind showed them to their pursuers and wild yells came to their ears.

They had before them only the last ascent to the water-cavern when Ennis stumbled and went down. He swayed up a little, yelled to Campbell. "Go on—get Ruth out! I'll try to hold them back a moment!"

"No!" rasped Campbell. "There's another way—one that may mean the end for us too, but our only chance!"

The inspector thrust his hand into his pocket, snatched out his big, old-fashioned gold watch.

He tore it from its chain, turned the stem of it twice around. Then he hurled it back down the tunnel with all his force.

"Quick—out of the tunnels now or we'll die right here!" he yelled.

They lunged forward, Campbell dragging both the girl and the exhausted Ennis, and emerged a moment later into the great water-cavern. It was now lit only by the searchlight of their waiting cutter.

As they emerged into the cavern, they were thrown flat on the rock ledge by a violent movement of it under them. An awful detonation and thunderous crashing of falling rock smote their ears.

Following that first tremendous crash, giant rumbling of collapsing rock shook the water-cavern.

"To the cutter!" Campbell cried. "That watch of mine was filled with the most concentrated high-explosive known, and it's blown up the tunnels. Now it's touched off more collapses and all these caverns and passages will fall in on us at any moment!"

The awful rumbling and crashing of collapsing rock masses was deafening in their ears as they lurched toward the cutter. Great chunks of rock were falling from the cavern roof into the water.

*   *   *   *   *

Sturt, white-faced but asking no questions, had the motor of the cutter running, and helped them pull the unconscious girl aboard.

"Out of the tunnel at once!" Campbell ordered. "Full speed!"

They roared down the water-tunnel at crazy velocity, the searchlight beam stabbing ahead. The tide had reached flood and turned, increasing the speed with which they dashed through the tunnel.

Masses of rock fell with loud splashes behind them, and all around them was still the ominous grinding of mighty weights of rock. The walls of the tunnel quivered repeatedly.

Sturt suddenly reversed the propellers, but in spite of his action the cutter smashed a moment later into a solid rock wall. It was a mass of rock forming an unbroken barrier across the water-tunnel, extending beneath the surface of the water.

"We're trapped!" cried Sturt. "A mass of the rock has settled here and blocked the tunnel."

"It can't be completely blocked!" Campbell exclaimed. "See, the tide still runs out beneath it. Our one chance is to swim out under the blocking mass of rock, before the whole cliff gives way!"

"But there's no telling how far the block may extend——" Sturt cried.

Then as Campbell and Ennis stripped off their coats and shoes, he followed their example. The rumble of grinding rock around them was now continuous and nerve-shattering.

Campbell helped Ennis lower Ruth's unconscious form into the water.

"Keep your hand over her nose and mouth!" cried the inspector. "Come on, now!"

Sturt went first, his face pale in the searchlight beam as he dived under the rock mass. The tidal current carried him out of sight in a moment.

Then, holding the girl between them, and with Ennis' hand covering her mouth and nostrils, the other two dived. Down through the cold waters they shot, and then the swift current was carrying them forward like a mill-race, their bodies bumping and scraping against the rock mass overhead.

Ennis' lungs began to burn, his brain to reel, as they rushed on in the waters, still holding the girl tightly. They struck solid rock, a wall across their way. The current sucked them downward, to a small opening at the bottom. They wedged in it, struggled fiercely, then tore through it. They rose on the other side of it into pure air. They were in the darkness, floating in the tunnel beyond the block, the current carrying them swiftly onward.

The walls were shaking and roaring frightfully about them as they were borne round the turns of the tunnel. Then they saw ahead of them a circle of dim light, pricked with white stars.

The current bore them out into that starlight, into the open sea. Before them in the water floated Sturt, and they swam with him out from the shaking, grinding cliffs.

The girl stirred a little in Ennis' grasp, and he saw in the starlight that her face was no longer dazed.

"Paul——" she muttered, clinging close to Ennis in the water.

"She's coming back to consciousness—the water must have revived her from that drug!" he cried.

But he was cut short by Campbell's cry. "Look! Look!" cried the inspector, pointing back at the black cliffs.

In the starlight the whole cliff was collapsing, with a prolonged, terrible roar as of grinding planets, its face breaking and buckling. The waters around them boiled furiously, whirling them this way and that.

Then the waters quieted. They found they had been flung near a sandy spit beyond the shattered cliffs, and they swam toward it.

"The whole underground honeycomb of caverns and tunnels gave way and the sea poured in!" Campbell cried. "The Door, and the Brotherhood of the Door, are ended for ever!"

The World with a Thousand Moons

ORIGINALLY PUBLISHED IN *AMAZING STORIES*, DECEMBER 1942

The World With A Thousand Moons

CHAPTER 1
Thrill Cruise

Lance Kenniston felt the cold realization of failure as he came out of the building into the sharp chill of the Martian night. He stood for a moment, his lean, drawn face haggard in the light of the two hurtling moons.

He looked hopelessly across the dark spaceport. It was a large one, for this ancient town of Syrtis was the main port of Mars. The forked light of the flying moons showed many ships docked on the tarmac—a big liner, several freighters, a small, shining cruiser and other small craft. And for lack of one of those ships, his hopes were ruined!

A squat, brawny figure in shapeless space-jacket came to Kenniston's side. It was Holk Or, the Jovian who had been waiting for him.

"What luck?" asked the Jovian in a rumbling whisper.

"It's hopeless," Kenniston answered heavily. "There isn't a small cruiser to be had at any price. The meteor-miners buy up all small ships here."

"The devil!" muttered Holk Or, dismayed. "What are we going to do? Go on to Earth and get a cruiser there?"

"We can't do that," Kenniston answered. "You know we've got to get back to that asteroid within two weeks. We've got to get a ship here."

Desperation made Kenniston's voice taut. His lean, hard face was bleak with knowledge of disastrous failure.

The big Jovian scratched his head. In the shifting moonslight his battered green face expressed ignorant perplexity as he stared across the busy spaceport.

"That shiny little cruiser there would be just the thing," Holk Or muttered, looking at the gleaming, torpedo-shaped craft nearby. "It would hold all the stuff we've got to take; and with robot controls we two could run it."

"We haven't a chance to get that craft," Kenniston told him. "I found out that it's under charter to a bunch of rich Earth youngsters who came out here in it for a pleasure cruise. A girl named Loring, heiress to Loring Radium, is the head of the party."

The Jovian swore. "Just the ship we need, and a lot of spoiled kids are using it for thrill-hunting!"

Kenniston had an idea. "It might be," he said slowly, "that they're tired of the cruise by this time and would sell us the craft. I think I'll go up to the Terra Hotel and see this Loring girl."

"Sure, let's try it anyway," Holk Or agreed.

The Earthman looked at him anxiously. "Oughtn't you to keep under cover, Holk? The Planet Patrol has had your record on file for a long time. If you happened to be recognized—"

"Bah, they think I'm dead, don't they?" scoffed the Jovian. "There's no danger of us getting picked up."

Kenniston was not so sure, but he was too driven by urgent need to waste time in argument. With the Jovian clumping along beside him, he made his way from the spaceport across the ancient Martian city.

The dark streets of old Syrtis were not crowded. Martians are not a nocturnal people and only a few were abroad in the chill darkness, even they being wrapped in heavy synthewool cloaks from which only their bald red heads and solemn, cadaverous faces protruded.

Earthmen were fairly numerous in this main port of the planet. Swaggering space-sailors, prosperous-looking traders and rough meteor-miners made up the most of them. There were a few tourists gaping at the grotesque old black stone buildings, and under a krypton-bulb at a corner, two men in the drab uniform of the Patrol stood eyeing passersby sharply. Kenniston breathed more easily when he and the Jovian had passed the two officers without challenge.

*   *   *   *   *

The Terra Hotel stood in a garden at the edge of town, fronting the moonlit immensity of the desert. This glittering glass block, especially built to cater to the tourist trade from Earth, was Earth-conditioned inside. Its gravitation, air pressure and humidity were ingeniously maintained at Earth standards for the greater comfort of its patrons.

Kenniston felt oddly oppressed by the warm, soft air inside the resplendent lobby. He had spent so much of his time away from Earth that he had become more or less adapted to thinner, colder atmospheres.

"Miss Gloria Loring?" repeated the immaculate young Earthman behind the information desk. His eyes appraised Kenniston's shabby space-jacket and the hulking green Jovian. "I am afraid—"

"I'm here to see her on important business, by appointment," Kenniston snapped.

The clerk melted at once. "Oh, I see! I believe that Miss Loring's party is now in The Bridge. That's our cocktail room—top floor."

Kenniston felt badly out of place, riding up in the magnetic lift with Holk Or. The other people in the car, Earthmen and women in the shimmering synthesilks of the latest formal dress, stared at him and the Jovian as though wondering how they had ever gained admittance.

The lights, silks and perfumes made Kenniston feel even shabbier than he was. All this luxury was a far cry from the hard, dangerous life he had led for so long amid the wild asteroids and moons of the outer planets.

It was worse up in the glittering cocktail room atop the hotel. The place had glassite walls and ceiling, and was designed to give an impression of the navigating bridge of a space-ship. The orchestra played behind a phony control-board of instruments and rocket-controls. Meaningless space-charts hung on the walls for decoration. It was just the sort of pretentious sham, Kenniston thought contemptuously, to appeal to tourists.

"Some crowd!" muttered Holk Or, looking over the tables of richly dressed and jewelled people. His small eyes gleamed. "What a place to loot!"

"Shut up!" Kenniston muttered hastily. He asked a waiter for the Loring party, and was conducted to a table in a corner.

There were a half dozen people at the table, most of them young Earthmen and girls. They were drinking pink Martian desert-wine, except for one sulky-looking youngster who had stuck to Earth whisky.

One of the girls turned and looked at Kenniston with cool, insolently uninterested gaze when the waiter whispered to her politely.

"I'm Gloria Loring," she drawled. "What did you want to see me about?"

She was dark and slim, and surprisingly young. There were almost childish lines to the bare shoulders revealed by her low golden gown. Her thoroughbred grace and beauty were spoiled for Kenniston by the bored look in her clear dark eyes and the faintly disdainful droop of her mouth.

The chubby, rosy youth beside her goggled in simulated amazement and terror at the battered green Jovian behind Kenniston. He set down his glass with a theatrical gesture of horror.

"This Martian liquor has got me!" he exclaimed. "I can see a little green man!"

Holk Or started wrathfully forward. "Why, that young pup—"

Kenniston hastily restrained him with a gesture. He turned back to the table. Some of the girls were giggling.

"Be quiet, Robbie," Gloria Loring was telling the chubby young comedian. She turned her cool gaze back to Kenniston. "Well?"

"Miss Loring, I heard down at the spaceport that you are the charterer of that small cruiser, the *Sunsprite*," Kenniston explained. "I need a craft like that very badly. If you would part with her, I'd be glad to pay almost any price for your charter."

*   *   *   *   *

The girl looked at him in astonishment. "Why in the world should I let you have our cruiser?"

Kenniston said earnestly, "Your party could travel just as well and a lot more comfortably by liner. And getting a cruiser like that is a life-or-death business for me right now."

"I'm not interested in your business, Mr. Kenniston," drawled Gloria Loring. "And I certainly don't propose to alter our plans just to help a stranger out of his difficulties."

Kenniston flushed from the cool rebuke. He stood there, suddenly feeling a savage dislike for the whole pampered group of them.

"Beside that," the girl continued, "we chose the cruiser for this trip because we wanted to get off the beaten track of liner routes, and see something new. We're going from here out to Jupiter's moons."

Kenniston perceived that these bored, spoiled youngsters were out here hunting for new thrills on the interplanetary frontier. His dislike of them increased.

A clean-cut, sober-faced young man who seemed older and more serious than the rest of the party, was speaking to the heiress.

"Unhardened space-travellers like us are likely to get hit by gravitation paralysis out in the outer planets, Gloria," he was saying to the heiress. "I don't think we ought to go farther out than Mars."

Gloria looked at him mockingly. "If you're scared, Hugh, why did you leave your nice safe office on Earth and come along with us?"

The chubby youth called Robbie laughed loudly. "We all know why Hugh Murdock came along. It's not thrills he wants—it's you, Gloria."

They were all ignoring Kenniston now. He felt that he had been dismissed but he was desperately reluctant to lose his last hope of getting a ship. Somehow he *must* get that cruiser!

A stratagem occurred to him. If these spoiled scions wouldn't give up their ship, at least he might induce them to go where he wanted.

Kenniston hesitated. It would mean leading them all into the deadliest kind of peril. But a man's life depended on it. A man who was worth all these rich young wastrels put together. He decided to try it.

"Miss Loring, if it's thrills you're after, maybe I can furnish them," Kenniston said. "Maybe we can team up on this. How would you like to go on a voyage after the biggest treasure in the System?"

"Treasure?" exclaimed the heiress surprisedly. "Where is it?"

They were all leaning forward, with quick interest. Kenniston saw that his bait had caught them.

"You've heard of John Dark, the notorious space-pirate?" he asked.

Gloria nodded. "Of course. The telenews was full of his exploits until the Patrol caught and destroyed his ship a few weeks ago."

Kenniston corrected her. "The Patrol caught up to John Dark's ship in the asteroid, but didn't completely destroy it. They gunned the pirate craft to a wreck in a running fight. But Dark's wrecked ship drifted into a dangerous zone of meteor swarms where they couldn't follow."

"I remember now—that's what the telenews said," conceded the heiress. "But Dark and his crew were undoubtedly killed, they said."

"John Dark," Kenniston went on, "looted scores of ships during his career. He amassed a hoard of jewels and precious metals. And he kept it right with him in his ship. That treasure's still in that lost wreck."

"How do you know?" asked Hugh Murdock bluntly.

"Because I found the lost wreck of Dark's ship myself," Kenniston answered. He hated to lie like this, but knew that he had no choice.

*   *   *   *   *

He plunged on. "I'm a meteor-miner by profession. Two weeks ago my Jovian partner and I were prospecting in the outer asteroid zone in our little rocket. Our air-tanks got low and to replenish them, we landed on the asteroid Vesta. That's the big asteroid they call the World with a Thousand Moons, because it's circled by a swarm of hundreds of meteors.

"It's a weird, jungled little world, inhabited by some very queer forms of life. In landing, my partner and I noticed where some great object had crashed down into the jungle. We discovered it was the wreck of John Dark's ship. The wreck had drifted until it crashed on Vesta, almost completely burying itself in the ground. No one was alive on it, of course."

Kenniston concluded. "We knew Dark's treasure must still be in the buried wreck. But it would take machinery and equipment to dig out the wreck. So we came here to Mars, intending to get a small cruiser, load it with the necessary equipment, and go back to Vesta and lift the treasure. Only we haven't been able to get a ship of any kind."

He leaned toward the girl. "Here's my proposition, Miss Loring. You take us and our equipment to Vesta in your cruiser, and we'll share the treasure with you fifty-fifty. What do you say?"

The blonde girl beside Gloria uttered a squeal of excitement. "Pirate treasure! Gloria, let's do it—what a thrill it would be!"

The others showed equal excitement. The romance of a treasure hunt in the wild asteroids lured them, rather than the possible rewards.

"We'd certainly be able to take back a wonderful story to Earth if we found John Dark's treasure," admitted Gloria, with quick, eager interest.

Hugh Murdock was an exception to the general enthusiasm. He asked Kenniston, "How do you know the treasure's still in the buried wreck?"

"Because the wreck was still undisturbed," Kenniston answered. "And because we found these jewels on the body of one of John Dark's crew, who had been flung clear somehow when the wreck crashed."

He held out a half-dozen gems he took from his pocket. They were Saturnian moon-stones, softly shining white jewels whose brilliance waxed and waned in perfect periodic rhythm.

"These jewels," Kenniston said, "must have been that pirate's share of the loot. You can imagine how rich John Dark's own hoard must be."

The jewels, worth many thousands, swept away the lingering incredulity of the others as Kenniston had known they would.

"You're sure no one else knows the wreck is there?" Gloria asked breathlessly.

"We kept our find absolutely secret," Kenniston told her. "But since I can't get a ship any other way, I'm willing to share the hoard with you. If I wait too long, someone else may find the wreck."

"I accept your proposition, Mr. Kenniston!" Gloria declared. "We'll start for Vesta just as soon as you can get the equipment you'll need loaded on the *Sunsprite*."

"Gloria, you're being too hasty," protested Hugh Murdock. "I've heard of this world with a Thousand Moons. There're stories of queer, unhuman creatures they call Vestans, who infest that asteroid. The danger—"

Gloria impatiently dismissed his objections. "Hugh, if you are going to start worrying about dangers again, you'd better go back to Earth and safety."

Murdock flushed and was silent. Kenniston felt a certain sympathy for the young businessman. He knew, if these others did not, just how real was the alien menace of those strange creatures, the Vestans.

"I'll go right down to the spaceport and see about loading the equipment aboard your cruiser," Kenniston told the heiress. "You'd better give me a note to your captain. We ought to be able to start tomorrow."

"Pirate treasure on an unexplored asteroid!" exulted the enthusiastic Robbie. "Ho for the World with a Thousand Moons!"

Kenniston felt guilty when he and Holk Or left the big hotel. These youngsters, he thought, hadn't the faintest idea of the peril into which he was leading them. They were as ignorant as babies of the dark evil and unearthly danger of the interplanetary frontier.

He hardened himself against the qualms of conscience. There was that at stake, he told himself fiercely, against which the safety of a lot of spoiled, rich young people was absolutely nothing.

Holk Or was chuckling as they emerged into the chill Martian night. He told Kenniston admiringly, "That was one of the smoothest jobs of lying I ever heard, that story about finding John Dark's treasure. Take it from me, it was slick!"

The Jovian guffawed loudly as he added, "What would their faces be like if they knew that John Dark and his crew are still living? That it was John Dark himself who sent us here?"

"Be quiet, you idiot!" ordered Kenniston hastily. "Do you want the whole Patrol to hear you?"

CHAPTER II
Discovered

The *Sunsprite* throbbed steadily through the vast, dangerous wilderness of the asteroidal zone. To the eye, the cruiser moved in a black void starred by creeping crumbs of light. In reality those bright, crawling specks were booming asteroids or whirling meteor-swarms rushing in complicated, unchartable orbits and constantly threatening destruction.

For three days now, the cruiser had cautiously groped deeper into this most perilous region of the System. Now a bright, tiny disk of white light was shining far ahead like a beckoning beacon. It was the asteroid Vesta—their goal.

Kenniston, leaning against the glassite deck-wall, somberly eyed the distant asteroid.

"We'll reach it by tomorrow," he thought. "Then what? I suppose John Dark will hold these rich youngsters for ransom."

Kenniston knew that the pirate leader would instantly see the chance of extorting vast sums by holding this group of wealthy young people as captives.

"I wish to God I hadn't had to bring them into this," Kenniston sweated. "But what else could I do? It was the only way I could get back to Vesta with the materials."

His mind was going back over the disastrous events since the day three weeks before, when the Patrol had caught up to John Dark at last.

Dark's pirate ship, the *Falcon*, had been gunned to a helpless wreck. It had, fortunately for the pirates, drifted off into a region of perilous meteor-swarms where the Patrol cruisers dared not follow. The Patrol thought everybody on the pirate ship dead anyway, Kenniston knew.

But John Dark and most of his crew were still alive in the drifting wreck. They had fought the battle wearing space-suits, and that had saved them. They had clung grimly to the wreck as it drifted on and on until it finally fell into the feeble gravitational pull of Vesta.

Kenniston could still remember those tense hours when the wreck had fallen through the satellite swarm of meteors onto the World with a Thousand Moons. They had managed to cushion their crash. John Dark, always the most resourceful of men, had managed to jury-rig makeshift rocket-tubes that had softened the impact of their fall.

But the wrecked *Falcon* had been marooned there in the weird asteroidal jungle, with the alien, menacing Vestans already gathering around it. The ship would never fly space again until major repairs were made. And they could not be made until quantities of material and equipment were brought. Someone must go for those materials to Mars, the nearest planet.

John Dark had superintended construction of a little two-man rocket from parts of the ship. Kenniston and Holk Or were to go in it.

"You *must* be back with that list of equipment and materials within two weeks, Kenniston," Dark had emphasized. "If we stay castaway here longer than that, either the Vestans will get us or the Patrol discover us."

The pirate leader had added, "The moon-jewels I've given you will more than pay for a small cruiser, if you can buy one at Mars. If you can't buy one, get one any way you can—but get back here quickly!"

Well, Kenniston thought grimly, he had got a cruiser in the only way he could. Down in its hold were the berylloy plates and spare rocket-tubes and new cyclotrons he had had loaded aboard at Syrtis.

But he was also bringing back to Vesta with him a bunch of thrill-seeking, rich, young people who believed they were going on a romantic treasure-hunt. What would they think of him when they discovered how he had betrayed them?

*   *   *   *   *

"That's Vesta, isn't it?" spoke a girl's eager voice behind him, interrupting his dark thoughts.

Kenniston turned quickly. It was Gloria Loring, boyish in silken space-slacks, her hands thrust into the pockets.

There was a naive eagerness in her clear, lovely face as she looked toward the distant asteroid, that made her look more like an excited small girl than like the bored, jewelled heiress of that night at Syrtis.

"Yes, that's the World with a Thousand Moons," Kenniston nodded. "We'll reach it by tomorrow. I've just been up on the bridge, telling your Captain Walls the safest route through the meteor swarms."

Her dark eyes studied him curiously. "You've been out here on the frontier a long time, haven't you?"

"Twelve years," he told her. "That's a long time in the outer planets. Most space-men don't last that long out here—wrecks, accidents or gravitation-paralysis gets them."

"Gravitation-paralysis?" she repeated. "I've heard of that as a terrible danger to space-travelers. But I don't really know what it is."

"It's the most dreaded danger of all out here," Kenniston answered. "A paralysis that hits you when you change from very weak to very strong gravities or vice versa, too often. It locks all your muscles rigid by numbing the motor-nerves."

Gloria shivered. "That sounds ghastly."

"It is," Kenniston said somberly. "I've seen scores of my friends stricken down by it, in the years I've sailed the outer System."

"I didn't know you'd been a space-sailor all that time," the heiress said wonderingly. "I thought you said you were a meteor-miner."

Kenniston woke up to the fact that he had made a bad slip. He hastily covered up. "You have to be a good bit of a space-sailor to be a meteor-miner, Miss Loring. You have to cover a lot of territory."

He was thankful that they were interrupted at that moment by some of the others who came along the deck in a lively, chattering group.

Robbie Boone was the center of the group. That chubby, clownish young man, heir to the Atomic Power Corporation millions, had garbed himself in what he fondly believed to be a typical space-man's outfit. His jacket and slacks were of black synthesilk, and he wore a big atom-pistol.

"Hiya, pal!" he grinned cherubically at Kenniston. "When does this here crate of ours jet down at Vesta?"

"If you knew how silly you looked, Robbie," said Gloria devastatingly, "trying to dress and talk like an old space-man."

"You're just jealous," Robbie defied. "I look all right, don't I, Kenniston?"

Kenniston's lips twitched. "You'd certainly create a sensation if you walked into the Spaceman's Rendezvous in Jovopolis."

Alice Krim, a featherheaded little blonde, eyed Kenniston admiringly. "You've been to an awful lot of planets, haven't you?" she sighed.

"Turn it off, Alice," said Gloria dryly. "Mr. Kenniston doesn't flirt."

Arthur Lanning, the sulky, handsome youngster who always had a drink in his hand, drawled. "Then you've tried him out, Gloria?"

The heiress' dark eyes snapped, but she was spared a reply by the appearance of Mrs. Milsom. That dumpy, fluttery woman, the nominal chaperone of the group, immediately seized upon Kenniston as usual.

"Mr. Kenniston, are you sure this asteroid we're going to is safe?" she asked him for the hundredth time. "Is there a good hotel there?"

"A good hotel there?" Kenniston was too astounded to answer, for a moment.

*   *   *   *   *

Into his mind had risen memory of the savage, choking green jungles of the World with a Thousand Moons; of the slithering creatures slipping through the fronds, of the rustling presence of the dreaded Vestans who could never quite be seen; of the pirate wreck around which John Dark and half a hundred of the System's most hardened outlaws waited.

"Of course there's no hotel there, Aunty," Gloria said disgustedly. "Can't you understand that this asteroid's almost unexplored?"

Holk Or had come up, and the big Jovian had heard. He broke into a booming laugh. "A hotel on Vesta! That's a good one!"

Kenniston flashed the big green pirate a warning glance. Robbie Boone was asking him, "Will there be any good hunting there?"

"Sure there will," Holk Or declared. His small eyes gleamed with secret humor. "You're going to find lots of adventure there, my lad."

When Mrs. Milsom had dragged the others away for the usual afternoon game of "dimension bridge," the Jovian looked after them, chuckling.

"This crowd of idiots hadn't ought to have ever left Earth. What a surprise they're going to get on Vesta!"

"They're not such a bad bunch, at bottom," Kenniston said halfheartedly. "Just a lot of ignorant kids looking for adventure."

"Bah, you're falling for the Loring girl," scoffed Holk Or. "You'd better keep your mind on John Dark's orders."

Kenniston made a warning gesture. "Cut it! Here comes Murdock."

Hugh Murdock came straight along the deck toward them, and his sober, clean-cut young face wore a puzzled look as he halted before them.

"Kenniston, there's something about this I can't understand," he declared.

"Yes? What's that?" returned Kenniston guardedly.

He was very much on the alert. Murdock was not a heedless, gullible youngster like the others. He was, Kenniston had learned, an already important official in the Loring Radium company.

From the chaffing the others gave Murdock, it was evident that the young business man had joined the party only because he was in love with Gloria. There was something likeable about the dogged devotion of the sober young man. His very obvious determination to protect Gloria's safety, and his intelligence, made him dangerous in Kenniston's eyes.

"I was down in the hold looking over the equipment you loaded," Hugh Murdock was saying. "You know, the stuff we're to use to dig out the wreck of Dark's ship. And I can't understand it—there's no digging machinery, but simply a lot of cyclotrons, rocket-tubes and spare plates."

Kenniston smiled to cover the alarm he felt. "Don't worry, Murdock, I loaded just the equipment we'll need. You'll see when we reach Vesta."

Murdock persisted. "But I still don't see how that stuff is going to help. It's more like ship-repair stores than anything else."

Kenniston lied hastily. "The cycs are for power-supply, and the rocket-tubes and plates are to build a heavy duty power-hoist to jack the wreck out of the mud. Holk Or and I have got that all figured out."

Murdock frowned as though still unconvinced, but dropped the subject. When he had gone off to join the others, Holk Or glared after him.

"That fellow's too smart for his own good," muttered the Jovian. "He's suspicious. Maybe I'd better see that he meets with an accident."

"No, let him alone," warned Kenniston. "If anything happened to him now, the others would want to turn back. And we're almost to Vesta now."

But worry remained as a shadow in the back of Kenniston's own mind. It still oppressed him hours later when the arbitrary ship's-time had brought the 'night.'

Sitting down in the luxurious passenger-cabin over highballs with the others, he wondered where Hugh Murdock was.

The rest of Gloria's party were all here, listening with fascinated interest to Holk Or's colorful yarns of adventures on the wild asteroids. But Murdock was missing. Kenniston wondered worriedly if the fellow was looking over that equipment in the hold again.

*   *   *   *   *

A young Earth space-man—one of the *Sunsprite's* small crew—came into the cabin and approached Kenniston.

"Captain Walls' compliments, sir, and would you come up to the bridge? He'd like your advice about the course again."

"I'll go with you," Gloria said as Kenniston rose. "I like it up in the bridge best of any place on the ship."

As they climbed past the little telaudio transmitter-room, they saw Hugh Murdock standing in there by the operator. He smiled at Gloria.

"I've been trying to get some messages through to Earth, but it seems we're almost out of range," he said ruefully.

"Can't you ever forget business, Hugh?" the girl said exasperatedly. "You're about as adventurous as a fat radium-broker of fifty."

Kenniston, however, felt relieved that Murdock had apparently forgotten about the oddness of the equipment below. His spirits were lighter when they entered the glassite-enclosed bridge.

Captain Walls turned from where he stood beside Bray, the chief pilot. The plump, cheerful master touched his cap to Gloria Loring.

"Sorry to bother you again, Mr. Kenniston," he apologized. "But we're getting pretty near Vesta, and you know this devilish region of space better than I do. The charts are so vague they're useless."

Kenniston glanced at the instrument-panel with a practiced eye and then squinted at the void ahead. The *Sunsprite* was now throbbing steadily through a starry immensity whose hosts of glittering points of light would have made a bewildering panorama to laymen's eyes.

They seemed near none of those blazing sparks. Yet every few minutes, red lights blinked and buzzers sounded on the instrument panel. At each such warning of the meteorometers, the pilot glanced quickly at their direction-dials and then touched the rocket-throttles to change course slightly. The cruiser was threading a way through unseen but highly perilous swarms of rushing meteors and scores of thundering asteroids.

Vesta was now a bright, pale-green disk like a little moon. It was not directly ahead, but lay well to the left. The cruiser was following an indirect course that had been laid to detour it well around one of the bigger meteor-swarms that was spinning rapidly toward Mars.

"What about it, Mr. Kenniston—is it safe to turn toward Vesta now?" Captain Walls asked anxiously. "The chart doesn't show any more swarms that should be in this region now, by my calculations."

Kenniston snorted. "Charts are all made by planet-lubbers. There's a small swarm that tags after that big No. 480 mess we just detoured around. Let me have the 'scopes and I'll try to locate it."

Using the meteorscopes whose sensitive electromagnetic beams could probe far out through space, to be reflected by any matter, Kenniston searched carefully. He finally straightened from the task.

"It's all right—the tag-swarm is on the far side of No. 480," he reported. "It should be safe to blast straight toward Vesta now."

The captain's anxiety was only partly assuaged. "But when we reach the asteroid, what then? How do we get through the satellite-swarm around it?"

"I can pilot you through that," Kenniston assured him. "There's a periodic break in that swarm, due to gravitational perturbations of the spinning meteor-moons. I know how to find it."

"Then I'll wake you up early tomorrow 'morning' before we reach Vesta," vowed Captain Walls. "I've no hankering to run that swarm myself."

"We'll be there in the morning?" exclaimed Gloria with eager delight. "How long then will it take us to find the pirate wreck?"

Kenniston uncomfortably evaded the question. "I don't know—it shouldn't take long. We can land in the jungle near the wreck."

His feeling of guilt was increased by her enthusiastic excitement. If she and the others only knew what the morrow was to bring them!

*   *   *   *   *

He did not feel like facing the rest of them now, and lingered on the dark deck when they went back down from the bridge. Gloria remained beside him instead of going on to the cabin.

She stood, with the starlight from the transparent deck-wall falling upon her youthful face as she looked up at him.

"You *are* a moody creature, you know," she told Kenniston lightly. "Sometimes you're almost human— then you get all dark and grim again."

Kenniston grinned despite himself. Her voice came in mock surprise. "Why, it can actually smile! I can't believe my eyes."

Her clear young face was provocatively close, the faint perfume of her dark hair in his nostrils. He knew that she was deliberately flirting with him, perhaps mostly out of curiosity.

She expected him to kiss her, he knew. Damn it, he *would* kiss her! He did so, half ironically. But the ironic amusement faded out of his mind somehow at the oddly shy contact of her soft lips.

"Why, you're just a kid," he muttered. "A little kid masquerading as a bored, sophisticated young lady."

Gloria stiffened with anger. "Don't be silly! I've kissed men before. I just wanted to find out what you were really like."

"Well, what did you find out?"

Her voice softened. "I found out that you're not as grim as you look. I think you're just lonely."

The truth of that made Kenniston wince. Yes, he was lonely enough, he thought somberly. All his old space-mates, passing one by one—

"Don't you have anyone?" Gloria was asking him wonderingly.

"No family, except my kid brother Ricky," he answered heavily. "And most of my old space-partners are either dead or else worse—lying in the grip of gravitation-paralysis."

Memory of those old partners re-established Kenniston's wavering resolution. He mustn't let them down! He must go through with delivering this cruiser's cargo to John Dark, no matter what the consequences.

He thrust the girl almost roughly from him. "It's getting late. You'd better turn in like the others."

But later, in his bunk in the little cabin he shared with Holk Or, Kenniston found memory of Gloria a barrier to sleep. The shy touch of her lips refused to be forgotten. What would she think of him by tomorrow?

He slept, finally. When he awakened, it was to realization that someone had just sharply spoken his name. He knew drowsily it was 'morning' and thought at first that Captain Walls had sent someone to awaken him.

Then he stiffened as he saw who had awakened him. It was Hugh Murdock. The young businessman's sober face was grim now, and he stood in the doorway of the cabin with a heavy atom-pistol in his hand.

"Get up and dress, Kenniston," Murdock said sternly. "And wake up your fellow-pirate, too. If you make a wrong move I'll kill you both."

CHAPTER III
Through the Meteor-Moons

Kenniston went cold with dismay. He told himself numbly that it was impossible Hugh Murdock could have discovered the truth. But the grim expression on Murdock's face and the naked hate in his eyes were explainable on no other grounds.

The young businessman's finger was tense on the trigger of the atom-pistol. Resistance would be senseless. Mechanically, Kenniston slipped from his bunk and threw on his slacks and space-jacket. Holk Or was doing the same, the big Jovian's battered green face almost ludicrous in astonishment.

"Now perhaps you'll tell us what this means," Kenniston said harshly, his mind racing. "Have you lost your senses?"

"I've just come to them, Kenniston," rapped Murdock. "What fools we all were, not to guess that you two belong to Dark's pirates!"

Kenniston's lips tightened. It was clear now that Murdock had actually discovered something. From Holk Or came an angry roar.

"Devils of Pluto, I'm no pirate!" the big Jovian lied magnificently. "Whatever gave you this crazy idea?"

Murdock's hard face did not relax. He waved the atom-pistol. "Go into the main cabin," he ordered. "Walk ahead of me."

Helplessly, Kenniston and Holk Or obeyed. His mind was desperate as he shouldered down the corridor. The throbbing of the rockets told him the *Sunsprite* was still forging through the void. They must be very near Vesta by now—and now this had to happen!

The others had been awakened by the uproar and streamed into the main cabin after Murdock and his two prisoners. Kenniston glimpsed Gloria, slim in a silken negligee, her dark eyes round with amazement.

"Hugh, have you gone crazy?" she exclaimed stupefiedly.

Murdock answered without looking toward her. "I've found out the truth, Gloria. These men belong to John Dark's crew. They were taking us into a trap."

"Holy smoke!" gasped Robbie Boone, his jaw sagging as the chubby youth stared at Kenniston and Holk Or. "They're pirates?"

"I think you must be losing your mind!" Gloria stormed at Hugh Murdock. "This is ridiculous."

Holk Or yawned elaborately. "Space-sickness hits people in queer ways, Miss Loring," the Jovian told Gloria confidentially. "Some it just makes sick, but others it makes delirious."

"I'm not delirious, and you two know it," Murdock retorted grimly. He spoke to Gloria and the others, without taking his eyes or the muzzle of his pistol off his two captives.

"I thought from the first that this Kenniston's story of finding the wreck of Dark's ship on Vesta was a thin one," Murdock declared. "And yesterday my suspicions were increased when I went down and looked over the cargo of equipment they brought. It's not equipment to dig out a buried wreck. It's equipment to *repair* a damaged ship— John Dark's ship!

"Suspecting that, last 'night' I sent a telaudiogram to Patrol headquarters at Earth. I gave full descriptions of Kenniston and this Jovian and inquired if they had criminal records. An answer came through an hour ago. This fellow Holk Or has a record of criminal piracy as long as your arm, and was definitely known to be one of John Dark's crew!"

There was an incredulous gasp from the others. Murdock still grimly watched Kenniston and the Jovian as he concluded.

"The Patrol hasn't yet sent through Kenniston's record, but it's obvious enough that he's one of Dark's men too, and that his story that he and the Jovian are meteor-miners is a flat lie."

"I can't understand this," muttered young Arthur Lanning, staring. "If they're Dark's men, why should they induce us to go to Vesta?"

"Can't you see?" said Hugh Murdock. "John Dark's ship did crash on Vesta after being wrecked—that must be true enough. But Dark and his pirates weren't dead as the Patrol thought. They had to have machines and material to repair their ship. So Dark sent these two men to Mars for the materials. The two couldn't get a ship there any other way, so they made use of our cruiser by selling us that treasure yarn!"

*   *   *   *   *

Kenniston winced. He knew now that he had underestimated Murdock, who had put together the evidence quickly when his suspicions were roused.

Gloria Loring, looking at Kenniston with wide dark eyes, saw the change in his expression. Into her white face came an incredulous loathing.

"Then it's true," she whispered. "You did that—you deliberately planned to lead us all into capture?"

"Aw, you're all space-struck," growled Holk Or, bluffing to the last.

Murdock spoke over his shoulder. "Call Captain Walls, Robbie."

"No need to—here he comes now!" yelped the excited youth.

Captain Walls, entering the cabin in urgent haste, had eyes only for Kenniston in the first moment.

"Ah, there you are, Mr. Kenniston!" the captain exclaimed relievedly. "I was just coming for you. We've reached Vesta! I've ordered the pilot to slow down, for I want you to pilot us through the swarm—"

The captain's voice trailed off. His eyes bulged as for the first time he perceived that Murdock was covering the two men with a gun.

"We're not going in to Vesta, captain," rapped Murdock. "John Dark and his pirates are on the asteroid—*alive!*"

Captain Walls' plump face went waxy as he heard the name of the most dreaded corsair of the System.

"Dark—living?" he stuttered. "Good God, you must be joking!"

Mrs. Milsom, her dumpy figure shivering and her teeth chattering with terror, pointed a finger at Kenniston and the Jovian.

"They're two of the pirates!" she shrilled. "They might have murdered us all in our beds! I knew this would happen when we left Earth—"

Kenniston's mind was seething with despair as he stood there with hands upraised. His whole desperate plan was ruined at this last moment.

He wouldn't *let* it be ruined! He would get this cargo of machines and materials to John Dark if it meant his life!

"Turn back at once toward Mars, captain," Gloria was saying quietly to the stunned officer. Her face was still very pale.

Kenniston, standing tense, had had an idea. A desperate chance to make a break, in the face of Murdock's atom-gun.

The captain had said that he had just ordered the pilot to slow down the *Sunsprite*. In a moment would come the shock of the braking rocket-tubes firing from the bows—

That shock came an instant after the wild expedient flashed across Kenniston's mind. It was only a jarring vibration through the fabric of the ship, for the pilot knew his business.

It staggered them all on their feet, for just a moment. But Kenniston had been waiting for that moment. As Hugh Murdock moved his gun-arm involuntarily to balance himself, Kenniston lunged forward.

"The bridge, Holk!" he yelled as he hurled himself.

Kenniston's shoulder hit the captain and sent him caroming into Murdock. The two men sprawled on the floor.

Holk Or, with instant understanding, already had the door of the cabin open. They plunged out into the corridor together.

"Our only chance is to make the bridge and grab the controls!" Kenniston cried as they raced down the corridor. "We can keep them long enough to land on Vesta—"

Hiss—*flash!* The crackling blast of the atom-gun tore into the lower steps of the ladder up which he and the Jovian frantically climbed. Murdock was running after them as he fired, and there were shouts of alarm.

Kenniston and Holk Or burst into the glassite-walled bridge. Bray, the pilot, turned for a startled moment from his rocket-throttles.

Beyond the pilot, the transparent front wall framed a square of black space in which bulked the monstrous sphere of the nearby asteroid.

The World with a Thousand Moons! It loomed up only a few hundred miles away, a big, pale-green sphere encircled by the vast globular swarm of hundreds on hundreds of gleaming little meteor-satellites.

"Why—what—" stammered the pilot, bewildered.

Kenniston's fist caught his chin, and the man sagged to the floor.

"Bar the door, Holk!" yelled Kenniston as he leaped toward the rocket-throttles.

"Hell, there's only a catch!" swore the Jovian. He braced his brawny shoulders against the metal door. "I can hold it a little while."

* * * * *

Kenniston's hands were flashing over the throttles. The *Sunsprite* was moving at reduced speed toward the meteor-enclosed asteroid.

The cruiser shook to the bursting roar of power, as he opened up all the tail rockets. It plunged visibly faster toward the deadly swarm around Vesta, picking up speed by the minute.

Rocking, creaking, quivering to the dangerous rate of acceleration Kenniston was maintaining, the little ship rushed ahead. But now there was loud hammering at the bridge-room door.

"Open up or we'll burn that door down!" came Captain Walls' yell.

Kenniston didn't turn. Hunched over the throttles, peering tensely ahead, he was tautly estimating speed and direction. His eyes searched frantically for the periodic break in the outer meteors.

There was a muffled crackling and the smell of scorched metal flooded the bridge-room. A hoarse exclamation of pain came from Holk Or.

"They got my arm through the door, damn them!" cursed the Jovian. "Hurry, Kenniston!"

Kenniston was driving the *Sunsprite* full speed toward the whirling cloud of meteors around the asteroid. He had spotted the break in the cloud, the periodic opening caused by the gravitational influence of another nearby asteroid.

It was not a real opening. It was merely a small area in the swarm where the rushing meteors were not so thick, and where a ship had a chance to worm through by careful piloting.

Kenniston only remotely heard the struggle that Holk Or was putting up to hold the door against the hammering crowd outside. His mind was wholly intent on the desperately ticklish piloting at hand.

He cut speed and eased the *Sunsprite* down into that thinner area of the meteor-swarm. Space around them now seemed buzzing with rushing, brilliant little moons.

The meteorometers had gone crazy, blinking and buzzing unceasing warning, their needles bobbing all over the direction-dials. Instruments were useless here—he had to work by sight alone. He eased the cruiser lower through the swarm, his fingers flashing over the throttles, using quick bursts of the rockets to veer aside from the bright, rushing meteors.

"Hurry!" yelled Holk Or hoarsely again, over the tumult. "I can't—hold them out much longer—"

Down and down went the *Sunsprite* through the maze of meteor-moons, twisting, turning, dropping ever lower toward the green asteroid.

A last gasping shout from Holk Or, and the door crashed off its burned-through hinges. Kenniston, unable to turn from the life-or-death business of threading the swarm, heard the Jovian fighting furiously.

Next moment a hand gripped Kenniston's shoulder and tore him away from the controls. It was Murdock, his eyes blazing, his gun raised.

"Raise your hands or I'll kill you, Kenniston!" he cried.

"Let me go!" yelled Kenniston, struggling to get back to the throttles. "You *fool!*"

He had just glimpsed the jagged moonlet rushing obliquely toward them from the left, bulking suddenly big and monstrous.

Crash! The shock flung them from their feet, and the *Sunsprite* gyrated crazily in space. There was a blood-chilling shriek of outrushing air from the fore part of the ship, and the slam-slam-slam of the automatic air-doors closing, down there.

The cruiser's whole bows had been crushed in by the glancing blow of the meteor. Now, ironically, the ship was falling clear of the meteor-swarm for Kenniston's piloting had almost won through it before the impact. But the *Sunsprite* was falling helplessly, turning over and over as it plunged down toward the green surface of the jungled asteroid.

*   *   *   *   *

"My God, we're struck!" came Captain Walls' thin yell.

"This is your fault!" Murdock blazed at Kenniston. "You damned pirates will die for this!"

"Let me at those controls or we'll all die together in five minutes!" Kenniston cried. "We'll crash to smithereens unless I can make a tail-tube landing—"

Heedless of Murdock's gun, he jumped to the controls. His hands flew over the throttles, firing desperate quick bursts of the tail rocket-tubes to bring them out of the spin in which they were falling.

The brake-rockets in the bow were gone. The ship was crippled, almost impossible to handle. And the dark green jungles of Vesta's surface were rushing upward with appalling speed.

Kenniston's frantic efforts brought the *Sunsprite* out of the spin. By firing the lateral rockets, he kept it falling tail-downward.

"We're goners!" yelled someone in the stricken ship. "We're going to crash!"

Air was screaming outside the plummeting ship. Kenniston, his hands superhumanly tense on the throttles, mechanically estimated their distance from the uprushing green jungles.

He glimpsed a little black lake in the jungle, and near it the big circle of an electrified stockade. He recognized it—John Dark's camp!

Then, a thousand feet above the jungle, Kenniston's hands jerked open the throttles. The tail rockets spouted fire downward.

Sickening shock of the sudden check almost hurled him away from the controls. His hands jabbed the throttles in and out with lightning rapidity, checking their further fall with one quick burst after another.

A sound of rending branches—a staggering sidewise shock that flung him from his feet. A jarring thump, then silence. They had landed.

CHAPTER IV
The Vestans

Kenniston picked himself up groggily. The others in the bridge had been thrown against walls or floor by the shock, but seemed no more than bruised. Holk Or was nursing his burned arm. But Hugh Murdock, staggering in a corner, still held his atom-pistol trained on Kenniston and the Jovian.

"My God, what a landing!" exclaimed Captain Walls, his plump face still white. "I thought we were done for."

"Maybe we still are," Murdock said grimly. He said savagely to Kenniston, "You think you've won, don't you? Because you've managed to crash us on this asteroid where your pirate boss is waiting?"

"Listen, Murdock—," Kenniston began desperately.

"Keep your hands up or I'll kill you both!" blazed Murdock. "March down to the main cabin."

Kenniston and the Jovian obeyed. The *Sunsprite* was lying sharply canted on its side, and it was difficult to scramble down through the tilted passageways and decks to the big main cabin.

The cabin was a scene of confusion, for it was impossible to stand upright on its tilted floor. Young Arthur Lanning had been stunned, and Gloria Loring and the scared blonde girl, Alice Krim, were bathing his bruised forehead. Robbie Boone was peering wildly through a porthole at the sunlit tangle of green jungle outside. From Mrs. Milsom came a shrill, steady wail of terror.

"Stop that screeching," Murdock told the dumpy dowager brutally. "You're not hurt. Gloria, are you others all right?"

Gloria raised her white face from her task. "Only bruised, Hugh."

She did not look at Kenniston or the big Jovian as she spoke.

Robbie Boone's teeth were chattering. "Murdock, what are we going to do? We're wrecked, on this hellish jungle asteroid—"

Murdock paid the frightened, chubby youth no attention. Captain Walls, Bray, and four of the crew were entering the cabin. The captain and pilot had belted on atom-pistols.

Captain Walls' plump face was paler. "Two of the crew were killed and our telaudio wrecked by that meteor," he reported. He glared at Kenniston. "You damned pirate! You're responsible for this!"

"If you hadn't dragged me away from the controls, the cruiser wouldn't have been struck," Kenniston denied. "And I'm not a pirate—"

Murdock interrupted. "We'll settle with those two later," he told the enraged captain. "Right now, we'll have to get out of the ship. We can't stay in here until we get it righted on an even keel."

Holk Or rumbled a warning. "Better be careful about going outside. Those cursed Vestans are thick in these jungles."

"I'll have no advice from you two pirates!" flamed the captain. "Bray, you and Thorpe keep your guns on them every minute."

The heavy main space-door was opened. Pale sunlight and warm, steamy air laden with rank scents of strange vegetation drifted in. Outside lay a raw clearing the falling ship had crushed out of the jungle.

Captain Walls supervised as they all donned lead-soled weight-shoes to compensate for the weaker gravity. Then they emerged, young Lanning being supported by Murdock and Robbie. Kenniston and the Jovian were last to emerge, under the watchful guns of their guards.

The crew and passengers were looking around with wonder and revulsion. The silvery bulk of the *Sunsprite* lay awkwardly heeled on its side. The symmetrical torpedo shape of the cruiser was now badly marred by the crumpled condition of its bow.

*　　*　　*　　*　　*

All around them in the thin sunlight rose slender trees whose enormous green leaves grew directly from the trunks. This grotesque forest was made more dense by festoons of writhing "snake-vines," weird rootless creepers which crawled like plant-serpents from one tree to another. Each stir of wind brought white spore-dust down in a shower from the trees.

The few living creatures of this forbidding landscape were equally alien. Big white meteor-rats scurried on their eight legs through the brush. Phosphorescent flame-birds shot through the upper fronds like streaks of fire. In the pale sky overhead, there were ceaseless gleams and flashes of light as the spinning meteor-swarm reflected the sunlight.

"What a horrible place!" shrilled Mrs. Milsom. "We'll all die here—we'll never get back to Earth. I knew this would happen!"

"This is certainly a mean spot to be cast away," muttered Captain Walls. "God knows what queer creatures inhabit it, not to speak of the mysterious Vestans everybody talks about. And John Dark and his crew are somewhere here. And the telaudio wrecked, so we can't call for help."

Kenniston realized that none of the others had glimpsed Dark's camp as they fell. They didn't know the pirate encampment was only a few miles away in the jungle.

"What are we going to do, captain?" Gloria was asking, her face still pale but her voice quite steady. "Can we get away?"

Captain Walls looked hopeless. "We can't take off with the whole bow of the *Sunsprite* crushed in."

"We can repair it, can't we?" Hugh Murdock suggested. "Remember, in the hold is the cargo of machinery and repair-materials that Kenniston was bringing to repair Dark's ship. Can't we use that equipment?"

The captain looked more hopeful. "Maybe we can. Bray and the crew and I ought to be able to do an emergency job of patching the bow and installing new rocket-tubes there. But we'll have to work fast to get away before Dark's outfit learns we're here."

He pointed vindicatively at Kenniston. "Better lock up that fellow and his partner to make sure he doesn't signal somehow to his fellow-pirates."

Kenniston tried again to explain. "Will you all listen to me? I tell you, I'm no pirate!"

Murdock eyed him sternly. "Do you deny that John Dark sent you to Mars for repair-equipment, and that you told us that lying treasure-story to get the equipment here in our ship?"

"No, I don't deny that," Kenniston admitted. "But I'm not one of John Dark's crew—I never was! I was a prisoner on his ship, captured by the pirates before they themselves were attacked by the Patrol."

"Do you expect us to believe that?" Murdock said incredulously.

"It's true!" Kenniston insisted. "My kid brother Ricky and I were captured by John Dark's outfit several weeks ago. We were prisoners on his ship when it was wrecked by the Patrol. After the wreck drifted onto Vesta here,

Dark wanted to send someone to Mars for repair-equipment. He wouldn't send one of his own men in charge, for fear the man would double-cross him and never come back.

"So he sent me, his prisoner, on that errand. Holk Or came along to help me navigate a ship back. And I had to obey Dark and get the equipment back here at any cost. For Dark kept my brother Ricky prisoner here with him, and told me that if I didn't bring back that equipment, Ricky would be shot!"

Holk Or spoke up. "It's true, what Kenniston's telling you," rumbled the Jovian. "Me, I'm one of Dark's pirates and I don't care a curse who knows it. But Kenniston did this only to save his brother."

"I don't believe it," said Captain Walls flatly. "It's another of the smooth lies this fellow Kenniston makes up so easily."

*   *   *   *   *

Gloria spoke to Kenniston, her dark eyes still accusing. "If what you say is true and you're not a pirate, then you brought all of us into this danger simply to save your own brother?"

Kenniston looked at her miserably. "Yes, I did. I was willing to lead you all into capture to save Ricky. But I had a reason—"

"Sure, you had a reason," Murdock said bitterly. "What did the safety of strangers like us mean to you, compared to your precious brother?"

Captain Walls motioned Kenniston and Holk Or angrily toward the ship. "Bray, take them in and lock them under guard in a cabin," he said.

Holk Or suddenly yelled. "Look out! There's a Vestan!"

Kenniston, his blood chilling with alarm, glanced where the Jovian pointed. At the west edge of the clearing, a small animal had suddenly emerged from the dense green jungle.

It was a six-legged, striped, catlike beast, not unordinary as interplanetary animals go. But its head looked queer, seeming to have a bulbous gray mass attached behind its ears.

Captain Walls uttered a scoffing exclamation. "That's only an ordinary asteroid-cat."

"That *is* a Vestan!" Kenniston cried. "Shoot at its head—"

His warning was too late. The catlike beast had launched itself in a spring toward their group.

As its striped body shot through the air, Walls triggered his atom-pistol. The crackling blast of force tore into the body of the charging asteroid-cat, and the beast fell heavily a few yards away.

But as it fell, the small gray mass upon its neck suddenly detached itself from the dead animal and scuttled swiftly forward. It moved with blurring speed toward Bray, the nearest to it of the group.

The little gray creature was no bigger than a man's clenched fists together. It was a gray, wrinkled featureless thing, except for pinpoint eyes and the tiny clawlike legs upon which it scurried. It reached Bray and ran swiftly up his legs and back as he swore startledly.

Kenniston, made reckless of danger by his horror, yelled and lunged toward the pilot. Bray was swearing and trying to slap at the gray thing running up his back. But the little creature had now reached his neck. Clinging there, it swiftly dug two tiny, needle-like antennae into the base of his neck.

"Hold him!" Kenniston shouted hoarsely. "The Vestan has got him!"

Bray had undergone a sudden metamorphosis as the gray creature dug its antennae into his neck. His face stiffened, became masklike.

The pilot turned and began to run stiffly toward the jungle. Kenniston's leap almost caught him, but Bray lashed out a fist that sent Kenniston sprawling.

"Don't let him get away!" Kenniston yelled, scrambling up.

But the others were too stricken by amazement and horror to interfere in time. Bray had already plunged into the jungle and was gone.

"My God, what happened?" Captain Walls exclaimed dazedly. "Bray went clean crazy!"

His gun was pointing at Kenniston and Holk Or as though he held them responsible for what had occurred.

"He didn't go crazy, but he's lost now," Kenniston said heavily. "That little gray creature was one of the Vestans."

"But what did it *do* to him? That thing wasn't big enough to harm anybody."

"That's all you know about it," said Holk Or ominously. "Those little Vestans are the most dangerous creatures in the System."

"The Vestans," Kenniston added dully, "are semi-intelligent *parasites*. The live by attaching themselves to and taking control of some other creature's body. They do it by jabbing in those tiny, needle-like antennae to contact the victim's nervous system. Thereafter, the Vestan controls the victim's body absolutely. When the victim dies or is hurt, the Vestan simply detaches himself and fastens upon a new victim."

*   *   *   *   *

Horror was on the white faces of the others. Murdock gulped and asked, "Then Bray—"

"Bray is beyond saving now," Kenniston said. "The Vestan parasite will control his body till he dies. The Vestans always like to attach themselves to human beings—they know that a man's body is more versatile in its capabilities than an animal's."

Twilight was beginning to descend upon the little clearing in the jungle, for the sun had gone down during the last few minutes. In the gathering dusk, the jungle loomed dark and brooding about them.

Overhead, the sky of this World with a Thousand Moons was burgeoning into its full glory. The hundreds of meteor-moons that spun across the heavens were shining brighter and brighter in the deepening dusk.

Captain Walls broke the spell of horror and dread. "We'd better get back inside the ship for tonight," he said nervously. "We can't do anything about repairs until tomorrow, anyway. By then we'll have figured out some way to deal with those devilish creatures."

Murdock said bitterly to Kenniston, "Bray's end is your fault, Kenniston. You brought him and us and these women into this place, all for the sake of that brother of yours."

"He'll stand trial for that when we get back to Mars," the captain vowed. "Even if he wasn't one of Dark's crew originally, by helping them he's made himself a space-pirate, liable to execution."

Kenniston made no attempt to defend himself. He knew they wouldn't understand why he had sacrificed them for Ricky's sake, even if he told them.

He and Holk Or were locked in one of the little cabins, after it had been carefully searched. The crewman Thorpe was stationed as a guard outside their bolted door.

Holk Or, who had bandaged his burned arm, looked around the dark little cabin disgustedly. "This is a devil of a fix to get into!" swore the Jovian. "Here we've reached Vesta with the stuff, but can't let the chief know."

Kenniston asked him earnestly, "Holk, would John Dark really shoot Ricky if I didn't deliver the equipment? He said he would, but you know he needs Ricky."

Kenniston was clinging to this last shred of hope for his brother. John Dark and his pirates did need Ricky. For Ricky was a physician—Doctor Richard Kenniston of the Institute of Planetary Medicine.

That was why John Dark had spared the lives of the two brothers when he had captured them in the freighter in which they were returning to Earth from Saturn. Ordinarily, the pirate leader would have ruthlessly killed them as he killed all prisoners who were not rich enough to pay ransom.

But the fact that Ricky was a physician had saved them. The pirates needed a doctor. They had kept the two brothers prisoner on their ship for that reason. Kenniston and Ricky had still been on the *Falcon* as prisoners, when the Patrol had finally caught up to it and wrecked it.

"Dark knows that Ricky is a fine doctor and he needs a doctor," Kenniston repeated hopefully, to the Jovian. "Surely he wouldn't be foolish enough to shoot Ricky, even if I don't deliver the equipment."

"Kenniston, don't fool yourself," warned Holk Or. "The chief said he'd shoot him if you weren't back with the stuff in two weeks, and shoot him he will. John Dark never breaks his word."

That assurance sank the iron deeper into Kenniston's tormented soul. If that was true, and he knew in his heart it was, Ricky would die two days from now unless he'd delivered the repair-equipment to Dark.

He mustn't *let* Ricky die! Too much depended on his young brother's life. He must save Ricky even if it did mean the capture of Gloria and the others by the pirates. Better that they be held for ransom, than for Ricky to be killed!

*   *   *   *   *

Kenniston got to his feet, rigid with decision. "Then we've got to get out of here," he muttered. "We've got to escape and take word to Dark that the equipment is here."

He continued quickly, "Holk, Dark's camp is only a few miles north of here. I spotted it as the *Sunsprite* fell."

Holk Or uttered an exclamation. "Why the devil didn't you tell me so! I figured it was on the other side of the asteroid, maybe, and that we'd never find it in the jungle even if we did get away."

"It still won't be easy for us," Kenniston warned. "The Vestans may get us in the jungle between here and Dark's camp. And anyway, how can we get out of this cabin?"

The big Jovian grinned. "That'll be easy. I'd have been out of here before now, only I was waiting for the ship to quiet down."

Kenniston stared. "That door is bolted. And there's no tool or weapon in the cabin. They didn't forget a thing when they searched it!"

Holk Or's grin deepened. "They forgot one thing. They forgot how strong a Jovian is on a little, weak-gravity asteroid like this!"

CHAPTER V
Night Attack

Kenniston caught desperately at the hope implied by the Jovian's words.

"What do you mean, Holk?"

"I mean that I'm a hundred times stronger on this little asteroid than I am on my own world, Jupiter. I can break the bolt of that door any time I want to."

"But there's an armed guard stationed outside it."

"I know, and that's where you come in, Kenniston. When I rip the door open, you be ready to jump the guard."

Kenniston considered swiftly. The chance of their getting out of the ship and safely through the jungles to the pirate camp, even if they escaped this cabin, seemed a slim one. Yet it presented the only possibility of delivering the equipment in the hold to John Dark.

The bitter irony of it struck Kenniston, for the hundredth time. He, Lance Kenniston, honorable space-man for a dozen years, working desperately to aid the most notorious pirate in the void! Even drawing into danger the girl for whom he felt—

He shut Gloria out of his mind. He mustn't think of her now. He must think only of Ricky, and of what would be lost if Ricky died. He must risk everything, sacrifice everything, to prevent that loss.

"We might as well try it now," he told the Jovian in low tones. "The ship seems quiet."

"I'll do my best to make as little noise as possible," Holk Or muttered. "Are you ready?"

The Jovian's big hands grasped the knob of the door. Kenniston crouched a little behind him, every muscle tense.

Holk Or suddenly put all his gigantically magnified strength into a tremendous tug at the door. Its bolt snapped with a crack like that of a pistolshot, and it swung wide open.

The man on guard outside turned startledly, his hand darting to the atom-gun at his belt and his mouth open to yell. But Kenniston had launched himself like a human projectile as the door was torn open.

Kenniston's fist smashed the space-sailor's chin and the man sagged limp and unconscious with no chance to utter the cry on his lips. Hastily, Kenniston took his atom-pistol and eased him to the floor.

He and Holk Or listened tensely. The single sharp crack of the snapping bolt had apparently aroused no one. The ship was silent. All aboard were sleeping exhaustedly.

"Come on," Kenniston murmured tensely to the Jovian. "We've got to hurry to get to Dark's camp before night is over."

Holk Or chuckled. "The chief will welcome us with open arms when he learns we've got the equipment here for him."

Kenniston gripped the atom-pistol as they stole through the dark ship and out of the space-door. Outside, they paused in the darkness.

The scene was one of magic, unearthly beauty. The metal bulk of the cruiser and the towering jungle around the clearing were washed by brilliant silver light that fell from the wonderful night sky of this World with a Thousand Moons.

A thousand moons indeed seemed blazing in the canopied heavens overhead! The whole dark sky was crowded by the shining moonlets that rushed ceaselessly across the firmament with the spinning of the meteor-swarm of which they were part. It was like the glorious vista of a world seen in dreams.

But Kenniston was familiar with the unearthly spectacle. He led the way rapidly toward the northern edge of the jungle.

"We'll just have to plunge in and head north," he told the Jovian. "If we reach that little lake, we can soon find Dark's camp."

They started into the dense jungle, a fairyland of silver beams sifting through the choking fronds. Something scurried close by.

"Kenniston, shoot!" cried Holk Or instantly.

* * * * *

Kenniston had already glimpsed the white beast scurrying toward them across a little patch of moonlight. It was one of the big meteor-rats. On its neck bunched one of the little gray masses—a Vestan.

The horror inspired by the hideous parasites tightened Kenniston's finger convulsively on the trigger of the atom-pistol. The crackling bolt of fire from the weapon ripped into the Vestan on the meteor-rat, and both parasite and animal victim were instantly a scorched, smoking heap.

"Hell, that's torn it!" cried the big Jovian. "We've roused the whole ship!"

Men awakened by the blast of the atom-gun were pouring out of the *Sunsprite*, rushing after the two escaped men. Kenniston heard Captain Walls shouting.

"They're in the jungle here! Spread out and surround them!" the officer was ordering.

Kenniston and the Jovian plunged forward, seeking to escape northward. But they had come up against an impenetrable abatis of brush.

Before they could find a way around it, they heard men crashing all around them. They were completely encircled.

"Kenniston, you and that Jovian walk back into the clearing with your hands raised or we'll blast every inch of the brush till we get you!" came the stentorian shout of the captain.

"The devil—they've got us boxed!" exclaimed Holk Or furiously. "We'll try to fight our way through."

"No!" Kenniston declared. "We couldn't make it anyway. And I'm not going to shoot innocent men."

Holk Or angrily grabbed for the atom-pistol, but Kenniston promptly threw it away. Not even in this last extremity could he bring himself to kill.

"You're a fool!" gritted the Jovian. "Now there's nothing for it but surrender."

With their hands raised, they walked out of the jungle into the brilliant silvery light of the clearing. Instantly they were surrounded by Captain Walls, Murdock and the other armed crew-men.

The girls and their scared chaperon, and young Lanning and Robbie Boone, were emerging in alarm from the *Sunsprite*. Kenniston did not look toward them.

Captain Walls' face was grim in the moonslight, as he and his men covered the two captured fugitives. "Kenniston, you and this Jovian were going to make your way to John Dark and tell him of our presence here, weren't you? You needn't deny it—it's plain enough."

"Sure we were!" exclaimed the angry Jovian. "We'd have made it, too, if a Vestan hadn't jumped us in the jungle."

"That would have meant capture of us all by Dark's pirates," said the captain grimly. "You two are a danger to us all, while you live. I'm going to remove that danger. As master of a space-ship, I have legal right to order summary execution of any space-pirates I capture. I'm going to order that now."

"You're going to kill them?" exclaimed Gloria. "Oh, no—you can't!"

"It's absolutely necessary, before they betray us to the pirates, Miss Loring," defended the captain. "They'd be sentenced to death by the courts if we took them back to Mars, anyway. But we daren't take a chance on keeping them prisoned that long."

"But just to shoot them down!" said Gloria horrifiedly. "I won't stand for that!"

Murdock took her by the arm. "It's space law, Gloria," he told her earnestly. "You'd better go back into the ship."

Kenniston stood silent in the moonslight, for he realized from the finality of Walls' voice that appeals would be utterly useless. There was no use trying again to explain why he'd been willing to betray them all to save Ricky. Even if they listened, they wouldn't understand.

He felt tired, crushed, old. He'd gone a long way in the last dozen years, but every mile of it had only led toward this ending. He was going to die here under the hurtling meteor-moons of Vesta, and that meant that Ricky and Ricky's dream were going to die soon too.

"I *told* you you were a fool to throw away that gun," Holk Or was muttering.

*　　*　　*　　*　　*

"You two march over there to the edge of the clearing," Captain Walls ordered grimly, gesturing with his gun. "Anything you want to say first, Kenniston?"

"Nothing that you would listen to or understand, you people," Kenniston answered dully. "No, I've got nothing to say."

A crackling voice came out of the dark jungle at that moment.

"*I* have something to say! Drop those guns, every man of you, and get your hands up!"

Walls spun around with an oath, levelling his atom-pistol. But out of the jungle crashed a streak of fire that hit the captain's arm and sent him reeling.

One of the girls screamed. Another of the *Sunsprite's* crew had tried to aim his weapon and had been cut down by a second bolt of atomic fire that had hit his leg.

"I *don't* want to kill you unless you force me to," came that crisp voice from the darkness. "You have ten seconds to drop the guns."

"That's the chief, Kenniston!" yelled Holk Or excitedly. "It's John Dark himself!"

The dreaded name of the pirate, a synonym for cold ruthlessness, reinforced the threat from the darkness.

Murdock let his weapon fall and shouted, "Drop the atom-guns, men! If we try to fight, the women will be hurt!"

The *Sunsprite's* men dropped their atom-pistols. Instantly out into the brilliant light from the jungle rushed a score of armed pirates. Martians, Earthmen, Venusians and others—this horde represented the criminal under-world of every planet in the System.

In a moment they had those in the clearing completely disarmed and lined up against the ship. All except Holk Or, who was loudly greeting his pirate comrades.

Kenniston saw John Dark coming across the moonlit clearing toward them. The notorious pirate was a tall, bulky Earthman, but he walked with the lightfootedness of a cat in his moonshoes. His black hair was bare, and in the silver light his black-browed, intelligent face was coldly calm as his eyes searched the row of prisoners.

"So you finally got here, Kenniston. What about the repair-equipment?" he asked sharply.

Kenniston nodded toward the *Sunsprite*. "It's in the hold. We got everything you listed."

"Good!" Dark approved. "We saw your ship crash-landing today, and started this way at once. We've been beating through the jungle, fighting off the damned Vestans, until we heard the uproar going on here. What happened? Who are these people?"

Kenniston explained briefly how he had induced Gloria Loring's party to come on a pretended treasure-hunt. He was careful to stress the wealth of the party, and John Dark reacted as he had expected.

"If they're that wealthy, their families can pay big ransoms. You've done very well, Kenniston."

"What about Ricky?" asked Kenniston tensely. "He's all right?"

"Sure he's all right—he's up at the camp," Dark answered.

Gloria said bitterly to Kenniston, "You can congratulate yourself. You've managed to save your brother."

John Dark addressed her. "Miss Loring, I presume you and your companions are willing to pay ransom for your crew also? I never take prisoners, unless they promise a good profit."

"Yes, of course we'll pay the ransom of the crew!" Gloria agreed hastily.

"Good!" said the pirate calmly. "You'll not find your captivity any more irksome than necessary."

Mrs. Milsom, the dumpy chaperon, was goggling at the notorious pirate in an extreme of terror. A sardonic gleam came into Dark's eyes as he glanced at her.

"You're a handsome wench," he told the plump dowager with mock admiration. "I've half a mind to keep you and let the ransom go."

"No, no!" shrieked the terrified woman.

Dark burst into a roar of laughter. "All right, my shrinking beauty, we'll accept ransom for you."

He turned and shot efficient orders to his subordinates, who by now had gathered behind him.

"Get that stuff out of the hold, rig up power-sledges, and start freighting it up to the camp. You'll have to cut a path through the jungle—use atom-blasters to burn one out."

One of the pirates, a hard-faced Martian, said uneasily, "That will make a racket that'll bring every Vestan on the asteroid down on us."

"You can keep the Vestans off if you keep your eyes open," Dark retorted. "Get to work, now! We've got to get the stuff up there and repair the *Falcon* at once. I'll take these prisoners up to camp."

Kenniston was grouped with the other prisoners. With a strong escort of armed pirates guarding them, and Dark and Holk Or ahead, they started through the jungle toward the pirate camp.

CHAPTER VI
Asteroid Horror

The pirate encampment was a big clearing hacked from the jungle a mile west of the little lake. In this space lay the long, looming black mass of the most dreaded corsair ship ever to sail the void. The *Falcon* had been righted to even keel, but its crippled condition was evident in the fused, wrecked condition of its tail rocket-tubes.

The whole camp was enclosed and protected by a shimmering blue dome of electric force. This emanated from a heavy copper cable that completely encircled the clearing, and which drew its power from insulated cables that led into the ship to generators driven by the few cyclotrons still functioning. This protective electric wall had been set up at John Dark's orders to keep out the dreaded Vestans.

John Dark raised his voice as he and his men with their prisoners approached the shimmering wall of the camp.

"Kin Ibo! Drop the wall for us!"

They saw the hard-looking Martian who was Dark's second-in-command dive into the ship to turn off the power of the electric barrier. It died, and Dark's party entered the clearing. Then the electric wall sprang into being again behind them.

Kenniston looked swiftly around. There were a score more of the motley pirates here in the camp. Also, near the side of the looming black *Falcon*, were the small, rough log huts that Dark's men had constructed.

Dark's black eyes were triumphant as he told his Martian lieutenant, "Kenniston and Holk Or brought back the equipment all right, and also brought some people who'll bring big ransom. Their wrecked ship is a few miles south. You go down there with half the men here and help the others bring up the equipment."

Kin Ibo, looking a little apprehensively out at the jungle, obeyed. Dark motioned Kenniston and the other captives toward one of the huts by the big ship.

"That hut will be your quarters until we get the *Falcon* repaired," declared the pirate leader. "Any of you who try to leave it will be shot at sight. I hope you'll not be foolish enough to attempt escape."

"That's right, folks, you wouldn't have a chance," Holk Or told them earnestly. "Even if you could get out through the electric wall, the Vestans would get you. They're thick in the jungle around here."

They silently entered the hut. Its broad open windows admitted enough of the dazzling moonlight to brighten its interior.

A dark, eager-looking young Earthman sprang up as they entered, and rushed to pump Kenniston's hand.

"Lance, you got back safely!" he exclaimed. "Thank the Lord—I've been worrying myself almost crazy about you."

"How about you, Ricky?" Kenniston asked his young brother anxiously. "You're all right?"

Ricky Kenniston nodded quickly. "Sure, I'm okay. But things haven't been so good here, Lance. The Vestans have got a half-dozen pirates who ventured outside the wall in the last few days. These creatures literally haunt the jungles around here now—I think they've been drawn here from all over the asteroid."

Ricky looked wonderingly at Gloria and the others who were entering the hut. "Lance, who are all these people? Are they prisoners of Dark too?"

"Yes, we're prisoners," Hugh Murdock told him bitterly, with a savage glance at Kenniston. "We're prisoners because your brother sacrificed us all to get back here and save *your* neck."

"Lance, you didn't do that?" Ricky exclaimed in distress.

"I had to, Ricky," Kenniston protested. "It meant your life if I didn't."

"Of course," Murdock agreed ironically. "What importance are we, compared to saving your young brother's life?"

Kenniston spoke slowly, to Murdock and Gloria and the others. "It wasn't merely Ricky's life at stake that made me sacrifice you all. It was more than that. I tried to tell you before, but you wouldn't listen."

*   *   *   *   *

Kenniston went across the hut and brought back the square black medicine-case of his young physician-brother. He opened it, and out of the vials and instruments inside he took a square bottle of milky fluid.

"This is what I sacrificed everything to save," Kenniston said simply.

They all stared. "What is it?" Gloria asked, puzzled.

"It's Ricky's discovery," Kenniston said. "It's a preventative and cure for gravitation-paralysis."

Captain Walls, himself an old-time space-man, was first of the group to appreciate the significance of the statement. The captain gasped.

"A preventative for gravitation-paralysis? Kenniston, are you *sure*?"

Kenniston nodded gravely. "Yes. Ricky had been working on the problem a long time, back in the Institute of Planetary Medicine. He thought he'd found a way to prevent gravitation-paralysis, the most awful scourge of all the outer System, the thing that's doomed so many space-men. But his formula required rare elements found only in the outer planets.

"Ricky and I," he continued, "went out there and secured those elements. He made up this formula, and tried it on a gravitation-paralysis case—a space-man who's lain paralyzed for years. The formula was designed to strengthen the human nervous system against the shock of varying gravitations, to re-establish an already damaged nerve-web. And it worked."

Kenniston's voice was husky as he concluded. "It worked, and that living log became a man again. The formula was a success. Ricky and I started back for Earth, where he intended to announce the discovery and arrange for its manufacture on a big scale. But, on the way back, Dark's pirates captured us."

Kenniston flung out his hand in a tortured gesture. "*That's* why I went to any lengths to save Ricky's life! It's because Ricky is the only person who knows the intricate formula of this serum. If he were to die, the secret of the cure would die with him. And that would mean that thousands on thousands more of space-men would be stricken into living death by gravitation-paralysis in the future, just as so many thousands of old friends and shipmates of mine have been stricken in the past!"

Captain Walls was the first to speak. Quietly, the plump master of the *Sunsprite* extended his hand.

"Kenniston, will you shake hands with me? And will you forgive me for everything? You did absolutely right. I'm an old space-man and I *know* what gravitation-paralysis is."

Gloria's dark eyes were glimmering with tears. "If we'd only known," she murmured to Kenniston. "No one could blame you for sacrificing a lot of worthless idlers like us, for a thing like this."

"But you're going to be all right—all of you," Kenniston assured her. "John Dark will make you pay a big ransom, but you can afford that and you'll get back safely to Earth."

"Thank Heaven for that!" exclaimed Mrs. Milsom. "I can't understand all this scientific talk of yours, but I do know that that pirate chief means no good to me. Didn't you see the lustful looks he gave me?"

The laugh that greeted this lessened the tension. Kenniston turned as Ricky plucked at his arm.

"What about ourselves, Lance?" Ricky asked quietly. "Dark still won't let us go, you know. He still needs me as a doctor."

Hugh Murdock stepped forward. "Dark would let you both go, for a big enough ransom. I'd like to pay it for you."

The handsomeness of Murdock's gesture moved Kenniston. He was only able to mutter his thanks.

*   *   *   *   *

While Ricky was treating Captain Walls' burned arm, the officer kept looking fascinatedly at that square bottle of milky fluid.

He said hesitantly, "I've a son—back on Earth. For five years he's lain in a cot from the gravitation-paralysis that hit him out on Jupiter. Do you suppose—"

Ricky nodded. "Yes, Captain. I'm sure that we can cure him, now."

There was an uproar out in the clearing. Kenniston went to the door and looked out.

The electric wall had temporarily been dropped, and Kin Ibo and the main body of the pirates were hastily entering the camp with their improvised power-sledges that bore heavy loads of machinery and materials.

Kenniston heard Kin Ibo reporting shrilly to John Dark, "We lost two men to the Vestans on the way here— and nearly lost two more! All this activity has drawn them from all over the asteroid! Look at that!"

Outside the electric wall, which had been hastily re-raised, could be glimpsed the shapes of lurking asteroidal animals. Meteor-rats, big striped cats, flame-birds—and every one of those lurking animals bore attached to its neck one of the little gray Vestan parasites.

John Dark was saying harshly, "We've got to have the rest of those materials to repair the *Falcon*."

"I tell you, it'd be suicide to try another trip through those jungles!" expostulated the Martian. "Those Vestans are devils!"

"Bah, you Martians are all alike—no good when your superstitions get aroused," snorted Dark contemptuously. "I'll take the men down myself. Come on, men—unload those sledges and we'll go back to the wreck."

His indomitable personality drove the scared, unwilling pirates into the task. Again the electric wall was faded out for a moment to let them out.

When they returned some time toward morning, Kenniston heard the crash of atom-guns heralding their approach. And when the wall was momentarily dropped, John Dark and his men stumbled into the camp with their loaded sledges in sweating haste.

"Turn on the wall again—quick!" bellowed Dark's bull voice. "The jungle's swarming with the gray devils now—they got five of us on the way back!"

Ricky, looking over Kenniston's shoulder, spoke appalledly. "Good God, Lance—look at them! I didn't know there *were* so many Vestans!"

Outside the barrier of shimmering electricity, scores of animals and birds dominated by the dreaded little gray parasitical creatures were now swarming. And their number seemed growing every minute.

"All this activity of the night has drawn the Vestans from far and wide," Kenniston muttered. "I don't like it. If that electric wall should fail, the creatures would be in on us in a moment."

Dark himself seemed to feel something of the same apprehension, for he was shouting urgent orders. "Hook up those atomic welders, and start putting the new plates into the *Falcon's* tail. Kin Ibo, have your gang fit in the new rocket-tubes. I'll see to installing the new cycs. If we work, we can get the job done by tomorrow night and get out of here."

Through the day, the pirates toiled with an energy that showed their earnest desire to leave the asteroid. That desire was reinforced by the ever-larger number of Vestans that now swarmed outside the wall.

There were literally hundreds of the gray parasites now outside the barrier. To have tried going outside the wall now would have been sheer suicide. The creatures were apparently driven by unholy eagerness to possess themselves of human bodies.

Gloria, looking out with Kenniston, shuddered deeply. "This horrible world! It's like a nightmare."

"We'll soon be away from it," Kenniston reassured. "See, they've almost finished repairing the *Falcon*."

* * * * *

The urgent toil of the pirates was showing results. By the time night came again, and the meteor-moonlets blazed forth with magic beauty in the dark heavens, the task of repair was almost done.

Kenniston and his companions had not ventured forth from the hut. Pirates were everywhere in the clearing, and all had heard John Dark's strict order to blast down the captives if they left their prison.

But from the hut, Kenniston and the others could see that the horde of Vestan-dominated animals around the camp had further increased. With ghastly avidity, they kept circling the shimmering, electric wall.

Kenniston turned in alarm at a ripping sound from the back of the log hut. Two of the logs were being torn out bodily. The battered green face and giant shoulders of Holk Or came through the opening.

"Kenniston, I came in this way because I didn't dare let Dark see me talking to you!" the Jovian exclaimed. His face was urgent in expression. "I've found out that Dark doesn't mean to let your friends here get away from Vesta alive."

"What?" exclaimed Kenniston. "That's impossible! Dark said he was going to hold Gloria and the others for ransom."

Holk Or nodded hastily. "I know, and he meant it, then. But since then, he's found out something that's changed his plans. He found it out from me—like a big fool, I told him everything when he questioned me."

The Jovian continued rapidly. "I told him that Murdock had sent that telaudio message back to Patrol headquarters, asking about my record. Now Dark figures that the Patrol will come out here to find out if that message meant that some of John Dark's outfit had actually escaped.

"Dark wants the Patrol to keep thinking that he and his outfit were destroyed—so he can slip out to Pluto and prepare a new base. So Dark, when he leaves here, is going to drop Miss Loring and her friends by the wrecked

Sunsprite, so the Patrol will find 'em dead by the wreck and will believe their cruiser crashed accidentally. That way, they won't go on searching as they would if Miss Loring's party was all missing. And Dark will have a chance to get out to Pluto without an alarm going out."

Kenniston was suspicious. "Why do you tell us this, Holk? You're one of the pirates yourself."

"I know, but I'm afraid Dark means to drop *me* with the others by the *Sunsprite*!" Holk Or exclaimed. "He didn't say so, but I believe he figures on doing it so that the telaudio inquiry about me would be explained when I was found dead with the others by the wreck."

Murdock said swiftly, "The Jovian's right, Kenniston. All this is just what Dark *would* do, to hide his trail, now that he knows my telaudio message may have aroused the Patrol's suspicion."

Holk Or said emphatically, "I'm with you if you can figure out any way to take the *Falcon*, Kenniston!"

Kenniston paced to and fro. His whole mind was suddenly in a wild turmoil of stark fears. This meant death for Gloria and the others, and the ultimate responsibility for that death would be his.

"There is one possible chance for us to take the *Falcon*," he muttered finally. "But my God, it seems like an insane idea—"

"Wait a minute!" Captain Walls interrupted. "Dark won't drop you and your brother to die, Kenniston. He still needs your brother as a physician. You two will be safe even if we are killed."

"What of that? I can't let Gloria and the rest of you be murdered! I was willing to sacrifice you when I thought it was only a question of your being held for ransom, but this changes everything," Kenniston said wildly.

"It doesn't change anything," the captain said firmly. "Your duty is to keep your brother alive at all costs, to save that formula that means life and hope for thousands of gravitation-paralysis victims like my son."

"You mean—I should let you all be killed so Ricky and I can be saved?" Kenniston cried. "I'm damned if I will!"

"We'll never do that!" Ricky Kenniston agreed warmly. "No formula in the world is worth that."

"*This* formula is," Gloria said earnestly to Kenniston. "The captain is right."

"I won't do it," Kenniston repeated. "I have an idea by which we might be able to take the *Falcon*. We're going to try it."

"Be reasonable, Kenniston," pleaded Hugh Murdock. "None of us except Holk Or has a weapon. What chance would we have against half a hundred armed pirates?"

* * * * *

Kenniston looked at his brother. "Ricky, your formula strengthens the nervous system against any form of shock or damage, doesn't it? You said it did it by sheathing the nerves themselves with an impenetrable coating."

Ricky nodded puzzledly. "Yes, that's the principle. But how is that going to help us?"

"The Vestans," Kenniston reminded, "seize control of their victims by inserting those tiny needle antennae of theirs into the victim's nerve-system to establish contact. Wouldn't your formula insulate the nerves against such contact? Wouldn't it make a man immune to Vestan attack?"

"Why, it would!" Ricky declared wonderingly. "I never thought of it, yet it's entirely logical."

"Then," Kenniston said swiftly, "I want you to give every one of us, including yourself, an injection of the formula right now."

The driving purpose in his voice brushed aside all their bewildered questions and objections. Hastily, Ricky prepared his hypodermics and rapidly made an injection of the milky fluid into the big nerve-centers in the neck of each of them. Kenniston did the same for Ricky himself.

"We *should* be immune now to Vestan attack," Kenniston said prayerfully.

"But what good's that going to do us?" Holk Or demanded. "Are you figuring to try an escape into the jungle?"

"No, I'm figuring on taking the *Falcon*—by using the Vestans," Kenniston replied. "Holk, can you get into the ship and turn off the power that keeps the electric wall going? Can you drop the wall?"

The Jovian's jaw dropped. "Why, sure, I could do that, but if I did, all those hordes of Vestans outside the wall will burst in here—"

He stopped, his eyes bulging. "Good God, then that's your plan? To let the Vestans in?"

"That's it," Kenniston said tightly, his face grim. "To let the Vestans in on the pirates. That'll give us a chance to take the ship—if the formula really makes us immune to the Vestans."

The terrible nature of the proposal stunned them all. But in a moment a flame of purpose lit in the Jovian's eyes.

"I'll do it!" he swore. "It's better than waiting for Dark to kill me like he's planning. You be ready!"

The Jovian slipped out of the opening in the back of the hut. They saw him presently, casually approaching the door of the *Falcon*.

John Dark stood, a tall, dominant figure in the moonlight, barking orders to the scores of pirates who were bolting in the last of the new rocket-tubes. Kenniston's eyes swung toward the shimmering electric wall, and the horde of Vestan-dominated animals outside it.

The wall suddenly died! And as the electric barrier vanished, into the clearing came rushing the swarm of asteroidal animals.

"The wall's down!" John Dark yelled, his atom-gun leaping into his hand. "Get back into the ship—get back—"

The crash of his atom-gun drowned his own shout. Other pirates were firing wildly at the hideous creatures assailing them.

For the little gray Vestans had detached themselves from their animal victims and were swarming upon the pirates, clambering with blurring speed up their legs and backs, sinking into their necks the tiny antennae.

Kenniston glimpsed John Dark, with a hideous little gray bunch now fastened to the back of his neck, drop his gun and stalk stiffly away toward the jungle. His face was an unhuman, lifeless mask—he was a human automaton, dominated utterly by the alien creature.

"Come on!" Kenniston yelled to his friends. "Now's our chance to get into the ship!"

*   *   *   *   *

They plunged out of the hut into the gruesome melee. Screaming pirates were now running into the jungle in vain effort to escape the hordes of Vestans. More than half the corsairs were now overcome.

Kenniston heard a scream from Gloria as they ran, felt a swift scurrying up his back, then the needle-like stab of antennae sinking into his neck.

But the parasitic creature did *not* overpower his will! He reached around, grasped and tore loose the hideous little thing, and with strong revulsion flung it to the ground.

"Your formula works, Ricky—we're immune to them!" he gasped. "But hurry!"

Other Vestans were clambering up on them like ghastly gray spiders as they ran, but were powerless to overcome them. They tore away the creatures and plunged on.

Holk Or appeared in the door of the *Falcon*, his green face blazing as his atom-pistol pumped crashing fire into pirates inside the ship.

"I've got the ship cleared of them!" the Jovian shouted to Kenniston. "Let's get out of here!"

It was time they did so. Almost the last of John Dark's pirates had been possessed by Vestans and had become parasite-dominated robots stumbling off into the jungle. The remaining swarms of gray creatures were scurrying toward Kenniston's group.

They tumbled into the *Falcon* and slammed shut the space-door. The ship, completely if roughly repaired, was ready for take-off. Captain Walls and the men of the *Sunsprite* crew hastily started the newly-installed cyclotrons while Kenniston and the others raced up to the bridge.

Kenniston took the controls. He sent the big black pirate ship leaping up into the darkness upon flaming keel and tail-jets, and then it climbed steeply toward the wonderful sky of countless rushing moonlets.

By the time an hour had passed, the *Falcon* had groped out through the periodic break in the meteor-swarm around the asteroid. And it was throbbing at steadily increasing speed out into the vault of space, away from the World with a Thousand Moons.

"We'll head for Mars," Kenniston told the others. "We can report there to the Patrol."

"If you don't mind," Holk Or put in hastily, "I'd just as soon you dropped me at some asteroid before then. I've no desire to meet the Patrol."

Captain Walls told the Jovian, "Nonsense! After what you've done, you'll get a full pardon from the Patrol."

"You can count on it," Hugh Murdock told the doubtful Jovian. "We have some influence, back at Earth."

"Well, I guess I'll have to go honest, then," sighed Holk Or. "All the real pirate outfits are gone now, anyway." He shook his head heavily as he walked away. "The System sure isn't what it used to be."

Captain Walls was asking Ricky earnestly, "You're quite sure your formula will cure my son? All these years, I've hoped and prayed—"

"I'm certain," Ricky smiled. "Within a few weeks after we get back to Earth, gravitation-paralysis will be a thing of the past."

They moved off with the others. But Gloria lingered in the bridge with Kenniston.

"Where will you be going, after we get back?" she asked him quietly.

"Oh, back to space," he answered, a little uncomfortably. "There's nothing to hold me on Earth now that Ricky's work has succeeded."

"Nothing to hold you on Earth?" Gloria repeated. "That, I would say, is about the most ungallant speech on record."

He flushed. "You don't mean—that night on the *Sunsprite*—you weren't in earnest, surely—"

"Your passionate proposal is accepted," Gloria said calmly.

Kenniston was aghast. "But I didn't propose! I mean— I do love you, and you know it, but you're an heiress, and I—"

"We'll have all the way back to Mars to argue *that* out," she told him. "And I have an idea you'll lose."

Kenniston had the same idea.

And Now a Message . . .
By Greg Fowlkes

A short Story from the upcoming Book - *Back Road to the Stars*

And Now A Message . . .

For the third time that night Jack Olsen was about to nod off over the copy of *Statistical Information Theory* that he was attempting to read. Giving it up as a bad effort, he shut the book and looked out the window of the control room at the giant bowl of the Arecibo radio telescope. Theoretically he was running the huge instrument, but in reality all the controlling was being done by the computers in the room around him. For six months he had been working eight hour shifts every night, and his job had consisted of the five minutes a shift that it took to enter the coordinates to be examined on the control console. Other than that, he was on hand only for the off chance that the monitoring programs would recognize some pattern in the radio noise, in which case an alarm would sound. So far, in the six months, it hadn't happened.

He walked over to the coffee machine in the hopes that a cup would revive him enough so that he could continue his studies. He never made it, for as if to prove the lie of his earlier thoughts, the alarm sounded. For a moment Jack was frozen, the alarm beating raucously in his ears, then he pulled himself together and flicked off the switch on the bell. With the room returned to the relative quiet of the whoosh of the cooling fans on the equipment, Jack sat down at the console and keyed in an enquiry. Within seconds the computer had replied that it was receiving a strong periodic signal on the 42 centimeter band. Further questioning showed that it was not a program malfunction but a genuine signal.

Jack picked up the phone and dialed his boss's number. It was three in the morning, but his instructions had been clear. If anything was received that could possibly be an intelligent signal, he was supposed to contact his superior immediately.

Despite the long drive through the mountains in the cool Puerto Rican night, Professor Kraft showed up with his eyes still sleepy. Shuffling over to the coffee pot by the window he poured himself a large mug before he said anything. "You'd better have something good to get me up at this hour."

"I think so," Jack said, aware that his boss's irritation was only feigned. "I've been checking with the computer since I called you. It shows a strong periodic signal with a sharp pulse every fifty milliseconds. It runs on like that for about two and a half minutes before the signal fades below the background."

"Any chance that it might be a pulsar?" Kraft asked, referring to the radio signals of rapidly rotating neutron stars. "That's within the range of periods for them. When the first one was discovered, they thought that they had received intelligent signals."

"I thought of that, so I checked the record of the broad band receiver." Jack brought out a long strip of graph paper and pointed to the evenly spaced patterns of peaks on it. "Where the narrow band shows only a single repetitive pulse, the wide band gives us this fine structure. It's far too regular to be a pulsar and much too detailed. It's more like some sort of timing signal or spacer. And in between the pulses there is another signal. It's not as repetitive as the main pulse. That's why the program doesn't bring it out. But there definitely is some sort of transmission in between. It's weaker, but I think that we can write a processing program to pick it out from the noise."

Kraft looked at the trace in his hand thoughtfully. "I hate to make snap judgements. You can be suckered in too easily that way. But it does look like some kind of artificial signal. We'll get the team working on it in the morning. Have you received any additional signals?"

"No. I've kept the dish tracking the source, but all we get on 42 cm. is background noise. It's like there was a moment of freak atmospheric conditions that opened a window, and then it shut again. Just like you get with shortwave sometimes because of the ionosphere."

"Well, we should be grateful for what we've got. I don't think I can sleep anymore tonight, so I'll keep you company. I'd like to be here if we get any more messages from our friends out there," he said, pointing with his cup towards the star filled sky that loomed over the radio telescope's antenna.

"Frustrating, isn't it?" Prof. Kraft remarked to the team of graduate students and post doctoral fellows that were working under him on the interstellar communications project. And frustrating it had been. For six months they had continuously monitored the sky searching for signs of life finally to be rewarded by a two minute snippet of extraterrestrial conversation.

Now, another six months later, they had still made no sense of the signal, nor had they received any further transmissions from that part of the sky, though they had concentrated their efforts in that direction.

"Rumors have leaked out about our discovery, and I've been getting requests for the data. I'd sure hate to have someone else steal our thunder by deciphering the signal, but if we don't make some progress soon, we're going to have to release it." He looked around the table at the young faces of his assistants. At the moment they didn't look nearly as bright and intelligent as he knew they were.

"Why don't I summarize what we've found so far in hopes that it will give us some new ideas?"

"First, we've got this repetitive pattern of pulses every twentieth of a second as regular as clockwork. So regular, in fact, that we can't decide whether they serve as breaks in the message or were just put there to attract our attention. Remember, it was these pulses that were first recognized by the computer."

"But the pulses aren't the real message. That lays in the spaces in between. We've been able to deduce that the messages are digitized and the computer has been able to enhance them so that we have a fairly error free record of them. There is some repetitive structure to them, and they do vary in some sort of progression, but beyond that, we haven't been able to get the least notion of what they mean. Anyone have something to add?"

Bill Warden, one of the post docs, spoke up. "Well, we've tried mathematical analysis on the signals and have gotten zero results. It has already been assumed that any sort of interstellar communications would be based on sort of easily recognizable mathematical progression. Like one, two three. Something like that to show that they were rational. From there you can always build up more complicated concepts."

"With this message we don't have that, which leads us to one of two assumptions. One, we have only a fragment of a broadcast, and from a very advanced lesson at that. If that's the case, I don't see much hope of our being able to decipher the message until we can receive more signals to give us a broader base to work from."

"The other alternative is that they, whoever they are, just don't think like us. Their minds work in some fashion so that this mess we have makes sense to them. If so, I don't see any hope at all. Their minds may just be too foreign for us to hold a dialog with them."

"Thank you for that optimistic note," Prof. Kraft said wryly. "For the first time mankind has received a message from another species and we can't tell whether it is a cure for cancer, a means of achieving universal peace, or a recipe for sauerbraten. Any comments?"

"If it's sauerbraten, where do we go for a tablespoon of powdered bandersnatch egg?" quipped one of the grad students. They all laughed at the joke more than it deserved. Six months of unrewarded work had left them all a little giddy. After the giggles and comments had died down, Jack Olsen coughed, trying to get their attention.

"You've got something useful to say, Jack?" Kraft asked. "You might as well tell us. I don't think anyone else has anything useful to add," he said, pointedly looking at the wisecracker.

"I've been thinking about the signal, and I remember something that I said to you the night it came in. I don't know if you recall, but I called the pulses timing signals. Now there is one type of common transmission that has the same kind of pulses, and that's television. They use the pulses to synchronize the frames. It's possible that the message in between each pulse is a picture, and the whole transmission is meant to be viewed in sequence."

"How long have you been sitting on this while the rest of us were beating our brains out?" Kraft asked.

"It just came to me," Jack said, his face flushed. "I should have thought of it earlier, but like Bill said, we've all been conditioned to look for something like one plus one equals two."

"I think that we should all have seen it," Kraft said. "It makes as much sense as anything else that's been suggested. Do you think that you can get us a picture?"

"If it's there, I should be able to pick it out using the computer," Jack answered.

"Good. Then, since it was your idea, you're in charge. Dragoon anything or anybody that you need to help you."

Five days later they were all gathered around the conference room table again, but this time there was a TV set and a video recorder on a cart at its end. From the nervous stubbing of cigarette butts and fingers drumming on the table, it was obvious that all the members of the team were in a state of anticipation.

"It took some time to figure out exactly how the signal was put together," Jack began. "After all, we didn't know how many lines there were in each frame or how many bits made up each unit of picture. In the end, I had to have the computer run through all the likely possibilities for one of the frames. It took a lot of computer time, but I've finally got some recognizable pictures."

"It turns out that the original broadcast was in color. That threw us for a while, but we finally psyched it out. The aliens must have eyes structurally different from ours; there are only two colors, not three in the signal. Which colors they are is anybody's guess. They might be ultraviolet and infrared for all we can tell. Arbitrarily, I've assigned them red and bluish green, so keep that in mind. Also, because the video recorder uses thirty frames a second instead of the twenty in the transmission, it was necessary to compress the program a bit. This means that everything you'll be seeing has been speeded up about fifty percent.

"I guess you're all more interested in seeing the tape than in listening to me." A snort from Prof. Kraft indicated agreement. Jack flicked off the lights and started the tape. For a minute the screen showed only snow, then a face became recognizable. It was a sickly chartreuse, and there was no nose between the two large, oval eyes, but it was recognizable as a face. The figures movements were quick and jerky like an old silent movie, the result of the difference in frame speed, and the picture left a lot to be desired in clarity, the product of interstellar noise, but it was a picture, the first of an alien race.

As the tape played, a weird, sings song voice came from the speaker sounding something like a Chinese chipmunk. "I forgot to mention that there was also an audio track along with the signal. Again, it's only a reconstruction and may not bear much resemblance to the original, but then, we'll never know," Jack commented. They had determined that the source of the transmission was at least several dozen light years away. It would take twice that number of years to send a message and receive a reply, by which time they would all be dead.

They continued to watch the tape. The camera had drawn back to show the alien from the waist up revealing rounded shoulders and a pair of six fingered hands. Apparently he was standing behind a low lectern or a table of some sort. The fuzzy picture and camera angle made it hard to tell which. As he, or her, or it, spoke, the alien pointed at a chart or poster suspended on the backdrop. A pattern of red and blue that hurt the eye with violent contrasts seemed to be some sort of text. The voice continued as the picture disappeared in a sea of snow and then it broke into static. The transmission had ended.

"You've done a fine job, Jack," Prof. Kraft said after they had played the tape through a half dozen times. "It's actually far better than I thought it would be, and I think we can accept any of the shortcomings that you mentioned."

"So, we've got a face and body of what certainly is a rational creature. He seemed to be giving us a lesson or lecture of some sort, though I for one don't have the faintest idea of what he was talking about. We have an idea of what they look like which I am sure will give the biologists a lot to speculate on, so I guess that we should be thankful for small favors, but I still don't see how we're going to learn any more about them without receiving further signals."

"I wouldn't hold out much hope of that," Jack interjected. "I think that it's clear now that the signal we picked up was not meant for interstellar communication. Any such signal would have been designed with much greater noise immunity. We were able to receive it only because of an accident of atmospheric conditions. It was actually just a local TV broadcast. As we haven't received anything since, those conditions must be rare."

"So," Kraft said, "we have a message of great potential import, that at the very least could provide us with insights on a totally alien culture, and no way to decipher it."

"I've got an idea," Bill said. "We've all been looking at the problem from the point of view of hardware and computer programs. That's natural because of our backgrounds, but now that we have what amounts to an artifact, maybe we should call in a specialist. We need someone who is trained in resurrecting a culture from its fragments. I suggest that we show the tape to some archeologists and get their opinions."

Convincing an archeologist to look at the tape was harder than it had sounded. Most of them were more interested in ancient rather than alien civilizations. Jack suspected that they felt out of their depth with the computers and electronics. With some pressure and pleading, a group finally agreed to view the tape, but after the showing, only one evinced any interest in following up on it.

A visiting lecturer from Norway, she was reputed to have a good background in languages, though Jack lacked the knowledge to judge her qualifications. However, as she was young, blond, and attractive, he was quite willing to spend the time required to familiarize her with the tape and the equipment they had used to come up with it. Together, they spent hours viewing the tape, studying it frame by frame attempting to pick out the slightest piece of information.

The project team had been assembled in the conference room, and this time it was the archeologist's turn to address them. For three weeks Cristina Peterson had been studying the tape almost constantly, and now she was ready to give her opinion. With the exception of Jack, who had been working closely with her, they were all, even Prof. Kraft, eagerly awaiting the report. There had been a great deal of speculation about what her findings would be.

"First," she began, "before I get your hopes up, I want to say that I have not been able to get a word for word translation of the voice on the tape. The sample of speech is just too brief for that to be possible. If the scene had contained more action, I might have been more successful, but we were not that fortunate. I have, however, been able to form a hypothesis based on the spoken word as well as visual clues such as facial expression, setting, and so on."

"An important point to remember is that the aliens, despite certain differences in appearance, are not too dissimilar from ourselves. They are bipedal, intelligent, and possess opposable thumbs. They have binocular vision and a form of color perception as well. Brain size is about the same in relationship to total body size as in humans, and I would be greatly surprised if they were much larger or smaller than ourselves. That much can be guessed on the basis of physiology from the picture and the nature of the signal. From this information, I think that we can draw the conclusion that their planet is, within limits, earthlike."

"Probably more relevant is their state of culture. They obviously have a technology and one that is recognizable in terms of our own. That we can receive their signals is proof of that. Also, they speak, they wear clothing, we can even guess at the purpose of some of the objects visible in the tape. I might add that this is more than we can do for some of the artifacts of primitive human cultures. In some ways we have more in common with the aliens than we do with the Tasadi or Bushman."

"I want you to bear in mind that these beings are not greatly different from ourselves. If we are to properly analyze the contents of the message, we must remember that they are influenced by the same drives and forces as humans." There was an uneasy shifting in their seats on the part of the team members as they took in the meaning of her statement.

"If we accept this premise, and replace the alien with a human, we can make an educated guess as to what we are seen on the tape. I'll run it again for you so that you can make the substitution." Jack tapped the switch, and for the next minute and a half they watched the now familiar scene replay itself.

"Before I give my own opinion, would anyone else like to make a guess?" Cristina asked.

Kraft looked around the room, but it appeared as though no one had the courage to be the first to put his own views forward. To break the silence he said, "It's only a guess, but to start the discussion, I'd say that the alien might be a lecturer. He's obviously standing at some sort of podium or speaker's table."

"He seems a little too impassioned for a lecturer, at least in the physical sciences," one of the grad students remarked. "I've never seen you that excited before a class." Kraft smiled at the reference to his own low keyed classroom delivery.

"Maybe it's a political science class. They get more aroused."

Bill Warden broke in, "Why a class? It looks to me more like he's a politician trying to persuade the voters. He must be up for reelection. The sign in back could be an election poster." That brought a couple of laughs and a few less than serious comments.

"We've all had a crack at it," Prof. Kraft said. "You obviously have your own interpretation, and I think that we've been kept in suspense long enough. From the look on Jack's face, it must be a good one. Let's hear it now. After all, the communication between two species is one of the most important events in human history."

She smiled at the jibe. "All your suggestions are plausible, but I've spent more time analyzing the tape than you have. I'll play it again for you and point out the features that have led me to my interpretation."

"The first thing that caught my attention was the fact that the word 'gratach' was mentioned fourteen times, an unusually high incidence in such a brief speech. Furthermore, at least four of those times the speaker pointed to the symbols on the chart behind him. I think that we can assume that 'gratach' is a name, and the symbols form the written version."

"Now here's something that I want you to see." She froze the picture on the television. "Note the artifacts on the table, a bowl filled with a substance and a box or container. There appears to be some writing on the box, but the resolution of the picture isn't good enough to allow us to make it out. However," she said as the tape began to roll again, "as the alien points to the box and says 'gratach' it is likely that the symbols again spell out the name in the chart behind the alien. Note, too, the expression on his face. Despite the lack of a nose, the face is surprisingly human, and if that expression was on a human face, it would be one of approval or pleasure."

"I think that if you put all the clues together, you can come to only one conclusion. Dr. Warden was not far off when he suggested a political campaign. The speaker is definitely trying to persuade his audience, but it is the package, not himself, that he is trying to sell."

"Oh, god," Kraft sputtered. "You can't mean it. The first communication from another planet and it's only . . ."

"Yes, I'm afraid so," Cristina said. "The first and only signal received from another world is nothing more than a breakfast food commercial."

Special Preview!

THE LAWS OF MAGIC
BY GREG FOWLKES
© 2010

Now available from The Fictional Press
www.TheFictionalPress.com

THE LAWS OF MAGIC
WITHOUT LICENSE

☆　　☆　　☆　　☆　　☆

As Egil Njalsson climbed the steps of the criminal courts building he wondered if it was really worth it. Eighteen months of practicing law on his own and here he was in his only suit, about to attend the preliminary hearing in a petty case for which with luck he would be able to recover his expenses. It wasn't even a paying client. The state would be picking up the tab for this one, and he'd ended up being the lawyer appointed by the court. At the moment it wasn't clear who would benefit most from the charity, the client or the lawyer. He hadn't had a case in three months and he'd just been eking out a living writing briefs for other lawyers. He could do that well enough. His technical background gave him a depth of knowledge most lawyers lacked when it came to cases involving points of science as well as law. If he hadn't had that he'd be starving.

He'd been thinking about that a lot lately; whether he had made the right decision giving up science and going into the law. At the time, with the aerospace industry in a depression in the early seventies, it had seemed like a good idea. Engineers were pumping gas and PhD's in physics were selling insurance. Being a lawyer had seemed like a good way to make money. A stable income, no ups and downs. He'd put in his time at law school and done well. After the grind at CalThaum, law school had been a snap. So here he was a lawyer barely making ends meet and his school mates, the ones who had stuck with science were all making it rich designing personal calculating engines and disk storage units.

He tried to put all these thoughts out of his mind as he passed through the big brass doors of the court house. After all, he did have a client to defend, and a duty to him. It wasn't easy, though. It wasn't, after all, a very important case. Just a charge of fortune telling and practicing the Art without a license. Minor offenses, probably not even any jail time involved. This wouldn't even be a trial today, just a plea and arranging of bail.

It wouldn't even have amounted to that if his client hadn't instisted on pleading not guilty. He'd met him at the county jail, an old man, one Jake Schmidts. He'd tried to talk him out of pleading not guilty, too. A guilty plea, a small fine, and they both could be done with it. His client, though, had turned out to be something of a character. So here he was.

It took an hour and a half before their case came up. The judge looked at him questioningly when he had pleaded not guilty, but thankfully had released his client on his own recognizance when he indicated he had a permanent address. It was over in five minutes.

They got the release papers and the court date from the bailiff. Egil started to head out when he noticed that his client seemed lost and disoriented by it all. "Do you have car fare home?"

"No," Schmidts said. "I didn't have any money on me when they came and arrested me. Not a cent."

"Which way do you live?"

The old man gave an address on Fair Oaks Street. It wasn't far out of his way. Neither one of them lived in the best part of town.

"I can give you a lift," Egil said.

"That's kind of you, Mr. Njalsson," Schmidts said. The mister was ironic. The arrest report hadn't given an age, just "somewhere around seventy." As far as Egil could tell that might have been off by a decade or two.

The address turned out to be a sort of second hand junk store. The operative word was junk. If the pieces in the dirty window were the best of the lot then Egil could see how Schmidts qualified as indigent.

"Thanks for the ride. I've a beer inside if you'd like."

Njalsson looked at his watch. It wasn't too early to start drinking, at least just a beer. The work at the office would wait. He had to talk to Schmidts anyway to prepare a case. Besides, the old man seemed to want to pay him back for the ride.

If anything, the shop was worse on the inside than it looked from the front. Odd bits of bric-a-brac were strewn around everywhere; most of it looking like it hadn't been moved or even dusted in twenty years. Broken down pieces of furniture were covered with moldering sheets.

The old man led him to the back and up some stairs to an apartment above the shop. The kitchen was cleaner, though still hardly spotless. Of course, Egil's own small apartment wasn't the neatest of place, either.

The refrigerator looked as old as Schmidt's, but the beer was cold. Schmidt's took out two and motioned him to a chair at the kitchen table.

"So what happens now, Mr. Njalsson?"

"The trial will be held on the date on the summons. The district attorney will call his witnesses and make his case. Then I'll make my case. The judge will then decide."

"No jury?" Schmidt's asked disappointedly.

"Not unless we've got a very strong case to present. This is a small matter. It's better left to a judge. A jury would be considered a waste of time, I'm afraid, and would probably result in a higher fine. Maybe even jail."

"So you think I'm guilty?"

"I don't think you have much of a case."

"That's different?"

"To a lawyer it is."

Schmidts snorted in disgust.

"I don't want to disillusion you, Mr. Schmidts, but you've got to face the facts. Do you have a license to practice Magic?"

"No."

"Did you tell the fortune of one Mrs. Einar Johnson?"

"Yes, and an ungrateful woman she is, too. Just because I told her the truth about that shifty salesman she thinks is going to marry her. He's just after her late husband's money."

Egil raised an eyebrow.

"It's the truth. I've been reading the cards longer than you've been alive, Mr. Njalsson, and I know what I'm doing. That salesman is the one that got her to swear out a complaint against me."

"It doesn't matter whether what you said was the truth or not. What matters is that you were practicing the Art without a license. Magic is a potentially dangerous business. It's not something that untrained people should be dealing with. That's what the law is about."

"What would you know about the Art, Mr. Lawyer?" Schmidts asked sharply.

"I know more than most, Mr. Schmidts. I studied applied metaphysics at the California Institute of Thaumaturgy for four years before going into the law. I've got a Bachelor's of Science degree. I've also got my practitioner's license from both the state of California and Wisconsin. I may not be the greatest practitioner of the Art, but I am competent enough to know what I am and am not capable of."

"So maybe you did study at a fancy school out west. Those scientists don't know everything. They think that they've discovered magic, but magic goes back. Way back. Back before Helmholtz and Gauss. Before the Egyptians and Babylonians. Magic is old, Mr. Njalsson, and the doctors and professors haven't learned half of it."

"And you have?" Egil asked sarcastically. He was getting annoyed at the old man's pretensions of knowledge. He was surprised, though, that Schmidts knew that the two physicists Helmholtz and Gauss had been instrumental in proving the scientific basis for magic.

"No. I'm no fool. I've been studying the Art all my life. I know what I know and I have a good idea of what I don't. What I do know is more than a youngster like you learns in four years at college, even if it is a fancy one."

"Look, Mr. Schmidts," Egil said. "This isn't working out. Maybe you should get yourself a different lawyer."

The old man looked at him in surprise, then shook his head. "No. I guess you were just telling me the way it is. I may not like it, but I can't fault you for telling the truth."

"Okay. Is there anything I can use in your defense?"

"Guess not."

"Well, where did you learn to tell fortunes, to read the cards?" Egil asked.

"From an old Romany woman," the old man answered.

"Where? Here in the city?"

"No, it was a long time ago. Bohemia, I think it was."

"Bohemia? You mean Czechoslovakia."

"Yes, that's what they call it now I think. Prague. I was a student there."

"A student? At a university? I thought you didn't believe in learning."

"I was younger then. I thought there were things I might learn. I was wrong."

"Did you get a degree, though? That might carry some weight, especially a foreign one."

"Wait a moment. I think I have one someplace. Let me go look." Schmidts went down to his shop. From below Egil could hear noises as if boxes were being moved around. He didn't quite know what to make of the old man's gypsy tale. Bohemia had become part of Czechoslovakia after the First World War in the breakup of the Austrian Empire. It hadn't been a separate country since the Hapsburgs.

There were footsteps on the stairway and Schmidts showed up with a small picture frame carrying a piece of parchment. It was certainly a degree, but not from the University of Prague. The writing had faded with age and Egil had never learned French, but it appeared to be a doctorate granted by the Sorbonne. It was also made out to one Jacques Krieger.

"This isn't your name."

"It was the name I was using then."

"Can you prove that?"

"Not that I can see."

"Oh well. Maybe we can use it. If you can find anymore old papers like this save them for me. We might have some defense if we can prove you had an education, particularly if it was before the current examination system went into effect."

"I'll do that, Mr. Njalsson."

"Well I've got to get going now. Can I take this with me?" the lawyer asked, holding up the sheepskin.

"Yes, if it will help."

Egil let himself out through the shop. He dumped the diploma on the car seat next to him and started the car. While the engine was warming up he glanced down at it. The date was written in Roman numerals. It took him a moment to figure out the year. It was 1847. Either the old man was lying to him or he might find himself defending him in a commitment hearing.

Also From Resurrected Press

Science Fiction Authors Resurrected

Fyfe Resurrected - The Stories of H. B. Fyfe

Stories from the Golden Age of Science Fiction by the author of D-99. dealing with the interaction of humans and aliens on far off worlds in ways that were as creative as they were imaginative.

Bone Resurrected - The Stories of J. F. Bone

More stories from the Golden Age of Science Fiction. Includes "The Issahar Artifact," "Assassin," "To Choke an Ocean" and more.

Nourse Resurrected - The Stories of Alan E. Nourse

Stories from the Golden Age of Science Fiction. Includes "Contamination Crew." "Coffin Cure," "The Link," and more.

Dick Resurrected - The Early Stories of Philip K. Dick

Early stories from the author of the novels that inspired "Blade Runner," "Total Recall," and through a scanner darkly. Science Fiction Authors Resurrected

OTHER CLASSIC SCIENCE FICTION NOVELS
BEING RESURRECTED SOON

TALENTS, INCORPORATED - BY MURRAY LEINSTER
When a Mekinese fleet conquers his home planet, Captain Bors turns to Talents, Incorporated for help using their collection of individuals with unusual abilities to defeat the enemy and save the galaxy.

THE PIRATES OF ERSATZ - BY MURRAY LEINSTER
Bran Hodden just wanted to be an electronic engineer and marry a delightful girl. But when he's framed by the powers on Walden he's forced to turn back to his family's trade, piracy. Also published as The Pirates of Zan.

EMPIRE - BY CLIFFORD SIMAK
Spencer Chambers and Interplanetary Power owned the Solar System because they controlled the source of power. It fell to Russell Page and Harry Wilson to challenge that control if they had to cross the universe to do it.

NIGHT OF THE LONG KNIVES - THE CREATURE FROM THE CLEVELAND DEPTHS - BY FRITZ LEIBER
Two classic novellas set in the not too distant future from a classic master of science fiction.

ARMAGEDDON - 2419 A.D. - THE AIR LORDS OF HAN - BY PHILLIP FRANCIS NOWLAN
The two novels that introduced the world to that intrepid hero of the 25th Century, Buck Rogers. Buck Rogers must save the world from the clutches of the insidious Han.

Other Classic Resurrected Science Fiction
Edited by Greg Fowlkes

RESURRECTED MARTIANS
Classic Stories about Mars and Martians from the Golden Age of Science Fiction

RESURRECTED ALIENS
Classic Stories of Aliens and Alien Encounters from the Golden Age of Science Fiction

RESURRECTED FLYING SAUCERS
Classic Stories of Flying Saucers and Alien Invasions from the Golden Age of Science Fiction

RESURRECTED ROBOTS
Classic Stories of Robots, Cyborgs and Androids from the Golden Age of Science Fiction

RESURRECTED SPACE SHIPS -
Classic Stories of Space Ships from the Golden Age of Science Fiction

RESURRECTED TIME TRAVEL
Classic Stories of Time Travel from the Golden Age of Science Fiction

RESURRECTED DIMENSIONS
Classic Stories of other Dimensions from the Golden Age of Science Fiction

RESURRECTED FUTURES
Classic Stories of the Far Future from the Golden Age of Science Fiction

RESURRECTED MAD SCIENTISTS
Classic Stories of Mad Scientists and their Creations from the Golden Age of Science Fiction

RESURRECTED MONSTERS
Classic Stories of Monsters and Mayhem from the Golden Age of Science Fiction

The Fictional Detective
by Greg Fowlkes

Who killed Ezekial O. Handler?

A beautiful dame, a hard-boiled private eye – and a dead body.

It started like any other case. When a famous writer dies in a mysterious car crash, private detective Frank Slade is called in to find answers, but all he finds is more questions. Who killed Ezekial Handler? Who is Janet Nielsen and why is she so interested in finding out? Who is leaving the neatly typed clues? And as Slade tries to find answers to these questions he starts to wonder if the ultimate answer will threaten his very existence.

Read about it in
The Fictional Detective

Visit www.thefictionaldetective.com

About Resurrected Press

A division of Intrepid Ink, LLC, Resurrected Press is dedicated to bringing high quality, vintage books back into publication. See our entire catalogue and find out more at www.ResurrectedPress.com.

About Intrepid Ink, LLC

Intrepid Ink, LLC provides full publishing services to authors of fiction and non-fiction books, eBooks and websites. From editing to formatting, from publishing to marketing, Intrepid Ink gets your creative works into the hands of the people who want to read them. Find out more at www.IntrepidInk.com.

www.ingramcontent.com/pod-product-compliance
Lightning Source LLC
Chambersburg PA
CBHW070858250626
47159CB00003B/1110